GAELS ON THREE

Don Schlenger

INK START MEDIA
5710 W Gate City Blvd Ste K #284
Greensboro, NC 27407

GAELS ON THREE

Jersey, Girls, Basketball

A Novel

Donald Schlenger

For Jackie.
Nothing is possible without you.

Dedicated to my brother, Dr. William Edward Schlenger.

My life will never be the same.

—Terrence Patrick McEntee

You wanna be friends, or ya wanna race?

—Ramona Voytek

CHAPTER ONE

Late October 1982

I was a first year math teacher at St. Ethel of the Holy Oasis Junior High School (for girls) in the early eighties. Having enlisted in the army right out of high school in June 1976, I finished college in three and a half years and was pretty much a permanent sub here at St. Ethel in the spring semester of 1982, which turned into a summer job painting, cleaning, and doing repair work in the school.

Then one day, out of the blue, I was hired for a permanent math job. "Listen, Mr. Edwards," the monsignor told me, "we like the way ya been handlin' the lasses. Yer keepin' order, they're learnin,' we can see that. And they seem ta like ya. And that's a tall order for a sub. Good full-time subs are hard t' find, so we're gonna pay ya a full-time teacher's salary as a math teacher, beginning in September, with all benefits included. Waddaya thinka that, boyo?"

"I am very pleased and honored, Monsignor. In fact, I'm delighted. Thank you." A little groveling never hurt. "I won't let you and St. Ethel down."

He was an avid hoops guy and told me the school needed a good girls' basketball team to attract more students. And he did

1

not want to hire someone outside of the Ethel community as the coach. I had been on a Bergen County (New Jersey) High School Championship Basketball Team six years back that had gotten a lot of ink, and some of the parents, fathers anyway, knew my name. I had played jayvee basketball for two years at the local state college, and there were no candidates other than the somewhat elderly Sister Mary Begay, a retired Dominican nun, once of the Navajo Nation on the reservation in Ship Rock, New Mexico.

That left me, Bill Edwards, as the chosen one, hired as coach in mid-October. Sister Mary, relocated to New York City as a teenager, had been a whirlwind, unstoppable basketball player in her day then later in college as well, or so the myth went. Then a college coach. Allegedly.

So now here I was a full-time math teacher and basketball coach—two jobs I hadn't even sought out. I sort of had a minor in math, but no NJ teaching certificate, as Catholic schools were a bit more lenient than the state of New Jersey. And no breaks for veterans in those days either. No one ever said, "Thank you for your service." My "service" kind of came and went unremarkably. That's not a complaint.

Before he hired me as basketball coach, he asked me to come over to the rectory for lunch, served by his housekeeper, Agnes O'Toole. She was a native of county Kildare and came with the rectory. Not shy, very opinionated, but she liked me and I enjoyed her spunk. Monsignor and I had, upon several occasions, discussed our philosophies of basketball. He had hooped back in the day for the Fordham University Rams, before entering the seminary, when they still jumped center after every basket. He liked to call himself the George Mikan of the Bronx. He was a tall, broad-shouldered, former athlete who was battling his waistline. So far, the pints were inching ahead. He was a brilliant man, conversant in a lot more than basketball, as I was to discover. Out the blue, one time he asked me, "You were a guard at Rutherford High, Will?"

"Well, sir," I said, "we called what I played a combo 2 and 3, depending on who we were playing."

"Ah, the game surely changed, didn't it, then?" he stated. "I was a giant at six-four, you a guard at six-two."

"It's so much faster now, too, Monsignor, and more complex," I said.

He changed the subject. "What did you major in again, Will?"

"I majored in sociology, Monsignor. Loved it," I answered.

"Talcott Parsons or Marx-Engels?" he asked.

"Closer to Marx, I think, sir. More conflict than consensus," I said.

"And that's why there's religion, my boy." And he let out a big laugh.

"Y'mean it's not the opiate of the people?" I asked.

"That's a conversation for another time, Billy," he said somberly. "And Comrade Marx, while he had many interesting ideas, was way off line on that one. Speaking of which, why wasn't a good Catholic lad like yourself leading St. Mary's to a Bergen county championship instead of the Bulldogs?" St. Mary's was the Catholic Church and high school in Rutherford where I grew up.

He liked to catch me off guard. "Well, sir, I was baptized, made my first communion, was confirmed, and went all the way through CCD at St. Mary's. But my parents were not in favor of a Catholic education, even though they were Catholic," I said.

"I hope they have since seen the light and returned to the Lord's bosom. I will pray for them, William, and so should you," he suggested with a twinkle in his eye.

"As do I on a nightly basis, Monsignor. Pray for them, I mean," I said. His sideways glance demonstrated his lack of belief in my piety. Oh well, I wasn't going to roll over on everything.

Truthfully, though, I could never get on top of this guy, but then I was down about 40 IQ points, I think. Probably more. Someone over at St. Mary's, in my CCD days, had made clear to me the foolishness of trying to best a Jesuit in a debate or argument, and as a Jesuit, he had not let me down gently.

Many on the faculty thought the St. Ethel assignment was going to be his last posting before retirement. He had been a high school coach of some note, and then headmaster, at St. Peters Prep down the line somewhere, but at Rutherford High School, where I had played, we had never crossed their path. But they had been a known basketball powerhouse for years. He was quick to smile, his blue eyes lighting up his face when he did, but he could bellow like a bull. His name, I later learned, was Terrence McEntee. He was also alleged to have been born in Ireland, but Ms. O'Toole told me out of his hearing one time he was an escapee from Hell's Kitchen. She also referred to Monsignor as "himself," but in an almost reverential way.

Despite all the trappings of his office, he did retain the drive to win, as well as a brogue when it suited his purpose The big basketball question, of course, was: does every girl get to play every game? So we were both dancing around this dilemma when he blurted, "Jaysus, Mary, and Joseph, boyo! Don't start that Rec league stuff with me. They keep score, don't they? Foot on their troat, Billy boy! Kick 'em when they're down! We're playin' to win! Isn't that's why they keep score?"

In a rare example of good judgement on my part, I decided it was best not to respond.

* * *

A few days later, with the actual preseason and tryouts soon upon us, and me starting to panic, I asked Monsignor if I could hire an assistant. He thought this was funny. "Sister Mary will do just fine, 'Coach.'"

"I'll take care of compensation out of my pocket, sir," I pleaded while I'm thinking, *You're a rookie in a Catholic Junior High School, Edwards. You don't even have a pocket!* "There'll be no parents," he demanded.

"Definitely not!"

In the tried and true Catholic manner, I took his silence as consent.

4

CHAPTER TWO

Late October 1982

Late the next afternoon, after school, having downed a few Schaefers to "sharpen my judgement," I made a phone call to my high school girlfriend. "Ramona? Hi. This is Will Edwards. From Rutherford? Do you remember…?"

We had grown up together since we were four years old and were best friends throughout childhood. We were boyfriend and girlfriend throughout high school. A real tragic breakup toward the end of senior year, for me anyway. Hadn't seen or spoken to each other since. Over six years. My hand on the phone was shaking.

Ramona: "Will? Oh, for Chrissakes! Are you still at Mama's?"

This past April, her grandma had rented me a room near the school for the year and gave me Ramona's phone number. Mama's house, an old two-story frame, and the school were one town over from Rutherford where Ramona and I had grown up.

Will: "Yes, I am, Ramona. I've been here since April as you likely have known. In fact, I'm sitting here in her kitchen as we speak. I'm teaching math, and I'm gonna be the girls' basketball coach at St. Ethel Junior High School, y'know it? I was wondering if you would be interested in, uh, helping me out with the coaching."

I played two years of jayvee basketball in college; she had a four-year Division II ride at Bloomsburg State Collge in central Pennsylvania. We were both First Team All Bergen County in High School. She twice, me once.

Ramona: "Me help *you* out? You're kidding, right?"

She was a better basketball player than me, and this was her way of telling me, in case I had forgotten.

Will: "Why would I be kidding? Really, Ramona, why would I be kidding? No, actually, I wasn't kidding, but you know what?"

Ramona: "Tell me."

Will: "I can see this phone call was a big mistake, Ramona. Sorry to have wasted your time. It was nice talking to you. Really. You take care of yourself."

And I hung up. Oh, man, what a great feeling!

What the hell, maybe the monsignor was right and Sister Mary would work out. She had played and coached in college. Okay, it was a long time ago, but she and I had talked hoops and she had kept up with the game and she knew a lot of basketball. Or maybe my jayvee teammate from Montclair, Jake Walker, would be interested. He was around the area somewhere. I was a little bit insecure about it, thought I could use some backup.

The phone rang and Mama answered, completely ignoring my waving arms and "No! I'm not here!," or pretending to, and said, "Oh, hi, honey. Yes, he's right here. Vill, ees Ramona for you," and gave me a big smile.

Ray: "You hung up on me, you asshole! Whatsamattawithyou? After six years?"

Jersey forever.

Will: "Yeah, I did, Ramona. So what? It wasn't as hard as I thought. Did you want something?"

Ray: "You called *me*, rosebud!"

6

Will: "Well, *golly!* You're right, I did. I asked you a question, didn't I? Am I right on this, Ramona? It was 'Did you want to help me out coaching at St. Ethel?' And I got an answer, too, didn't I? 'Me help *you* out?' Now how do you suppose I took that? Well, Ramona, I took it as a solid 'Get lost!' Why, I surely did!

Like the great Ramona Voytek would stoop so low. I got the message, so yeah, I hung up. I'd say it's a QED, wouldn't you, Einstein? End of story? So like I said to you a few minutes ago, 'You take care of your—"

Ray: "Stop that right now! God, you're still such a wiseass. Can you just stop it for a minute? For an f—— minute? Six years go by and nothing? Then outathe blue 'Wanna help me coach basketball?' You need to work on your game, buddy...Could we just put down the weapons and get together for a while and talk? Fill in some blanks? I'm free tonight."

Will: "Well, I'm kinda of busy and I have to find an assistant coach, and I don't know where you live, Ramona."

Ray: "And I'm not telling you."

Me: "Jesus, Ramona, did I *ask*? What's the point anyway?"

Ball in Ramona's court.

Ray: "The point would be, sunny Jim, that after six—no, six and a half years—I would like to see you. Y'know, just out of curiosity."

Will: "Oh, I get it. Y'know what, Ramona, I'm too f—— busy to satisfy your curiosity like something in a zoo. So, no thanks, I'll pass."

Ray: "Oh, give it a rest, will you?"

Will: "I think I did that already." Pause. Deep breath. Time stopped. "Okay, listen. I'll be at Sullivans, remember where that is? Good. Tonight till 8:30, okay? If you're there, we'll talk, or at least you can look at me, right? I still look pretty much the same, maybe a bit taller. If not, I'll still be looking for an assistant." I hung up.

Not sure if this first encounter had a winner. I knew I folded, but I might still get an assistant coach. Okay, I wanted to see her. I really wanted to see her. But she wanted to see me just as bad. God, this was worse than bein' sixteen.

Sullivans was the local Irish pub in my neighborhood. I had become a regular and could walk there in one direction from Mama's, to the school in the other. I sat at the horseshoe oaken bar talking to Liam Dooney, a father of one of my students and foreman at B+D in East Rutherford. "So you'll be coachin' the girls is the word, Will."

"Looks like," I said, "been doin' some studying and thinking about it. Monsignor's gonna let me have an assistant, plus Sister Mary will help, too. She coached in college, y'know."

"Oh, really?" he asked, attention on the TV, not seeming all that interested.

"Yeah, like twenty years at Caldwell College, into the sixties. For Chrissakes, Liam, ya think she might know more than all of us combined?" I said, a little defensively, put off by his disinterest.

Liam shrugged and returned to the hockey on the TV. The Devils were on tonight from the Garden against the Rangers. I wasn't much for hockey, but the Irish guys loved it, and the bar was busy. They seemed to especially love the fights, and occasionally, one erupted at the bar, which is why Sully kept a 36" Louisville Slugger Mickey Mantle under the bar. Story was that the Mick had hit one with it back in the early fifties when he first came up, and its age attested to how long the bar had been here.

In truth, the *legend* was they had possessed one of the Babe's bats but had to sell it back in the twenties during Prohibition when they couldn't make the weekly contribution to Frank Hague's Widows and Orphans Fund, which also had the magic effect of keeping the Treasury Agents out of the neighborhood. While Sullivans was not within Hudson County, Hague's fiefdom, it was close enough for those enterprises willing and able to contribute. So that's *really* how old the place was.

And for those sticklers for punctuation, the missing apostrophe goes back to World War II. Five brothers named Sullivan were killed when their US naval ship was sunk in 1942 at Guadalcanal in the South Pacific. This tragedy led to a naval rule that siblings could not be assigned to the same ship. The story was also made into a Hollywood movie in 1944. The apostrophe was removed in late 1944 out of respect for the Sullivan family and as a patriotic gesture.

Looking at the bar clock, I saw it was past 9:15. "School night," I jokingly said to Liam. "Gotta hit the road. Night, lads."

Out the door and to the left, halfway down the block. "Get back in there, Willieboy," she yelled at me. "You're buying me a Smirnoff and a Schaefer back!"

"Nice to see you, too," I said.

Hollow leg, Ramona had. Going back in, all eyes on Ramona, a chorus of "School night" for me. I shrugged, gave them all the finger, and winked, like "Wish you were me, lads?"

I could see the cause of Ramona's lateness: clearly some time spent before the mirror doing whatever women do there. Yeah, last time I saw her she was a girl. Not no more, as we used to say in Ruddifid. Wow! Whatever it was, I was completely speechless. God, she was more beautiful than even I remembered. I had no plans of disclosing this to her tonight. But right then, she took my breath away.

The bar's reaction was her reward, like a standing O for a Broadway star. She was five-ten; dark, really dark brown hair with auburn streaks (a new touch); dark blue eyes; a lythe, athletic figure, and she moved like a panther, or a runway model, when she chose to. She drew attention when she entered any room, yet still had not grown comfortable with eyes on her..

Amidst hoots and whistles, I carried our drinks to a semiquiet corner booth.

Ray: "You were leaving? You were f——g leaving?"

Will: "Hold on there, Missy. You were due forty-five minutes ago. So I figured you blew me off. Not like it would be the first time. More your style, as I remember."

Ramona had a way of ignoring what she did not want to hear and charged ahead.

Ray: "You kind of took me by surprise today, Will."

Will: "What, no excuse for almost an hour late? Like I'm some piece of dog shit stuck on your shoe?"

Ray: "Oh, Willie, come on…"

9

Now it's "Willie," is it?

God, I hadn't realized how mad I still was at her. And hurt. Damn! I thought I was past all this.

Will: "Why is that anyway? That I took you by surprise? You knew I was at Mama's. You've known since April. You coulda come by, you coulda called. What the hell, Ramona? I just figured you were engaged or had a boyfriend. I think Mama woulda told me if you were married or had a kid."

Ray: "It's complicated."

Will: "Oh, gimme an f—— break, Ramona. Wait, why didn't you say that in the first place, that explains—"

Ray: "Oh, just shut up, Will. Can't we just do some catching up? We haven't talked to each other since forever. Don't you think it's time? Ve ah real peoples now? Remember when we used to say that? Don't you want to? It's over six years, for God's sakes. Put the knives away for a while, okay? I can if you can. I really mis—"

Will: "You go first."

Ray: "Okay." She smiled and looked me straight in the eye, took a dramatic deep breath, and said, "Here we go. Been waitin' a long time for this. Okay, back to high school. I got the full ride to Bloom. I loved the school. It was much bigger than I thought and harder. God, physics/ed double major nearly killed me, had to go an extra summer just to keep up."

Will: "C'mon, you were the smartest kid I ever knew."

Ray: "Yeah, but in college, in physics, they're *all* smart. And here, we, you and me I mean, didn't have any academic background or guidance at home. Neither of our parents had any books in the house, right? I loved science from the time we were little kids. We made it up as we went along, I worked my ass off, you glided—"

Will: "You know that's not true. I made people think that—"

Ray: "Anyway, the kids at Bloom were really nice, not wiseasses like us. I mean, not simpletons or hayseeds, but decent, open, just so not-Jersey. Bloomsburg is a nice town, y'could live there if it wasn't so damn cold in the winter. And it's all surrounded by cornfields. I mean—"

Will: "Boyfriends?"

Ray: "Not going there. Anyway, nothing serious."

Will: "Hoops?"

Ray: "That's the thing, Will. It's a job. Of course, I loved playing basketball, but the coaches are just looking for their next job. And, man, when the school is paying the freight, they got a lot to say about what you can and can't do. I almost left after freshman year."

Will: "Ooh, that sounds serious. Because?"

Ray: "They wanted me to put on fifteen pounds of muscle. I wasn't having it. I knew I had to lift, we all did, but fifteen pounds? Not happening. Told them I'd go home and play D III with Carol at Montclair. You remember Carol, right? I wasn't the best on the team, but I was close so I had some clout. If they benched me, I would have come home. I was going to start. Which I did. All four years. Scored a thousand. But it was a battle. I survived more than succeeded."

Will: "That's a hell of a story, Ramona. Really, congratulations."

Ray: "Anyway…Hey, it was my dream to play in college. It came true. And I got a free education. Not bad for a child of immigrants, eh? That's American dream stuff, right? I mean, really? You know what? I learned I was tougher than the PA kids, too. They gave in all the time to the bastard. I fought him for four years. Jersey, baby! Wasn't fun, though. Not like high school. Anyways…tell me about the army."

Will: "Okay, I'll give you the whole schpiel. You know how I wanted to go to what I thought then was a really good college, like one of those little Ivies in New England? 1180 SAT, top 10 percent of class, pretty good, but not full academic ride good? Not even close. No bucks at home. Couldn't swing the money. Folks were tapped out. I thought about it for months, finally said, f—— it, I enlisted in the army. Other reasons too, maybe."

Quick side-eye glance from Ray.

"Y'know, looking back, I never talked to Ms. Thompson about this, remember our senior English teacher? I loved her, she was great. I used to sneak in after school and talk to her. She put a story of mine in the literary magazine at the end of the year, no one could believe it. You didn't know that, did you? I shoulda talked to her about the whole mess. I was like a f—— zombie. I didn't talk to anybody."

Ray: "I read the story. It was good, made me cry. I didn't know you could write."

Will: "Anyway, raised some eyebrows, and my socialist US history teacher, Mr. Golden, remember him? Never spoke to me again, except for, "Ya'know, Willie boy, you been hangin' around with the tough guys too much, boychik. The dumbrowskis. You're cuttin' off your nose to spite your face? So you didn't get into some WASP paradise! You coulda kicked some serious ass in the city. The chicks are much better lookin' than those WASP shicksas, anyway. What the f——'s amattah with you?"

"Yeah, Mr. G, I coulda had class. I coulda been—"

"Get outa my sight, you goyisch schmuck! And I'm not signing your ferschluginah yearbook, either!"

"He had me all but enrolled in City College of New York. But what the hell, it was 1976 and Vietnam was over. I had older friends, you know, Al Stone and those guys, Meredith, Piccarelli, Smith, and them. The car guys who were always polishing their cars on Sundays at Lincoln Park and got all the hot girls. They gave me good advice. And I had killed the ASVAB, you know what that was?"

"Nah. Some army thing?" she asked.

"Army test for aptitude. Anyway, I scored really high, enlisted, and I was on the bus to Ft. Dix seven days after graduation.

Basic was culture shock, a real kick in the groin. Just do what the sergeant says, you understand it, you know it's stupid, shut up and grind. None of that made a dent. Fights. Race shit. Drugs. Still got my ass kicked. But I was a platoon leader, proudly marched in the graduation parade, ready to go. My parents were pissed that I had enlisted, but they still came down to Dix for graduation anyway. Good advice, as I said, helped a lot.

"After basic, the army sent me to Intelligence School in Ft. Huachuca, Arizona, got a lot of really cool training, a lot of IBM computer stuff. I worked as an analyst, mostly at Ft. Meade outside DC and some in the Pentagon, the rest is classified. Travelled the world, too, but that's classified as well. But I did see the world, and the USA, and I couldn't get enough of it. Made me want to see more. Met a lot of bright, interesting guys in the army, too. Especially in intelligence. Gave some serious thought to makin' a career of it. I don't know if you got to travel much, Ramona, but this is just a beautiful country.

"At Huachuca, we had a basketball league, and it was lots of fun playing. Once in a while, we'd play some of the local Indian teams and really get our asses kicked. They'd just run us to death. They never got winded or tired, and sometimes they'd show up with only five guys, didn't make a difference.

"When I had done my time, I used what GI money I had to go to Montclair, lived on campus, worked in a diner up on Rte. 46, had a lot of fun playing jayvee hoops for two years. Seriously, I had no prayer of making the varsity. I majored in sociology, loved it, really loved it. Majored in math. Not my best move."

Ray: "Seriously?" She laughed. "You majored in math?"

Will: "Yeah. What's so funny? I got Tony into FDU tutoring him in math."

Ray: "Nothing, Will. I'm sorry, just kidding."

Will: "Correction. I minored in math. Then I took Calc III and a beast called Boolean Algebra."

Ray: "Oh, for two there, right?"

Will: "Ended my math career. Had to drop out of both classes. Still don't know what a Boolean is. I was humiliated. And now I'm a junior high school math teacher. Had to go one summer to catch up."Ray: "The Lord works in mysterious ways."

Will: "His wonders to perform. Look, it's getting late. We're both serious adults. Waddayatheen about the coaching? That was question one. And how about dinner tomorrow night?"

Willieboy swings for the fences!

13

Ray: "Yes to coaching. Might be fun, and I'm missing basketball. Two conditions."

Will: "You are haffing my attention."

Ray: "Six of Schaefer and a package of pirogies delivered on demand."

Will: "No can do."

Ray: "What? Why not?"

Will: "Your place of living is not known to me."

Ray: "Oh god, Willie. Alright then, I'll pick 'em up at Mama's!"Will: "Second condition?"

Ray: "Might not be able to do games. Lotta stress."

Will: "Deal. Dinner?"

Ray: "No can do."

And misses. Not gonna ask twice, lady. You got the ball now.

Will: "Okay, then, I'll let you know about the basketball. We'll get together with Sister Mary, you'll love her. Thanks, Ramona."

Ray: "You're not gonna ask—"

Will: "Gettin' late. Drive safe. I'll call. Nice to see you again, Ramona."

Ray: "Nice to see you again, too."

Well, at least I tried, damn it, at least I did that.

As we were leaving, I stepped back into the bar, took a bow, and said, "Thank you, thank you very much. What's that you ask? My new assistant coach? Why, yes, it is. I'll see the schedules are available. No, yez don't get her name and number. Now, don't cry, lads, it doesn't become yez, not as grown men. Sorry, but Elvis is leaving the building."

"Booooo!"

"You suck, Edwards."

"Way outta your league."

CHAPTER THREE

Early November 1982

Apparently, the monsignor's messages to the school staff and parents came through loud and clear, as thirty-seven seventh and eighth grade girls, out of an enrollment of 180, showed up for tryouts. All shapes, all sizes. Several fathers volunteered to help out. They were gently redirected by Monsignor and Sister Mary. Ray agreed to coach and she, Sister Mary, and I met half a dozen times and put together a plan for practice and for the season. Sister was great, and she and Ray hit it off right away.

At our first meeting, in my classroom sitting around a work table, armed with our clipboards, we started by telling our stories.

* * *

Sister Mary Begay: "I was born in Ship Rock, in northwest New Mexico, on the Navajo Reservation. Delivered by Navajo midwives in the old ways. The Rez is enormous and most of it is in Arizona. My folks were Noah and Enid Begay, and they owned a little diner called the Netahni Nez. Daddy cooked and Mama waited tables. The diner was on the main drag in Ship Rock, a

15

dusty little town then, which was also US Rte 64, so we had a lot of traffic. Most of our local customers, though, were Navajo, as the whites were still very prejudiced against Indians then."

Ramona: "That's a long way from Jersey, Sister, and a long time ago. Must be a lot of stories in between, I bet."

Sister: "Oh there are, Ramona."

Ramona: "Please call me Ray, Sister."

Sister: "Well, that will be fine, Ray. We'll have lots of time to tell stories during the season, won't we, Coach Will?" Spoken with a mischievous smile.

Will: "That we will, girls, that we will. Especially if Jim joins us."

Sister: "Now, no tellin' about Jim, William. Just keep that between us." Again, the secret smile.

Ray: "Oh no. That'll be enough of that, bothaya. I thought there was only three coaches. Who's this Jim?'

Sister: "He couldn't make it tonight, right, William?"

Will: "Nah, but he'll be around next time we get together. How about we talk some hoops?"

I said to Ray, "Our kids have basically no skills except for two guards with some playground sense. Our home court is very small. We only have fifteen ancient unis. We have some good size. We haven't yet seen anybody play, really, except some of the girls trying to impress us on the playground. Okay, tell us what you think."

"Yeah, right," Ray shot right back at me.

"No, really, Ray," said Sister, "we're just throwing around ideas."

"Okay," Ray began, "First, forget playing man defense. First, teach them to pass and catch. How to move their feet correctly. Rebound and box out. If there are way too many girls trying out, run 'em to death. Other decisions depend upon team speed and athleticism."

Sister and I high-fived each other and gave Ray big smiles. I said, "Part one of meeting adjourned."

"Okay, so what's going on?" asked Ray.

"Part two of the meeting is at Sister's," I said. "That is, if you are able to attend."

"Works for me," said Ray.

I asked Sister if the absent Jim could stop over.

"He'll be there," she said.

Ray leaned over to me and whispered, "Who the hell is Jim?"

Sister Mary lived on the convent compound near St. Ethels, an easy walk. Sister Mary was small, willowy, and moved with a whisper. I loved her and soaked up her stories about life on the reservation anytime we were both free. We had been getting together for several months. She seemed both ancient and young, with a noble Navajo face like one from a Gorman painting. Yeah, I took art appreciation! She had long hair not seen by many, as it was usually braided or tucked in. "Just for a while, William, it's already past six."

"We can walk over with you, okay?" I answered. On the way, I said, "Can I ask you a question, Sister?"

"Sure, unless it's about how I can drink alcohol when you've heard Indians can't tolerate it," she shot me down. "Just kidding, William. Always in moderation, never alone, drink plenty of water after. I saw too many drunken Navajo men in Gallup and Santa Fe, and I was always angry at them and at the white men who sold them liquor. It is a terrible thing, all over the west, the stereotype drunken Indian. It's the devil's work, for sure."

I said, "It's a problem for the poor everywhere. For the Irish certainly in Ireland and here."

"Russians, too. Like my father," said Ray.

Once at Sister's, three glasses were produced, and Jim Beam made his appearance. Ray burst out laughing. "You two got me on that one. Well done. Some Dominican humor, Sister?"

"Well, we do our best, dear," Sister answered. "Will, could you call the Central and order a pizza delivered? Extra cheese, okay? I just love their pies! On me."

* * *

The Netahni Nez, with its four-stool counter and two four-top tables, was a successful business, and Enid was able to keep watch on Mary in the diner. When she was old enough, with Enid's tutelage, Mary learned her ABCs and could read, write, and do simple math by age four. Enid took her to her mother's house in the countryside on weekends so she could learn Navajo language, culture, and the ways of the Dineh, as the Navajo called themselves. Enid and her mother's family were insistent that Mary learn the Navajo ways and, as many Navajo, resist the government's efforts to assimilate them. The Navajo are matrilineal, so the clans are based on lineage through the mother's line. The husband joins and lives with the wife's clan.

Mary began school in the local Bureau of Indian Affairs Elementary School in Ship Rock when she was five. It was woeful experience. She was so far ahead that she bored easily, and the teacher was either disinterested or not qualified to deal with a gifted child. This caused endless fighting between her parents. Enid was convinced that Mary's life lay beyond the reservation. Her family, and Noah as well, were set in the Navajo ways. Both Enid and Noah had some education and spoke English fairly well, but this was not enough for Enid's daughter. Traditional Navajo families were resistant to the government's efforts and saw them as a dead end. Enid saw beyond that "dead end" for Mary.

One day in late October, she asked her brother, Ellis Chee, to drive her and Mary to Gallup, a fair-sized town, off the reservation, ninety miles south of Ship Rock, where she had cousins who had once lived in Ship Rock. She knew there was a Catholic Church there with a Navajo congregation. The church also had a six-grade elementary school. They found St. William Roman Catholic Church, called at the rectory, and spoke to a priest named Father Thomas, who talked them through the process. Mary could start school and catch up, but both mother and daughter would begin to take instruction in the Catholic faith. Mary was thrilled and excited to begin as soon as she could. Thanking Fr. Thomas profusely, Enid had Ellis drive her to their cousins' home a quarter mile away where they would be able to stay. Enid could get a job and pay for their room and board, as well as tuition and fees at the new school. The one setback was the transportation; the car was owned by many members of the Chee clan and not always available, so Enid would stay in Gallup and Ellis would hire a waitress. Business was good. Enid and Mary would spend the summers at home with the family in Ship Rock where she would be steeped in the Navajo ways.

With her mother's help, Mary excelled in her studies, most importantly in English. Her mother joined St. William, and she and Mary were both baptized. Enid got a part-time job waiting tables. Mary flew through her lessons and was allowed to complete six grades in five years. The principal at St. William school, Sister Theresa, as well as Father Thomas, spoke on her behalf at the Loretto Academy for Girls in Santa Fe, a seventh through twelfth grade school. Enid again found cousins she and Mary could stay with, and Mary got a job working in a grocery store.

The Loretto School gave Mary a reduced fee because of her academic prowess. It was here that her academic talent blossomed. Her native ability, interest in ideas, and curiosity about the world were insatiable. She was a brilliant and aggressive student. And though Loretto could be a harsh environment, especially for Navajo girls, Mary was determined to continue her journey, as her mother had called it, wherever it led. She learned to speak, read, and write Spanish and began Latin. She would not be deterred nor distracted from her goals.

As her seventh grade progressed, she discovered other Navajo girls, who became friends, and they in turn introduced her to what they called "rez ball," similar to basketball but played at a much faster pace. Mary had found her true love. There were two baskets, ten feet high on poles, about eighty feet apart, in the yard, and the Navajo girls played whenever they had time. Rez ball consisted of five on five, usually three on three, full court, full speed, pass, cut, screen, little dribbling, and shooting. It was up and down and up and down. They played with determination and joy and acquired skills, learning to pass and catch, dribble, screen, and shoot.

Sister paused and said, "That's it for me. Your turn, Ray."

* * *

When I was about four or five, my mother took me for a walk over to Washington School, a few blocks from our house, where we lived in a two-family house. There was a little playground there, and I wanted her to push me on the swings. Then another mother came into the park with her little boy and began pushing him on the swings, too, and she and my mother began chatting in Slovak, losing interest in the little boy and me. I jumped off my swing and ran over to him and said, "Wanna race? Bet I can beatcha."

"No way, Jose!" he shouted back.

I put my face right into his face and said, "My name's Ramona, not Jose! What's your name?"

He answered, "Billy."

"Okay, Billy, wanna be friends or ya wanna race?"

"Race first then be friends. Ready? One, two, three, go!" He ran about twenty yards, turned back to me, and yelled, "I won!"

"Hey, you cheated! I yelled at him."

"Now we're friends," he said back at me and laughed. Our first fight, our first makeup. We went around the playground stomping on puddles and getting each other soaked.

"Hey, Ramona," he acknowledged, "you're cool for a girl."

"Hey, Billy, are you Catlic?" I asked.

"I don't know," he answered. "What's a Catalic?"

"It's church, silly," she said.

"Yeah, my mom takes me to church," he said, "so I guess I am."

"See you tomorrow, Billy." And I ran over to my mother.

The next day, our mothers let us play for hours. It helped a lot that I didn't have dolls or Barbies, but we were only four, hadn't started school yet, so we had to use our imaginations and made up games and stories or watched cartoons. There was no Sesame Street or programs like that when we were little.

* * *

Ray and I ran the tryouts and practices. She would drive down each day from the northern part of the county where she taught physics in a new regional high school. We agreed that they had to learn to pass and catch first, learn the proper footwork second, and rebound third. The rest would come later. Having consulted former coaches, read books by Dean Smith and Bob Knight, and taken in some local college practices, Ray and I realized we had to winnow thirty-seven down to fifteen, the number of uniforms we had. Winnowing by running. And then more running. Passing and catching the ball, a detail kids are almost never taught. Then, of course, parents complained, "How could you have tryouts when no one even shot the ball?"

"Ah, Fitz, have some faith, the lad knows what he's doin', he does. Can't have thirty-seven lasses on the squad now, can he?" argued the monsignor.

Running was not just up and back. We had the girls play tag, amoeba, skipping, jumping the line, Simon Says, Red Rover. Taught them cariocas, drop steps, jump stops, stutter steps, and slides. They jumped rope. Did foot-speed stuff. Played four-player follow the pass (started out as the legendary Chinese fire drill). Mirror drills. Some of the drills were fun, and none involved standing around in lines. Moving all the time. A good number just stopped running, like in public high school PE class. So of course the girls were exhausted when it was over, and many felt their motivation to return the next day evaporating.

The next morning, I had fifteen notes on my desk explaining, with sorrow and regret, why Peggy or Bridget or Patty couldn't go out for basketball this season, family obligations, after school Irish dance classes, etc. So far so good. I made sure to smile sadly and be kind to them, easing their feelings of having let me, the team, or St. Ethel down. I had handled some unhappy parent phone calls last night, and I'm sure Monsignor had as well..

I had already designated a statistician. She was a small Polish girl, born in Krakow, a seventh-grade math wizard and NBA fanatic named Ludmila "Luddy" Woijahowicz. Luddy was convinced that Larry was Polish, hence the obsession. "That's not his *real* name!" Luddy actually wrote letters c/o the Boston Garden to Larry "Ptak" (the Polish word for bird) but got only autographed glossies back. Meanwhile, she had appropriated an assistant, Christine Harodetsky, to keep possession evaluations and shot charts. It turned out Mr. Harodetsky owned a multilingual stationers in Lodi, so they both carried special briefcases with "highly secret" team documents. Embossed with their names no less. Christine's older brothers made certain no one played with their briefcases. Eat your heart out, Dean Smith.

Tryouts still included running, but now skills were added: shooting, of course (opposite hand as well), but also rebounding, boxing out, passing and catching, dribbling, free throws, and always, footwork. A lot of basketball is making your feet do things that aren't natural.

Ramona was still hesitant about being on the bench during games, saying it would be too stressful, so she coached only in practice. I was hoping she would find she couldn't stay away. As the days went by, it was clear that she loved the girls, and they adored her. She gave clear instruction and was clearly in charge when she did. The only thing they didn't like was that she demanded opposite hand layups and dribbling. First one to make an opposite hand shot in a game got treated to an *Awful Awful*, a famous ice cream concoction known all over north Jersey, at Bond's, a place up in Clifton on Rte. 46.

Ramona had all the basketball skills and was a big-time shooter. The kids wanted us to play O-U-T after each tryout and sometimes we accommodated them. I could never beat her. And God knows I tried, using every playground and driveway shot in my arsenal. To no avail. I almost never lost to anyone in O-U-T. But always to Ray, going back elementary school.

At tryouts, we added competition to the skills, and now another five girls bit the dust. Ray or I spoke to each of them at the end of practice. Two to go. Sister Mary intervened and spoke privately to the pious Bidwell sisters, Maura and Laura, the girls most likely never to leave the bench. She pointed out upcoming retreats, prayer vigils, and pilgrimages to holy grottos. I think perhaps she saw Dominican potential in the girls. Silently thanking Sister Mary and praying for Maura's and Laura's souls, we now had our fifteen.

* * *

I was very happy in Ray's grandma's house, and I lived like a king. The house was a two-story, white-framed house with three small bedrooms, just off the main drag in East Rutherford. About three miles or so from where we had grown up in Rutherford. It had a little stoop in the front and a nice garden with some plum trees in the back. There was a side entrance to the big kitchen where Mama spent most of her day. She was Ray's maternal grandmother, Maria Ziska, and she could bake and cook any Eastern European dish you could name. She was short, round, dark gray hair, blue eyes, and with the soft loving demeanor that said "Gram" in any language. Some of the Eastern invaders in her face. Old school indeed. Just enough Slovak families around to visit with in this mostly Irish working-class area. Much of the town consisted of two-family homes and small apartment buildings. Factories, mills, and auto body shops were also common on the edges of town. Shops and stores were up the street.

Across the tracks and to the west, Rutherford had a much larger area of affluence with big houses on Ridge Road, east-west spine of the town. Also a shopping street, which had so far survived coming of the the malls and the outlets. Many commuters settled in Rutherford for the convenience of the commute to New York via either bus or train. The west end, by the Passaic River, was a lot of GI housing, then a lot of apartments, and where Ray and I grew up, near the tracks, lots of two families. State Rte. 17 was the eastern border of the settled part of both towns. On the other side of the highway was "the meadows," as it was called when we were kids, famous for the Bonny Dell Farms dairy and not much else besides rodents. Big ones. Now it housed warehouses, office buildings, Giants Stadium (1976), and Brendan Byrne Arena (1981). Its name had been upgraded to "The Meadowlands." As though it were somewhere desirable to be, like in the English countryside.

Donald Schlenger

CHAPTER FOUR

Mid-November 1982

When we first assembled our team, I walked them around the court pointing out names of things: the paint, the blocks, the elbows, top of the key, the foul line, the key, half-court line, backcourt, the baselines, with only two feet between the stripe and the brick walls. Then we had a test.

"Okay, who can go stand on the right elbow?" and so forth. Having finished that, we moved on.

"Okay, if the the entire court is all the knowledge possible about basketball, who do you think knows *everything* about basketball?"

If some wiseass, perhaps Ramona, had said, "Not you," I was screwed. No one did, but Ray was probably thinking it. Someone weakly said, "God."

I said, being we are in a Catholic school and I was a good Catholic boy, "Of course! Good answer. Now, let's take half-court. Whose knowledge is equal to half-court?"

Luddy, who attended practice, yelled out, "Red Auerbach!"

25

"No, no, it's Sister Mary," claimed Mary Catherine.

"Good answer, Luddie and Cat. You're both likely right," I said then had Luddie explain to those noncitizens of Celtic nation who Red Auerbach was. "Okay, how about the paint?"

Teagen whispered, "You and Coach Ray."

"Good answer, Teagen, that's right." Then I stood on a block and asked, "How about this block?"

Ramona said, "The girls eventually."

"Right," I said. (We had agreed on this ahead of time.)

"We can see that there is a lot to learn about basketball, can't we? Okay, now get up and come out here to the foul line."

In the exact center of every foul line in every regulation gym is an indentation, hardly visible, that marks the center of the line. Everyone got a look, some with their noses almost on the floor, and they sat back down. "Everyone saw the dot? Really? Pretty small, right?" Long pause…

"Well, that's how much your *father* knows about basketball! Any questions? Okay, everybody up. On the baseline. Cariocas, up and back."

I would likely live to regret it, but at least Ray cracked up. Sister smiled but shook her head.

Our gym was also the school cafeteria and auditorium. St. Ethel is an all-girls school—saddle shoes, knee sox, plaid skirts, white shirts, gray flannel blazers for all—and we didn't have to share with boys. But we did, after lunch, have to help clean the cafeteria and fold and push all the tables and bench seats under the stage at one end of the room before practice and replace them after. We pray the Lord accepts our sacrifice. Sooner rather than later.

As St. Ethel is an Irish parish school, many of our girls are of Irish descent, some born on the Emerald Isle, others first and second generation. Although we have lost some to the professional and businsess classes' migration to the newer and more exclusive outer suburbs, the Devlins, O'Neils, Rileys, Sheridans, and Kellys remained powers in the parish, still driving south down the Parkway or eastbound across Rte. 3 to St. Ethel for Sunday Mass. If it were the twelfth century, they would have been on horseback and caravans with knights and ladies in waiting, minstrel boys singing, and harlequins dancing alongside the big steeds. I somehow can't get Brave Sir Robin, Patsy, and shrubberies out of my mind whenever this subject comes up.

As two of the nearby parish schools, St. Cyril and Methodius (Polish), and St. Joseph (Slovak) have closed, we have assimilated many of their students, those who chose not to attend any of the other schools in the area, either public or parochial. After a Diocesan Admissions Test, student applicants and their families were interviewed by the monsignor. All knew by then, the spring before I arrived, that St. Ethel would be starting a basketball program. It's just possible that Monsignor was looking for talent, and he did have some financial aid at his disposal. He had a preference for athletic-looking lasses.

As for assimilating, well, not exactly. *Bohonk, Donkey, Dirty Commie, Shanty Irish, Polack, Hunky, and Mick* were still heard in the hallways. And those were the least offensive terms, likely stuff they heard at the kitchen table when Da or Papa or older brothers had knocked back one too many Schaefers or seven and sevens or shots of slivovitz. Reminded me of my father's views on ethnic diversity—he was not a fan. Wasn't big on irony either, given our own family's situation.

Our basketball team reflected this diversity. As follows, our roster, including the name I called each girl:

- Mary Margaret FitzGerald "Fitz"
- Patricia Ann McDonald "Patsy"
- Mary Alice Rafferty "Raffy"
- Teagan Marie McGuire "Teag"
- Mary Catherine Delaney "Cat"
- Stephanie Maria Masaryk "Steph"
- Mary Pat Flanagan "Mary Pat"
- Anna Sophia Plutarski "Greet"
- Mary Grace Dooney "Doons"
- Virginia Rose Norman "Ginna"
- Sarah Jane Johnson "SJ"
- Lizbet Maria Milak "Liz"
- Gertrude Bilotskivic "Trudy"
- Edna Mae Monroe "Eddie"
- Irina Maria Hdowanicz "Reenie"

I wonder if the girls had nicknames for us.

If nothing else this season, we will clearly lead the league in Marys. Preseason practices revealed some promising characteristics: we could rebound, we were fast, we were smart, our shooting would come along, and we were getting good at passing and catching. Four of our starters were tough kids, that would come in handy, as this was more city ball than suburban. Our gym was very small. The foul circles extended to almost half-court, the low ceiling encouraged layups, and room for only three rows of bleachers on one side and the teams benches on the other, or the kitchen/cafeteria, side. Scorer's table between the teams' benches.

The low ceiling was not uncommon in Catholic school gyms. A few miles east of us, in Union City, several generations ago, a lad named Tommy Heinsohn had perfected the "trolley wire jump shot" at a low-ceilinged Catholic high school in Hudson County and rode it to All American at Holy Cross and multiple championships with the Celtics. I learned this from Luddie, our authority on all things Celtic.

Fans also gathered on the stage, where folding chairs were set on risers, to cheer on the blue and gold of the Mighty Gaelettes. I know, a less than adequate nickname. The kids and coaches preferred just Gaels. At the other end of the room, the monsignor had a little two-seat balcony opening from his office, overlooking the court, from which he emerged during games, watching over and surreptitiously blessing his lasses. He didn't disagree when the opposing clergy accused him of sending signals to his young wet-behind-the-ears coach. Oy!

We cut a practice short to give out uniforms, which were used. Used hard. Gimme a break! Royal blue heavy shiny Tshirts with gold letters, piping, and *GAELS* across the chest and little chintzy numbers sewn below the letters. Larger numbers sewn on the back. Shorts were shiny satin with gold stripes down the sides and gold around the waist. And of course, white unis, with blue and gold trim, for home games. Likely first worn in the sixties. I hope we didn't play the previous owners.

Our girls were not spoiled suburban princesses, which I remembered in the nick of time, before saying to Ray, "Do you believe this shit?" I had forgotten how thrilled I had been when I got my first uniform. Didn't matter how crappy it was. It was all mine. These kids didn't even fight over numbers! Any fitting problems could be remedied by the moms; it was a badge of pride that your mom could sew. I let Ray be in charge of distribution as they insisted on trying everything on. Not my department, but it brought back memories.

I had asked that if they bought new sneakers they buy white ones but didn't quite make the cut, so we had multicolored Adidas, Nikes, Pumas, Converse, and some off-brands. I did demand white sox, though. Athletic white sox, not the kind they wore with Mary Janes.

CHAPTER FIVE

Early December 1982

We brought the parents in for socializing and "coffee-ands" one evening after practice before our first game. Mothers provided the "ands." Wow! It was as though they tried to outdo each other. Well, likely they did. Ray and I were a little nervous, being as we were only ten or so years older than the kids, but as Sister Mary pointed out to the parents, "these two really know their stuff and their hearts are in the right place. Your daughters are in good hands."

Ray and I talked about our basketball backgrounds, and they seemed duly impressed. Ray spoke about what the girls were learning and how hard they were working. I spoke briefly about building a winning program that our community could be proud of. Then we took questions. Inevitably came the one about "Why no shooting?"

"Basketball is a game of movement, not shooting," I answered. "If a girl plays all thirty-two minutes and takes ten shots, which is a lot, that takes, let's say, twenty seconds, two per shot. That's way less than 1 percent of the time she is in the game. What about the other 99-plus percent of the game? Those movements can't be random. We feel they have to be learned

31

because they're not natural. The fewer mistakes made in that 99 percent, the better the player, the better our chances to win. Shooting will take care of itself as time goes on."

Big smiles from Ray and Monsignor.

Liam Dooney wanted to know, "Are yez gonna let everyone play like in recreation, or are yez playin' to win?'

"Good question," I said. "If the girls want to play for fun and exercise, then Rec or even the YMCA is the place for them. We are playing to win. We will play as many girls as possible given that objective. And we plan to talk to each girl about her role on the team both for this season and next."

Then Mike McDonald said, "So girls will come to all the practices and put in the same amount of time as all the others but will hardly play at all. Based on your say so, and you've never coached. Is that right?" Pause. "*Coach*? Speakin' for those of us who don't know more than a dot about basketball, like it's rocket science." He said this

with an edge to his voice.

I could see where this was going, as Patsy, his daughter, would not see much floor time unless we had a lot of blowouts.

As I started to respond, the monsignor stepped in and said, with a more dangerous edge in his voice, "Now, Mike, let the coaches do their jobs. They certainly have made clear what this is all about. We'll be playin' to win, to be sure."

And he gave him one of his death stare smiles. I stared at him blankly and said, "Maybe you'd like to discuss this in a more private setting, Mr...what did you say your name was?"

The monsignor turned bright red, turned to me, and boomed, "I said that will be enough, both of you! Michael, you and Maureen go home. William, wait for me in my office."

Other questions were for Sister and Ray, ones which I would have trouble answering. The meeting broke into groups of males and females, storms on the horizon. McDonald went off and got their coats, as well as those of the FitzGeralds, and left. Their daughters were seventh graders not likely to see much action. Two self-important little blowhards who owned car dealerships. I'm sure that they felt this enhanced their status in the parish and entitled them to voice their opinions. I was also sure I hadn't heard the last of them. But damned if I was taking any lip from these two wannabes.

I had chatted earlier with the other fathers and was happy to find that many of them were vets, and they invited me to the (mostly Irish) Legion Hall for a beer, which is where I was heading after my meeting with the Monsignor. In he comes, furrowed brow, blue eyes blazing, staring at me, hands on hips and says with a smile "So it's a fighter you are, is it boyo? No, don't say a word. Just listen. Those two arses will be lookin' over yer shoulder and tryin' to provoke you. If they do, and you lose your temper, you'll be gone. No, no! Not only from coaching, but from teaching here. And likely the diocese. It will be out of my hands. No hearing, no appeal. Gone. The two gobshites are connected. To Paterson. There is nothing else to say. Indicate that you fully ken what I'm tellin' ya by noddin' yer head. Do it again. Yes, that's it. Now get out of my sight, tough guy!"

"Thank you, Monsignor. I'm sorry I embarrassed myself."

A second glance from him to see if I was sassing him and being sarcastic. I knew better. Altar boy caught in the wine chalice.

Later that evening, at the Legion, I was glad I had done military service. Some of the guys had served way back, forty years ago, in World War II and Korea, and some had served in and lost family and friends in Vietnam. All of them were decent and very quick-witted guys, not inclined to talk about their war experiences. A lot of North Jersey Irish ballbusting, much of it directed at me.

- "So tell us, Billy. What was your weapon of choice, a Papermate or a Ticonderoga?" Or
- "Did you ever have incoming on your way to work?" Or
- "Did ya ever walk point? Or pull guard duty?" Or
- "Get the clap in any o'them 'hoorhouses' in DC we heerd about?"
- But also,
- "McGuire, could ya bring my sox into work tomorrow? Left 'em under your bed the other day. There's a good lad" Or
- "Delaney, where do you get the peat yer still burnin' in yer stove? Me mam wants t' get some." Or
- "Wait, now, this is true, lads, heard it from the doc himself. Dooney was so ugly when he was born the doc slapped his ma" Or

33

- "Can't be true. None of us was born in a hospital. I know Dooney sure as shit wasn't, neither was I." Or
- "Rafferty, we'll be over tomorrow after work to show yez how to use yer new water closet. The kids'll love it."

"Listen, Coach, don't worry about those arseholes. They're eedjits. They both got cut from jayvees at Pope Pius years ago by Gallagher and have been trying to make up for it ever since," offered Pat Rafferty. "Dog turds on your brogans, nothing more."

Me: "I'm glad to see, by comin' to this establishment, that yez are all as fulla shyte as I imagined yez t'be. Me da warned me about this place. Spent a few evenin's here, elbows to the bar, he did."

"Are ye not Frankie's kid then?" one of the old-timers asked.

"That I am, Rutherford VFW, he was, and a proud son of Eire, born in County Sligo, where he spent his first decade. Tired of the carbo diet though. Came to the Golden Door, better known as Red Hook, Brooklyn, age ten. Now residing in the Sunshine State."

And all raised a glass to Frankie Edwards, who was stationed in postwar Berlin where he met, courted, and married one Czechoslovakian DP, Evelyn Rudenko, my sainted mother.

"Listen to the young harp, soundin' like he's right off the boat, he does," shouted McGuire, and they all laughed.

Seemed to be the group's take, all good-natured. I decided to take a risk.

* * *

Since you lads have treated me so well, I'm gonna tell yez a story about life in today's army, okay?

When I was at Fort Meade, there were a lot of sports leagues, and I was on a baseball team. The level of play was pretty good, better than high school; some of these guys had been in the service for years and were seasoned baseball vets. Anyway, our team was the Microdots, and we were playing an Air Force Intelligence team called the Overflights. Note now that this is Army and Air Force G-2, or Intelligence for you younger guys, so not a lotta harps on the field a play. Our pitcher was a speedballer named Ken Tredinnick, and the veteran control pitcher Mel Famy on the mound for the Air Force.

We're up first. Three up, three down. While they're at bat, Famy is on the bench sucking down two beers. I know, I was in left field watching him. Their dugout was on the third base side. They get a single and a triple way deep in left center. One zip. Second inning, Famy walks two guys. This never happens. Then he gets frustrated and gives up a double, tie game.

Game goes on. He's polishing one or two beers every inning, walking one or two men every inning until finally he walks in two runs in the top of the ninth. Ken strikes out the side in the bottom of the ninth. Had no fast ball left but a change up and curveball they couldn't touch. Final score: Microdots, 3; Overflights, 1.

Famy has now knocked off two six-packs in nine innings. Now we've played these guys before, and it's almost a written rule: Don't expect Famy to walk anyone. So how to explain this? Our manager, Sgt. Jimmy Elko, always quick to figure things like this out, tells us, "You know, it was the beer that made Mel Famy walk us."Boooooo!" They threw napkins, pretzels, cheetos at me. More boos.

"Come on," I said, "I had you sucked in."

"We'll grant you a conditional, provisional, part-time membership." Dooney shouted "All in favor?"

Silence

"All opposed?"

"Noooo!"

"Motion carried. Meeting adjourned. Well done, lads."

They were all laughing their asses off.

Me too.

* * *

CHAPTER SIX

Mid-December 1982

Sister Mary would be my bench coach, spiritual advisor, team chaplain, and mandatory female on the bus/bench/locker room. Occasionally, she would drop by practice, discreetly making helpful suggestions, or whispering in one of her favorite's ears. Sister Mary was the brains behind our pressure 1-1-3 defense. After practice, some of the girls would challenge her to foul shooting. To no avail. She remained undefeated throughout the season against the kids.

Once a week, she would take all the big girls into a corner and work on balance, stretching, footwork, and slow motion movement, almost like tai chi. The kids thought it was a hoot until Ray came and joined in. When it was apparent she could do all the things they couldn't, their approach got more serious; and by the end of January, they were mastering most of the movements. I could see it in the hallways and in the lunchroom.

After a December practice, we agreed to have a coaches' meeting at Sullivan's, dinner and drinks on Sister Mary, who won the rock, paper, scissors. We ordered Smirnoff rocks, Jim Beam, and a Guinness. Sister and Ray put their heads together and started giggling.

Then she asked me to take a walk to the church and make sure the gym was locked. "Sister, I know I locked the gym," I said indignantly.

"Yes, William," she answered and nodded toward the church as Ray was doubled over laughing.

When I got back, Sister was explaining to Ray that "she never drank alone. Always drank plenty of water. "I saw too many drunken Navajo men in Gallup and Santa Fe and I was always angry at the white men who sold them alcohol. Alcohol wasn't allowed to be sold on the Reservation. It's a terrible thing and it's all over the west, whichever tribe you mention, the drunken Indian. It's the devil's work."

"Okay, wanna tell me what the trip to the church and all the giggling was about, girls?" I asked.

They looked at each other, each started to speak, then both burst into laughter. "We'd rather not say. It's girl stuff," Ray said, trying hard to keep a straight face.

Okay, I thought, *I can play this game*. "Sorry to interrupt. Ramona, you were saying?"

"I saw it with my Russian father and his friends, Sister," said Ray. "He was a terrible drunk. Not often, but mean and nasty when he drank."

"That was when he—," I said.

"Not now," she cut me off, shaking her head.

They looked at each other again then Sister picked up on it, changed the subject, and said, "Come on, Will. You know it's really bothering you to know what we were laughing about, isn't it? We'll tell, but you have to ask us nicely."

"Dream on, Sister." Man, I have always wanted to say that!

* * *

When Mary was a ninth grader, a Dominican nun, Sister Louise from the Mother House in Long Island, New York, spent an academic year at Loretto. She was so taken by Mary's scholastic aptitude and excitement in learning that she inquired of the headmistress and teachers if they thought Mary would be equal to finishing her education with the Dominican sisters at their secondary school in New York City and eventually enter the convent in New York State. She made this approach only after writing to the Mother House and to the Dominican Academy in New York City, making sure there was a place, as well as funds for Mary. Sister was very skilled at this recruiting and travelled every year for the order all over the country searching for girls like Mary.

Having consulted with all the adults involved, both in Santa Fe and New York, Sister Louise was certain her plan was a good one. Enid and Mary were nervous, excited, and heartbroken, recognizing that Mary's life would lead her far away from the Dineh and her family.

Her years at Loretto had done much to reduce but not eradicate the Navajo side of Mary's inner life. They were not easy years, as the goal of the church and the state remained assimilation, but Mary was clever enough to carry off her mission. She was a spiritual girl with deep internal resources that, aided by Enid, saw her through dark times at Loretto She was determined to retain her Navajo identity. When she boarded the train for New York with Sister Louise, she was thirteen. It was May 1931 when she waved goodbye to her mother, not knowing if she would ever see her again.

Sister paused, took a deep breath, and said "My mother sacrificed her life for me, children. I knew then that God would direct me, and I put my life in his hands."

Due to an excessive and unanticipated time overrun on storytelling, the segment of the coaches' meeting allotted to basketball planning was postponed. It wasn't the only time it happened that season, but there were a lot of good stories.

* * *

"It's killin' you not to know what we were laughin' about, isn't it, Willie?" asked Ramona.

"When was that, Ramona? A coupla days ago?" I said. "Guess I forgot. Sorry. See you tomorrow, girls. Good stories. Good meeting." Nice try, girls.

Donald Schlenger

CHAPTER SEVEN

Mid-December 1982

We had two African American girls starting in the backcourt: Edna Mae Monroe and Sarah Jane Johnson, each of whom had more than a little playground hoops in them. They were really neat kids, good-natured, small and quick, like water beetles on a lake's surface, though SJ was by far the most talented and advanced player on the team. Their mothers, Mavis Monroe and LaShonda Johnson, both devout Catholics, were the cooks in the school cafeteria and watched over their daughters like hawks. SJ and Eddie, as they were called, allowed us to play an attacking, chaser defense, one of them hounding the ball, the other looking to intercept a pass or double team the dribbler, while the three bigger girls defended the paint, feet spread, hands up.

The other three starters—Mary Alice Rafferty, Mary Grace Dooney, and Gertrude Bilotskivic—were big. Trudy was tall and athletic, but the other two were hippy and took up a lot ot space and were very hard to "box out." They also set breathtaking picks. Literally. As shy and diffident as Trudy was, Mary Alice (Raffy) and Mary Grace (Doons) laughed easily, were always chirping, but brooked no insolence from the opposition. Mary

41

Grace had older brothers (the widely feared Dooney boys) and had learned some things in the physical aggression sphere not usually available to the fairer sex. Being the only girl and the youngest of the Dooneys, she was fearless. But Trudy was the most talented of the bigs.

Nevertheless, we had to coach aggressiveness into them. Each of the girls must feel they are getting as much coaches' attention as the others and no one is being slighted or favored. At the same time, they learn that they are competing, so we make as much of practice time as competitive as possible. Rebounding is contact, boxing out is contact. But if done in drills where there is a winner and loser, everyone pays more attention. And as always, losers pay a penalty. But we also worked every day on pivoting, getting the ball off the board, and Wes Unselding[1] it out to one of the breaking guards.Backing up Eddie and SJ were Virginia Rose Norman, our little English rose, born in Cornwall, who was lethally quick, but whose vision was suspect. The other backcourt backup was Mary Catherine Delaney. Our offense was pretty much predicated upon the bigs rebounding a miss and whipping the ball out to one of the breaking guards. Two dribbles and a hoop. Ginna, however, would have to pass off as her long vision would fail her in such moments. Anyway, in and around St. Ethel, the four of them were inseperable. They were funny and irrepressible. I'm not sure that they carried news of these relationships to their homes. The ultimate victory would be, of course: sleepover! I was clueless, but Ray did not have a good feeling about that ever happening.

We had two backups for the big girls: Mary Pat Flanagan and Anna Sophia Plutarski. Mary Pat's face was the map of Eire, Anna Sophia's the map of Poland. They, too, were bffs. Big girls not afraid of contact could catch the ball off the backboard and pass it out. We spent a lot of time with the bigs.

One day just before practice was to begin, Dooney, then Rafferty, then all of them, started with "Ramona and Will, sittin' in a tree, K-I-S-S-I-N-G..."

Ray and I had been waiting for this and had agreed we would stamp in out quickly and mercilessly.

---

[1] . Wes Unseld was an iconic NBA center known for his fierce rebounding and his two-hand, over-the-head outlet passes, sometimes as far out as half-court.

"Coach Ray," I asked, "do you think the girls feel like doing some gassers? I thought that's what they were saying? G-A-S-S-E-R-S, right?"

"I am, like, sooooo certain I, like, heard that, Coach. Like, no doubt at all. Oh my god! One hundred percent, fers, here!" said Ray in her best Valley girl voice.

"No! It's not fair. Not fair!" they shouted back to no avail, they knew.

"Well, Gaels," I said, "fair has nothing to do it. On the baseline. It is our job, as adults, to teach you, as *children*, that actions have consequences."

"*We are not children—*"

"Of course you are," I said.

"Only children would do such a childish thing. Whose idea was this anyway?" asked Ray.

"It was my idea," said Dooney.

"No, it was mine," said Rafferty.

"No, it was mine," the rest piped in. As we hoped they would. Ray and I turned our backs and smiled.

"Spartacus," I said to her.

"What?" she answered.

Whistle shrills...Ran till gassed. We felt like we were successful in not only communicating our objectives, but in helping them connect actions with consequences, knowledge necessary for healthy adulthoods. A little team unity building as well. Against their mean coaches.

"Gee, Coach," Ray said, "waddaya think will happen the next time we hear that?"

"Oooh, Coach." I shivered. "I'm too frightened, truly I am, to even think about it."

Ray blew the whistle. "Rebound and outlet drill, both ends. *Move it!*"

CHAPTER EIGHT

December 19, 1982

After Mass at St. Ethel, I took Mama over to Wallington for a huge Polish breakfast at Wilczinski's. There's a whole bunch of Polish, Slovak, and Hungarian restaurants, beer and dance halls, nightclubs, groceries, and delis in Wallington and the little towns around it. I had friends growing up in Rutherford whose families shopped there religiously. I took Mama there for a treat once in a while. After we sat and got our food, she asked, "How is Ramona doing wit deh coaching, Vill? She is good coacher?"

"She's doin' great," I said. "Mama. Really. She likes it and the kids like her. And she's good at it."

"Eet vas good idea you asked her, yes, Vill?" she asked with a smile. Meaning "I made you answer the phone, didn't I, Will?"

I smiled back. "Sure. It's goin' great."

Back home, we did some cleaning up, and I told her I'd be gone for a few hours. I got on Rte. 3 Eastbound for Manhattan. One of my two best high school friends had been Tony Andolini. His father owned a great restaurant on the river, Jersey side, which is where I was headed. Tony was the best pitcher I ever saw. I used to tell guys that the School for the Blind would bring a bus full of their folks to our games to "hear" him pitch. Anyway, I was the left fielder, and we had a really good team when we were seniors. We won the county championship. Okay, enough of that.

As I had skated through math in high school up through trig, I had gotten Tony through Algebra II and helped him prep him for the SATs. Tony's father didn't trust the professional tutors, go figure, and had always taken a shine to me, something my own father wasn't that interested in or capable of. He slipped me a twenty every coupla weeks behind Tony's back. I could talk to Mr. A and run ideas past him, like joining the army at age eighteen. He told me many times, "Billy, if there's evah, *evah*, anything you need, you come see me."

I always told him it was like a scene from *The Godfather*, and he got a kick out of that. Not so much when I called him godfather. Only once, to be sure.

Tony and I had kept in touch on and off, not so much in the past year. He had gone to Fairleigh Dickinson University in Teaneck on a DI ride, studying accounting, and had signed with the Braves right after graduation, first Andolini to climb that mountain. Against all odds, he had gotten his degree. On time, well, almost. What the hell, the odds in baseball were against him as well, but play out the baseball dream while you can, right? He had lived on campus, away from Mama, and had grown up a lot during those years. Now he spent the summer riding buses all over the South. Any of the guys on our team at Rutherford High would have traded lives with him in a heartbeat.

So here I am, heading over to Weehawken, down to the bottom of the cliffs to this really cool and kind of swanky, for the likes of me anyway, restaurant on the river. The Hudson River. With a to-die-for view of Manhattan. Mr. Andolini had started there as a kid, bussing tables, and working whenever they needed him. He saved every penny, taking the subway to the ferry and the ferry to Hoboken every day and returning to the Village where he lived with his large family, every night. And now he owned it. And a big house on Ridge Road in Rutherford. I had called and asked if I could stop by.

He was a stocky man, full head of salt-and-pepper hair, and big mustache. He moved gracefully, like he had been born into the restaurant life, first as a servant, now as the boss. Gracious and attentive at all times.

"Billy, figlio mio, com' estare?"

Will: "I'm fine, Mr. A. How's the family?"

Andolini: "Everybody is good. Maria had twins, how'bout that? And Ant'ny was askin' for you when he was home for Thanksgiving, only for a day though. He told me you're teaching and coaching at St. Ethel, right? You liking it? You doing okay?"

Will: "Oh, man, I'm sorry I missed him. What's he doing now? Is he gonna give the dream another year?"

Andolini: "I think yes, if they let him start the season at Charlotte. He's got a girl. They live in Charlotte. Both in grad school taking classes to be a CPA. How 'bout my Ant'ny? All 'cause you helped him, Billy!"

Will: "Ah, he woulda got there, Mr. A. He's a smart guy, like his papa. I like the job fine, maybe not forever, but it's okay for now. I like the coaching better than the teaching."

Andolini: "Ah, Billy, you were such a wonderful basketball player. Even Mrs. Andolini used to love to come to the games. All County, right? And then you went into the army? Stunad!"

Will: "No, no, sorry, Mr. A, I have to beg to disagree, no disrespect. The army was good for me, it opened up the world. I saw the world, Mr. A, I mean the whole world, on Uncle Sam's dime, never had a shot fired at me. Anyway, I came to collect on that favor."

Andolini: "Hey, what'd I tell you? Anything, any time!"Will: "Well, this is really a tough one. How about an 8:00 reservation for two on New Year's Eve?"

His face fell, and he looked heartbroken.

Andolini: "Ah, Billy, if you had asked anything else." Pause. "Oh, you shoulda seen your face! Please tell me it's that beautiful girl, Ramona."

I nodded and he grinned from ear to ear.

I forgot to mention Mr. A was a major league ballbuster.

I was golden for the big night. Fist in air! Yess!

Of course, I hadn't yet figured how to approach the big challenge.

And I was scared already. Ramona!

CHAPTER NINE

I asked that they respect each other: no mocking, making fun, bullying, accept the responsibility for their mistakes, and give their teammates credit for good things they did. Never show up a teammate who has made a mistake; I will take you out of the game immediately. I never said anything about giving 110%, never called them ladies, both of which I thought were insulting and patronizing. They started finding each other at lunchtime and soon claimed their own lunch table, likely causing bad feelings among their former lunch mates. But eventually, I feared race or the tribal nature of their lives would rear their ugly heads in ways we could not yet know. It was indeed a bubble we lived in. I knew then it was idealistic to aim for this, but as a player, I had felt those things on the good, not necessarily winning, teams I had played on, and it always started with the coach. As Sister once told me, "It's not what's taught, William. It's what's caught."

We had worked on offense before the first game, and ironically, it was a watered-down variation of the offense coach Phil Rogers had used at Indiana State when Larry played there. It was called Rover, and we set up with four in a box or a diamond with the "rover" going from side to side, wherever she could get open, using screens, changing direction, stopping, and going. SJ was rover 1, Trudy was rover 2. As the season went along, we tinkered and adjusted, or used it as a misdirection, but it was about timing and setting picks, which Raffy and Doons actually enjoyed.

* * *

49

About Phil Rogers: In the spring of 1979, he and the Michigan State coach, Jud Heathcoate, were in demand on the coaching clinic circuit, which follows the NCAA Championship. Indiana State/Bird had lost to Michigan State/Magic in the NCAA finals. Phil Rogers was appearing at a coaching clinic at the Hilton on Rte. 17. My JV teammates friends Jake Walker, Dominic Sinopoli, and I, just after our own basketball season had ended, had a way in; Dom's mother's cousin's whoever was the banquet manager. So we listened to the coaches share their wisdom. I took some notes when Bob Knight and Dean Smith spoke; they had thought it all out so clearly and broken it all down so well and explained how to teach it with our players, not that I was coaching at that point. Thinking about it, maybe. It was hard for me, like many "terminal players," to accept there would be no more hoops.

After the conference, we all went to the bar upstairs for a beer and listened to all the coaches tell stories and to BS. I engaged a suspicous Coach Brown, a Jersey guy who was then coach of Atlanta in the NBA and later to be coach of the Knicks, but he lightened up when I told him my uncle had played played baseball for Rutherford against Fairlawn High when he coached baseball there. Then he went into basketball mode and told Jake, Dominic, and me some great stories.

Meanwhile, one of Phil Rogers's assistants kept throwing back the Cuervos and hustling one of the cleavages, scantily clad in a basketball official's tank top, tending bar. As he got more suggestive and nasty, some of the guys, John Thompson and Jim Boeheim, encouraged him to call it a night and took him to his room. Hard to argue with Big John, and it looked like the assistant coach wasn't ready to hang with the big boys. Phil Rogers took some ribbing for it. Ballbusting was the lingua franca for NCAA basketball coaches. Have to up my game if I was planning to move in that direction. I mean, I was competitive in the local VFW/Legion league, but not with these guys. Then, to top it off, the champ took the floor.

Jim Valvano, who had been very successful at Iona College, just outside of New York City, and was destined to win a national championship at North Carolina State in 1983, took center stage. He was better than a standup comic, and as the evening wore on, I was amazed at how bright and quick and funny these big-time guys were. "Jimmy V" held court at the bar and then the gathering broke in smaller groups in which the three of us, trying to pass as grad assistants trying to get an assistant's position, would begin to stand out, called it a night. But I was completely starstruck.

* * *

CHAPTER TEN

We had decided not to press, but we had little trouble handling pressure. No one would likely outrebound us. Our girls, those who weren't necessarily highly skilled, were brave. As the weeks passed and they became accustomed to contact, they stepped in rather than back. When they started boxing each other out in the hallways, however, the sisters drew the line and asked if they could "have a word." Some serious sprinting cut the roughhousing short. When I played, these were called "suicides," but realities in the world had changed their name to gassers or just sprints.

We practiced every nongame day from 3:30 till 5:00. School ended at 2:45. They had to be on the floor at 3:25. We practiced coming out of the locker room to music, pregame drills, jump balls, bench behavior, entering and leaving a game, time-outs. Everything. "*How to Act Like a Basketball Team.*" Spent a lot of time on inbounds plays, not that much time on offense. But we did work on setting screens, coming off screens, etc. We could use the rover as a one-size-fits-all. Not having to teach "plays" meant we could teach them how to play basketball. Pass down, screen across; pass across, screen down. How to come off a screen. And those led to counters. Having two coaches allowed us the luxury of avoiding kids standing in lines and, most importantly, maximizing repetitions and inducing muscle memory. The more athletic kids picked up skills that had seemed out of reach in mid-November.

51

If the girls had permission in writing from home, they could stay an extra half-hour and work on individual skills. A lot of them did, as this gave them individual attention from either Ray or me. Trudy especially liked to stay with Ray, Dooney and Rafferty with me. Go figure. We normally had games on Tuesday and Friday afternoons beginning at 4:00. For away games, I had a CDL and drove the bus: two coaches, fifteen players, and a "staff" of three, including our scorekeeper, a girl named Marcy O'Bannion, a name that surely deserved "winsome lass" in front of it. A name for 1950s brilliantly colored Technicolor westerns starring Rory Calhoun or Jeff Chandler, which my father absorbed each afternoon on Channel 9 or 11, local TV stations in New York on his brand-new Emerson color TV.

We were normally home by 6:30, as most of our opponents were located within forty-five minutes, and between us, Sister Mary and I knew all the shortcuts. The kids played music or sang on the way there and Stephanie Masaryk, she of the golden voice, always sang "Ave Maria" before we got off the bus. The game's outcome governed behavior on the way back. If I never hear "The Unicorn Song," "Hit Me With Your Best Shot," or any Queen song again, I'll be just fine. Or that TV theme song "Believe It or Not, I'm Walkin' on Air." All songs accompanied by loud altos and sopranos.

Our opponents were St. Bridget, Our Lady of the Harbor, St. Henrietta, St. Elizabeth, St. Hyacinth, Blessed Kateri, St. Ann, St. Cecelia, Mother Seton, Our Lady of Charity, and St. Ursula. We were scheduled for nineteen games, including a Christmas Tournament "downa shore." There might be a tournament at season's end.

CHAPTER ELEVEN

December 12, 1982

Our first game was at St. Bridget's, a tiny suburban school in the "better," more recently developed part of the county, north up the Rte. 17, with a regulation-sized gym. I was nervous. All the girls were nervous and didn't settle down until the middle of the second quarter when we were down by 7, playing your basic girls' basketball 2-3 zone. I called time-out, and we began playing our 1-1-3 scramble, which kind of ended the game, shutting down Bridget's offense. We had been happy with our first nine, and our confidence was rewarded in the Bridget's game, which we won by 17, and everyone got to play.

I had been afraid that our attacking defense was made for our postage-stamp-sized home court, but our bench helped, and Ginna and Cat got a lot of playing time, as SJ and Eddie got gassed early. Winning a first game blowout was great, but it also portended doom in a coach's mind; it could be all downhill from here. Like I knew what I was talking about; I'd coached one game.

St. Ethel, 41
St. Bridget, 24
Won, 1; Lost, 0

We had two fast kids and three big kids. All of them "could play." Sooner or later, we would meet a team with five big *and* fast kids. The girls, of course, acted as though we had won the NCAA. I practically had to beat them to get them through the shake hands line, but I loved the way, even in practice, their emotions were almost always on display, out there front and center, even when they thought they were being cool, like the boys. They got as excited for each other as they did for themselves and silly and girly just to piss me off. But I loved it, and they knew it.

After they dressed (too modest yet for showers, though Ray had nagged them about it), I knocked on the locker room door and was given permission to enter. They were still excited and started chanting, "We are Ethel! We are Ethel!"

I quieted them down and said, "Nice comeback tonight, girls. You showed some grit."

Anna, whose family was a more recent addition to our parish and to our shores, asked, "What does that mean? We 'showed some greet.' What is this 'greet'?"

"Oh, man, everyone knows what grit is, Anna. Get with the program!" This from Rafferty.

"I don't know what it means either!" piped up Mary Pat, sticking up for her buddy.

All of them were buzzing now.

I yelled, "Knock it off. All of you. Right now!"

Big dramatic eye-rolling from Patsy and Fitz. Sister caught it, glared at them, and asked, "Did you two want to contribute something?" Long pause. "Well? I didn't think so!"

Kind of took Raffy off the hook, but she wasn't about to escape a consequence. I said, "Everyone on the bus. Now! Rafferty, stay here with me!"

As the girls went out, I just tilted my head and gazed at Raffy, saying nothing. Finally, she said, "Okay, I'm sorry. I shouldn't have said it that way."

"Don't tell *me* you're sorry. And explain to Anna what 'greet' is. And apologize to your teammates."

A tiny almost smile and she said, "Got it, Coach."

Ray would have run her till she puked.

On the bus, Rafferty stood up and explained to Sophia, soon to be known to all as "Greet," "Grit is toughness, Anna, and I'm sorry for makin' fun. I apologize to yez all. Won't happen again." And she sat down.

As she got off the bus at Ethel, I pulled her over and whispered, "Good job there, lady. Well done." She turned crimson.

When we got back to St. Ethel, we had a surprise ready for the girls and whatever family members came along…a lot of secret planning had gone into this. Mavis and LaShonda had made us a soul food dinner, and this was the maiden postgame team meal, win or lose. The mothers and fathers had divided up the schedule so that many of the away games were covered, and we looked forward to some serious food. Now ah mean! Grits, cornbread, ribs, fried chicken, collards and bacon, sweet tea, biscuits, and butter beans. Both mothers were from down around Charleston where food and eatin' are serious bidness. Not every girl sampled every item, but they managed not to embarrass anyone or themselves. None of the white kids had ever heard of soul food, let alone seen or tasted it. Thankfully, Mavis and LaShonda had the good judgment to leave chit'lins off the menu.

But even the monsignor, his eye always out for a good low-cost meal, was impressed, and he revealed he knew all about soul food since he had grown up in Southern Ireland. South Bronx, maybe. He caught my eye and motioned me over and reminded me we had the "development" game coming up next month and what a delight it would be if five Irish girls were on the floor when the game began.

I asked him, while I had the chance, if we could do anything about Ginna's eyesight problems. I think she was nearsighted, but it might be worse. If I spoke to her parents, Nick and Celia Norman, and I could finesse them into accepting some help, would he back my play. "You go ahead and bring them in, Billy boy. It'll be grand. Don't worry." Like he already knew about it. What was I missing?

CHAPTER TWELVE

December 22, 1982

The next day, I called the Normans' house and asked if they could both come in and "have a word" after Wedneday's practice, which concluded with Rafferty entertaining us with running her gassers from yesterday. The "clericalese" is rubbing off on me.

Nick is a handyman, no machine he couldn't repair or rebuild; Cecelia a seamstress. Salt of the earth Cornish. They were both small, wiry, fair-haired, blue-eyed, attractive people. They had two other kids who lived with an aunt in the Pennsylvania countryside. But for Nick and Cecilia, the good-paying jobs were in North Jersey. They both did a lot of work for St. Ethel and got a big break on tuition.

Fearing the worst, I'm sure, they hesitantly came into the gym while Ginna waited outside. I got us coffees and we sat down, three of us nervous. They must have been frightened out of their minds. "You have a wonderful daughter, folks. Everyone on our team loves Ginna. Let's set that straight first."

"Oh, thank God. She does love the basketball. Talks about it all day long. We're football people ourselves, I mean soccer. Nick was a wonderful striker for the Cornwall team, weren't you, dear?" Nick turned crimson and mumbled something.

I said, "She is a lovely girl and an important member of our team. Here is my problem, and I'm not sure I know how to say this. She has an eyesight problem. I'm not sure what causes it, don't know if you have noticed it at home, because it doesn't seem to affect her reading or her schoolwork. She can't see from one end of the court from the other. Nearsighted maybe? Waddaya think?"

Nick looked across at his wife, his face a question mark. She said, "Yes, Coach, it's come on in the last year, but like you said, it didn't seem to bother her."

Nick asked, "Any ideas?"

"Would you consider an eye exam? Here at the school? For all the girls on the team, I mean. Would that be all right? The school will cover the cost." Sparing them having to ask, "How much?" I was tap-dancing around this and sensed that Cecelia realized it.

They both nodded their heads. Nick asked, "When?"

"Tomorrow after morning prayer. I'll keep an eye on her. She'd probably be mortified if you came in with her. They're at the age now, right? How about if I speak to the doc when he's done and call you right away, okay? You'll be home?"

"That's very kind of you, Coach. Yes, I'll be home."

As we were walking out, I asked them where they were from in Cornwall. "Nick is from Penzance, and I'm from a little village up in the hills. It was a tin mining village once." Pleased that I had asked.

"I'd really love to go there someday. Do you know any places around here that make good pasties? My aunt Mildred used to make them for us when we were kids."

"Now don't you be silly, Coach. I make better pasties than any shop in New Jersey. I'll be making a batch next week and will send some in with Ginna." Then she stepped back as Nick walked ahead. "And thanks for this, Bill." (Only one at Ethel who's called me Bill.) "Nick is a proud man."

Yesss! Silver lining strikes early. Thank you, Monsignor. He came up with the plan and used his long reach to gather in one of his former players at St. Peter's Prep, who he had also baptized and confirmed, and who was now an opthamologist and taught his boyo how things get done. Grand, indeed. And boyo, who felt he had been walking a tightrope, was greatly relieved.

* * *

On a beautiful spring day in May 1926, twelve-year-old Terrence McEntee left his family's flat on West 44th St., turned right, then right again on 9th Avenue, and headed for Sacred Heart of Jesus School for Boys on West 52nd St. He was a bright boy, big for his age, and his mother, Anne, kept a tight rein on him for good reason. She was the widow of Patsy McEntee, a known and feared underboss of Owney Madden, who had ridden the advent of Prohibition in 1918 to become the crime boss of midtown Manhattan's west side, known as Hell's Kitchen. One night, on a trip north of the border, Patsy's truck, loaded with the "finest" Canadian whiskey, was met by a squad of Treasury agent, whose objective was not the exchange of pleasantries. All of Owney's men were killed. Such were the risks of the trade. Owney had promised Patsy he would take care of Anne and her four children, Terrence being the oldest. Though not a religious man, Madden had stood for them at their wedding and for Terrence at his baptism. Say what you will, Owney was a man of his word.

Terrence excelled at Latin and Mathematics and was an excellent athlete at Sacred Heart. The older boys learned not to single him out as one of "Owney's Lot" or risk a word from one of Terrence's "sponsors." Otherwise, he was well-mannered and respectful to the priests and brothers and well-liked by his classmates. He was in the sixth grade and knew all the merchants and tradesmen up and down the avenues, and the ladies found him to be a darlin' lad, especially upon learning he was Mr. Madden's "nephew." He ran errands for his friends along his routes and got to see a side of life his mam had hoped to shield him from. Still, he kept to the straight and narrow. Almost. Once, on that aforementioned spring day, while running some numbers for "Fish" Dailey, a bartender on Eighth Avenue, on his way home from school, he was stopped by some street punks a year or two older and bigger than he was. "You'll be givin' us your money, sissy schoolboy."

"And ye'll be suckin' each others' dicks first is what I'm thinkin'," he countered and charged fearlessly into them, fists flying.

Receivin' a bit more than he dished out, to his good fortune, a local cop put an end to it. The punks never got Fish's money, the cop drank for free for a year at Owney's, then quit the force to work security for him. The punks got jobs for Owney in distant Staten Island and were never seen again. Owney and Ann boxed Terrence around a bit, but each secretly burst with pride at his courage. And he continued his errands unimpeded, especially those for the ladies.

With his final year at Sacred Heart nearing completion, the headmaster, Father Ed Gallagher, was approached by Monsignor Francis Xavier Costello of the Regis School, on the other side of Central Park, and mentioned they had a spot for a fine lad like Terrence in their seven through twelve secondary school. He didn't have to mention a generous donation from Mr. Madden to help with the completion of the school's new gymnasium. Terrence commenced his studies at the Regis School for Boys in September, 1926. He would spend the rest of his life as a student, acolyte, seminarian, and ordained priest in the Jesuit order, fulfilling his mother's most fervent dreams. God rest her soul.

CHAPTER THIRTEEN

December 23, 1982

Our second game, and home opener, was the next day, Thursday. It the last one before Christmas vacation, against Our Lady of the Harbor, from somewhere in Hudson County, on the river. Ginna had just had her eye exam, so no glasses yet to correct her shortsightedness. But we let her play anyway with parental consent. I'm guessing two hours of whining was all they could bear.

Harbor was pretty good, but we had a good game on our home court whose small dimensions would, hopefully, always give us an advantage. The Harbor coach, Suzanne Something, was a squat, sour-faced woman who reminded me of my freshman English teacher, Mrs. Minotti. She complained the whole game about the gym, as though the officials could change it. Nice example you're setting, Suzanne. Trudy had a good game, as did Eddie. Good to see that. Mighta been a little home cookin'. Not as good as Mavis's and LaShonda's though.

St. Ethel, 33
Our Lady of the Harbor, 31
Won, 2; Lost, 0

Dinner that night was FitzGerald/McDonald, who glared at me whenever possible. Sister asked me later, "What's their problem?"

"They think their darlings should have more playing time," I said.

"Of course they do, William. That's their job. Pay them no mind," she said.

They had ordered takeout from our go-to pizza place, Mikey's, over in Hasbrouck Heights but added pasta and calzones to the menu. All the kids, Luddie and her staff included, did secret Santa and got Sister Mary, Ray, and I each a little Christmas gift. It was sweet and we were delighted. Tomorrow was a half-day, and I told them we would practice then let them talk me out of it. I had planned to give in, to see if they would argue; and darn it, they *knew* I would. How could they know that? How is it that girls know about boys so much earlier in life than boys know about girls? That is, if they ever did? If there was a course on this in grad school, I'm all over it. So I didn't bring them in until the 27 and 28, as our games at the beach were on the 29 and 30.

CHAPTER FOURTEEN

December 24–26, 1982

It was nice to have a break as we had been at it since mid-November. I had gotten in touch with some guys from college, proposed a field trip, and we spent a few days in Boston where two of our buddies, brothers Luke and Ben Nelson, were in law school at Boston College and let us crash in their empty apartment. They had gone home to North Carolina for the break. We left early morning Christmas Eve. That night, during a light snowfall, we snuck into Fenway Park with balls, gloves, and bats; played a little ball; and ran around the bases, sliding safely into home, yelling, "Boston sucks!" at the top of our lungs until we got chased. Top ten in *best night ever!* We toured the town and Combat Zone, rode the T, caught a Celtics game on Christmas Day at the Boston Garden, and had a great all-around break.

While we were at the Garden, I asked a Celtic official to give an envelope to Larry and told him it was from my little sister, who idolized him. Who knows, maybe it will work. I loved Boston, a great place to be Irish (even half-Irish), but truth was I missed Mama, Sister Mary, and most of all, Ray. My parents had moved to Florida…upstate, inland, cattle country. So there was no going home for Christmas.

Who the hell does that? But thank God, they left me their '76 Chevy Malibu, metal flake, midnight blue, big sound system with cassette deck, passed anything but a gas station. But I had gotten presents for my brother's kids, and I would visit them when I got back to Jersey.

December 27, 1982

Early in the morning, I called Ray from Boston, and we made a date to get together that night at Mama's then called Sister Mary to join us in some storytelling and spirits. While I was in Boston, the snow had piled up a bit, so Ray and I went over and got Sister. After a few rounds, the stories started. Mama had run away from home in upstate New York and gone to live in Jersey and clean the homes of the rich on Fifth Avenue in Manhattan. She had also lived in Persia for a while with her grandfather. Ray mostly whined and complained about her rich, spoiled, and entitled students up in northern Bergen County and how hard college basketball had been.

* * *

Just gonna tell a story, okay? My father's family was from Sligo, a poor part of Ireland, and they moved to Brooklyn when he was ten. He grew up there in Red Hook. He went into the army in 1943, and he was assigned to APO, that's Armed Services mail, stationed in London. After the Allies took Berlin in the spring of 1945, he got shipped there, to Berlin. He met my mother, Evelyn Rudenko, a displaced person from Pilsen, in what's now Czechoslovakia, got her out of the camps by pulling some strings, and they got married. My mother never talked about her life before or her family in the old country. I was just a kid, never thought to ask.

When they got home in 1946, he got a job in the Rutherford Post Office, and she studied English. She eventually worked for the Rutherford School System as a bookkeeper, loved the United States, really. They had three kids. I was the youngest, born in 1958. We lived around the corner from the Voyteks, Ray's family, in a two-family house. Our mothers were friends. My parents were kind of worn out by the time I was coming up. I can't blame them. Anyway, when I got out of the army in '78, he got himself transferred to central Florida. He left me his car and haven't seen them since. Phone calls back and forth with my mom, but not much else.

My brother, Patrick, enlisted in the army out of high school in '64 and then got bounced with bad eyesight. He was heartbroken; he really wanted to serve his country. But the next few years, Vietnam really exploded, so maybe he lucked out. He's twelve years old'rn me.

Anyway, he went into the city and started at an ad agency. He worked his way up and took art and college courses at Parsons. I think he's an art director at BBD&O, a big ad agency in New York. Anyway, now he's a big deal there. He's got two kids and lives in Woodridge, just a few miles north of here. I'm really proud of him.

My sister, Cecelia—I still call her Cissy—was kinda wild. She got right into the scene when she was still in high school, went right into the Village and the drugs and the music—Doors, Airplane, Cream, Janis, all that and more. She graduated in 1970, that's like the middle of the drug scene when things got crazy ground zero year, man. She sang in a band like Jefferson Airplane, had the whole Grace Slack thing goin', but the band wasn't that good. They got some play in clubs in the East Village, but no record contract. They all hung out in the East Village, living the dream, but they weren't goin' anywhere.

She got out before it got really crazy, came home, got clean and sober, went to college at Newark Rutgers, lived home, got a degree in business, now she's works for Atlantic Records in New York. I think some bad shit—sorry—happened to her, but she'd never talk about it. I love her. She was always lookin' out for me. We talk every week or so on the phone. She's engaged to some designer guy, and they live in an apartment in Soho. Long way from LSD and whatever else they were into back then. I think maybe heroin, too.

* * *

Mama added her own story, maybe it was true: "I leev in Persia vhen I vas young girl. My grandpa Stephan come to Pilsen, in Czechoslovakia, vhere ve lived. I teenk vas mebbe Austria den. He told my mozzer and fazzer dey had to come to Persia to help veet his store. He vas trader on Silk Road. Eet vas ancient trade route to China and India, vhere deh long camel caravans carried goods back and forss from Europe to zeh East. Ve all lived in von room, no electreecity, no plumbing. So bad! Grandpa Stephan, *everyone zere call heem Smutsy, had a leettle suk, or shop, vhere he traded and sold tings like kerosene, contraband Breetish and Turkish cigarettes, Etiopian coffee, olive oil, salt, Scotch veeskey, sheepskins, hashish, money, at a little crossroads and oasis.*

Eet vas tricky business, and dere vas loud yelling and bargaining in many languages veet guys who carried veapons and looked like they'd slit your sroat for a shekel or ruble. As de voices got louder, I vas always afraid dey vould start fighting. And alvays zuh dogs vould come and start barking, adding to zeh noice. Very scary for leetle girl like me. Vhen zeh dealing vas feenished and both sides satisfied, zeh mens vould mount zeir camels or mules or horses and zeh caravan vould head out, but ze dogs vould keep on barking for long time. So I alvays tell dese childrens, you know, vhen day complaining about zumzing, "You know, zeh dogs bark, but zeh caravan moves on."

* * *

Sister Mary picked up her narrative: I was mostly in a trance my first few weeks in Manhattan. I boarded and was a student at the Dominican Academy on the east side of Central Park in the most beautiful part of New York. But I was dreadfully homesick. I found that there were other Indian girls there, some Navajo, but mostly from other nations—Commanche, Oglala, Cherokee—and we made fast friends. We had to speak English because we didn't know each other's languages, but some of us knew Spanish. We ate and studied together, but best of all, they knew how to play rezball! I was there until 1936 and then on to the convent for two more years. I think it's time to call it a night, children. What do you think, Maria?

"Ees time, Sister. I am sleepy."

* * *

At this, Ray and I walked Sister back to the convent. "We will have to hear some more details about rezball, Sister."

"Yes, I think we can use some of the principles," she said.

We walked, she glided. After she went in, Ray pulled out a joint and started to spark it up. "Not here!" I yelped.

"Oh, Willie, you didn't used to be such a Goody Two-shoes!" She laughed and ran away. I chased her down, fake tackled her into a snowbank, and gave her a snow facial. Thought about a noogie, thought about a kiss, used my better judgement. For a moment, we were seventeen again. It was joyous. When we got up, we stood very close together, but we both chickened out. I said to her, "Come on in, and I'll make you a cup of coffee for the road, waddaya say, Ramonushka? Mama'll already be upstairs asleep."

"I don't know, William. Can I trust you to be a gentleman?" the newly demure Ray asked demurely.

"I'm thinking there's no right answer, so I'll say, 'Let's see what happens.'" I gave it a shot.

"You done good, Snooky," she said. "Milk and lots of sugar."

When we got to Mama's, I put a tea kettle on to make some instant coffee, keeping busy and looking everywhere but at Ray. Trying to sound cool and nonchalant, I asked her if she were doing anything New Year's Eve. I was really nervous, not sure this was a good idea, and knew she knew it. Damn, she always knew it.

"And you're asking me this why?" she asked.

"Uh, I, uh…," I said, letting me swing for a few seconds. Saved by the screaming tea kettle, I got up and made our coffees, got out the milk and sugars, brought them to the table, and sat down.

"I was planning on going to a party in the city with friends," she said. Pause. "Why? What about you?" Another pause. "Got a date?"

This is Ramona at her world-class best, breaking my balls. I almost joined the fun and said, "Why, yes, I met somebody. I don't think you know her." But I choked and blurted out, "I know it's late, but how about dinner?"

"Yeah, it *is* late." Pause. "Dinner?" Pause. "You mean with you?"

Choking back a sarcastic response, I said, "Well, yeah, who'd you think? Y'know, Mickey D's or Rutt's or somethin' like that? Then you can go to your party."

"Excellent plan, William. If you'll take me to the party. In the Big City. You know your way around the city, don't you?"

Really rubbing it in now. "Well, I used to. As long as it's in Manhattan. What type of cuisine would suit your fancy?"

"Surprise me."

"Pick you up at seven. Dress nice. I'm wearing a suit."

"Oh my."

"Indeed."

"Jeez, William, it took you long enough!"

"And you made it so much easier for me." Maybe most nervous I've ever been.

We both burst out laughing, mostly with relief. It seemed like six years had melted away. But only for a moment. We had been as close as two children, then teenagers, could be for like fourteen years. Now we were afraid of each other. Afraid of getting ripped to pieces like we both had been six years ago. My hands weren't clean in that incident either. At some point, I hoped we could face it, deal with it, and get back together where I felt we belonged.

I walked her out to her shiny little red Honda coupe and said, "Now drive carefully, honey."

December 28–29, 1982

We boarded the bus for Belmar in the morning for our 2:00 game. As a big surprise, Ray showed up and jumped on the bus, saying she "might" come to the game. The Gaels cheered. The weather was perfect, sunny in the low fifties, and hopefully we'd get some beach or boardwalk time. We were scheduled to play St. Lucie's from down in the south Jersey pines. I know, right? Ethel vs. Lucie. The second game would be the host school, powerful St. Rose of Belmar vs. St. Rose of Phillipsburg in western Jersey. Some humor in the diocese here. Of course, when a team invites you to its tournament, it usually means they think they can whip you.

We did have a surprise when we walked into the big gym at St. Rose of Belmar High School. As we crossed the gym floor, a tall, blond, young woman ran down the bleachers shouting, "Ray! Ray!"

Ray turned and yelled back, "Emma! What are you doing here?" as she and the tall blonde hugged at mid court.

"Coach, this is my friend Emma Walker from Bloom. She was All American Division II LaCrosse. Graduated last year. I knew she lived somewhere around here. Emma, this is Will Edwards. He's the coach. We were friends in high school."

"Nice to meet you, Emma," I said.

"My pleasure, Will. Heard a lot about you." She smiled. "I'm actually here to see my niece play for St. Lucie, so I'll have to root against you guys."

"Hey, listen, old friend," I said to Ray, "why don't you and Emma catch up and I'll take care of pregame."

Of course, in the pregame locker room, all they wanted to know was "Was that girl with Coach Ray the actress 'what's her name'?" asked Dooney.

"She looks like a movie stah," said Trudy.

"No, I don't know," I said sharply "She's coach's friend from college. Now get your mind on what we came here for. Think you can do that?"

Turns out they could. We didn't have much trouble with St. Lucie, won by eighteen, good game for the second unit bigs, and even the shockers (as in "shock troops," the seventh graders at the end of the bench) played a full quarter. The starters were good about cheering for the subs when they scored or made a good play.

St. Ethel, 46
St. Lucy, 28
Won, 3; Lost, 0

The girls got dressed, and we headed home, having stopped at Point Pleasant on the way to Belmar. They ran around on the mostly empty boardwalk, and some ventured onto the beach. I think some of them had never seen the ocean, but I didn't press.

Not the Irish kids, as we were near that part of the shore known as the "Irish Riviera." All in all, it was a good day. Ray's presence made it better.

So did the eastern European feast awaiting us back at St. Ethel, prepared by our Polish and Slovak mothers: Mary Masaryk, Frances Plutarski, Janet Hdowanicz, Betty Milak, and Clara Bilotskivic. Pirogies, kielbasy, paprikash, potato pancakes, Golabki, Kolachi, Paczki. Again, some hesistancy with the cuisine, which most of the girls had never seen or tasted. Mothers clucking around making sure no kid said, "Ill, that looks disgusting!" Though Patsy and Fitz made some faces. Clearly, Mikey's was the first choice of the former Mighty Gaelettes, now the Gaels.

Our next game was the championship round against St. Rose of Belmar. They were a perennial shore powerhouse program, which fed the mighty St. Rose of Belmar Catholic High School Girls Basketball. We "got beat like a mule," as my Czechoslovakian mother would say. Wow! We were never in it and lost by 30. Five big *and* fast girls on the court at all times.

In the four games we had played, I saw parents filming, or I guess taping, the action. I'm surprised our two little leprechauns weren't taping, but if their girls were playing next year, they likely would be. The fact that I wasn't interested would be a nail in my coffin when they complained about my poor performance to whomever there was at the diocese to receive such vital information. Let's be honest here, taping middle school games? Really? If your kid has punched a ticket to Division I, okay. You are sitting with him or her and reviewing his or her mistakes/ successes if he/she can stand it. I know I couldn't have. I brought this up with Ray and she said what I thought she would say, "Yeah right! Me and Veector and Smeernof, dah?"

St. Rose, 58
St. Ethel, 28
Won, 3; Lost, 1

Postgame, I told them we would talk about it at tomorrow's shootaround, and we would learn what lessons getting blown out had taught us then move on. We stopped at a Parkway rest stop and the kids somberly ate burgers or Roy Rogers or Kentucky Fried. It was a quiet bus ride home, but I knew I would have everyone's attention tomorrow morning. I was glad we played and especially that we played at the beach. We drove up to Asbury Park, past the Casino, slowed down at the at the Stone Pony, where Ray and I and yelled, "BRRRUUUUCE!" And then tried to sing "Born to Run" but realized we had to be somber, having just gotten waxed by St. Rose. Rookie mistake.

December 30, 1982

When Ray and I were going over the practice plan as the kids were coming in, I stepped in closer to her and said, "I like it a lot better when you're in the locker room and on the bench, Coach Voytek. Obviously, the girls do as well. As Mama says, 'You are a good coacher.'"

"Well, why did you say that?" she asked. "Why do you think that is?"

"Take the compliment. We'll talk about it later," I said.

We brought them in at ten for an hour, as we wouldn't see them now until the fifth when we had a game. I've never been much of a screamer, nor do I think kids should be punished after a blowout. So the message was, "Hey, they were really, really good, weren't they? Better than us yesterday, for sure. But you girls are good about working hard and learning what we're teaching. So today, we're going to get loose, have some fun, do some walk-throughs, do a lot of shooting, and elect captains. Coach Ray will take over for a little while.

"But here's the thing. Do you want to get better? Do you want to be able to beat them if we run into them again? Do you want to keep working you're a—oops off? 'Cause that's what it takes. Well? *Do You?*"

"*Yeah!*"

"All yours, Coach," I said and went into the cafeteria to do some paperwork.

Monsignor had seen to it that we got a delivery of a dozen new Wilson basketballs. We put away six, inflated six, and now each girl had a ball, girl's size somewhat smaller and therefor easier to handle. Ray was a maniac on left-handed dribbling and shooting, and the girls were coming along. They did mirror drills at half-court, dribbling two balls, and they played "escape from practice." Dribbling from the opposite foul line, first running half-court shot to go in ends practice. Trudy usually saved the day, but this time it was Mary Pat, who burst out laughing when it swished through. "Nothin' but net, baby!"

Team huddle, right hands up and joined. "Gaels on three! One...two...three...Gaels!" We had quietly discarded the "Mighty Gaelettes" moniker, and the kids were happy with this one. And with that, the first part of our season was over. Except for Ginna delivering her mama's pasties wrapped in a towel in a basket. I said, "Ah, yer a darlin' girl, Ginna Norman from Cornwall. Thank ye. But dontcha know I won't be savin' ye any."

"That's okay, Coach. But wrong accent." She laughed and ran away.

"I knew that. I knew that."

* * *

My sister-in-law AnnMarie had called last week and asked me to come over for dinner and to see the kids tonight, and I was excited to see them all. Sarah, nine, was dark like her Italian mother, and Billy was fair like his daddy and favorite uncle. I knocked on their door, loaded down with Christmas goodies, including the pasties, at six sharp. Patrick answered the door and yelled back into the house, "Oh my god, Willie boy is on time. Call the networks! Wait, it might not be him!" He turned back to me and demanded, "Show me some ID there, buddy."

Then the kids came and grabbed me and the bags of gifts. I gave them each a big hug and said, "Merry Christmas! Oh my god, I forgot presents for the kids. Wait, I'll have to go to the deli."

"Nooo. Nooo!" they both shouted. "We saw the presents in the Macy's bag. You're tryin' to fool us, Uncle Bill! You lose!"

"Okay, I give. I gotchuz each a nice baloney sammich on white with mayo. What's better than that? And some Double bubble, too!"

"No, you didn't," said Sarah, by far the quickest of the two, "that's what we got *you!*"

"Well played, young Sarah," I said, getting a big smile back. I picked up the both of them and yelled to Ann Marie, "Isn't it past their bedtime? I can tell the little monsters are really tired."

"We're not monsters!" yelled Billy. "*You're* a monster!"

"You're right, little Willie," I whispered, setting Sarah down, "that is what I am. And I came to eat a seven-year-old boy for dinner. Seen anya them around?"

And I commenced to nibble his neck and ears and make him giggle and scream with laughter.

I put him down and said, "I can see, young Sarah, that you are beggin' your uncle for some dancin' steps, is this not so?"

"Why, yes, that would be most delightful," she said, and we whirled around the room in a waltz step, after which she curtsied and I bowed. Sarah took dancing lessons. Patrick said she was brilliant.

"You dance like a princess, fair Sarah," I said with a bow.

Big smile as she gave me her hand for a kiss. "Your grace," I said.

Turning to her parents, I begged, "*Now* can I have a drink?"

"Okay, darlins, give UB a little break, can yez?" said their father. Patrick was a little shorter than me, but stockier, and lifted weights in high school for football. Played defensive end and fullback for the Bulldogs. Loved the contact, took a lot of hits. Gave a lot as well. Sandy brown hair, a little red like mine, hazel eyes, much more serious than me. Ate up all that military stuff, was gung ho to join up. Now put that together with the art and design guy he grew into. That was probably from Mama's side.

The kids ran off to another room to play and the three of us sat and caught up. I hadn't seen or talked to my brother and sister-in-law since we went to a Yankee game in September. "Our two remind me of Cissy and you when you were little," Patrick said.

"Me too," I agreed. "Does Sarah look out for Billy like Cissy did for me?"

73

"Indeed," he said.

"I just love your kids, Ann Marie, They're so quick, especially Sarah. She remembers everything, doesn't she?" I said. "Is she gonna take Irish dancing?"

"Oh, she does. Remember everything. Every f-bomb Patrick ever said. No chance on the Irish dance though. None. Nunca. Over my dead body no," she said, looking at Patrick as she spoke, as though this had been discussed previously.

"And she's always bossing us all around and never stops asking questions. Why do you do it this way? How come it doesn't say this? If I'm still sane when she's fifteen, it'll be a miracle. But then she'll be a teenager and that'll be worse!"

AnnMarie was a New York City girl Patrick had met at P. J. Clark's on a blind date in 1969, fixed up by friends. She worked at Chase, he was at BBD&O. Married two years later, Sarah born two or three years after that. I think moving to the suburbs in Jersey was not something she took to easily. AnnMarie had developed a little home business doing taxes for friends and neighbors but didn't plan on going back to work till the kids were in high school. She was a dark brunette, brown eyes, voluptuous, looked like Sophia Loren, and warm and funny. Very bawdy funny.

"How's your business?" I asked her.

"Y'know, I took some classes at Bergen County Community just to get some skills? So I'm gonna see if I can branch out the business and do some accounting and bookkeeping and see how that goes. Then maybe finance. I gotta lotta contacts, maybe I can build a company, waddaya think, Willieboy?" she asked.

"Man, you go, girl! What a woman! That's great, really great, good luck with it. I knew one of the two of you had the brains," I said, looking at my brother, who flipped me off.

"So thank you, Willie. Anyway, are you married and didn't tell your brother? We woulda come to the wedding, wouldn't we, Pat?" AnnMarie was the only one I knew of who called my brother Pat.

74

"Nah," he said. "I woulda been playin' thirty-six holes that day, and you were takin' the kids to the shore, remember?" It was clear they had worked this out already, avoiding a wedding that never took place. "Anyway, Cissy said the bride was really fat and ugly and didn't speak English. But her old man owns a bar in Lyndhurst. Zat true?"

"Hope you're having a good time at my expense. No, my poor Fartsmella flew to Albania to spend Orthodox Christmas with relatives and was killed when her goat cart was run over by an ox. Very sad. She was just learning to shave with an electric," I said, getting up to get my coat and leave. "It was nice to see you and the kids." Now it was *high noon*." Who would fold first?"Don't forget your gift, Will," said AnnMarie, handing me a clearly used, decades-old *Archie* comic book.

"Oh, man," I said. "How did you know this is the one I've been looking for? Thanks, AnnMarie." And I gave her a big hug.

"Sorry I can't stay for dinner. There's a memorial for Fartsmella at the Albanian Rotary in Moonachie tonight," she said, opening the door. "You can keep the pasties."

"Don't go, Uncle Bill!" Billy and Sarah came screaming into the room. I looked back at Patrick and AnnMarie questioningly, palms up.

"Who's a fart smeller, Uncle Bill?" asked Sarah then she and Billy were rolling on the floor laughing.

"Nice, UB," commented their mother.

"Uncle Bill is!" said Billy joyfully. "UB's a fart smeller!"

"That'll be enougha that, William. I mean it," said his mother.

Patrick declared, "Tie game."

"I appeal the decision," I stated. "No contest. My comeback— clearly a winner. If only on my poor deceased bride's name alone. Come on! Is that not correct, Sophia?" My go-to name for my sister-in-law.

"I'm afraid the little creep is right, Patrick," she cooed, looking at me flirtatiously.

"I accept under protest and will take this to the Commissioner, but for now, done!" he exclaimed. "Possible loss of points for choice of bride's name. Bad influence on young'uns."

"Well played, all," I said.

* * *

"I just love this family to pieces," I told them after dinner, dessert, and coffee, and all presents were unwrapped, kids in their rooms. "I never thought any woman would ever pierce Patrick's armor—now just relax and shut up, my brother, and do what you've done, lady, but hats off to you. You still miss the Village though, don't you?"

"Yeah, but not so much, anymore. It all seems kinda crowded now, even at Mama's when we're all there. And this is a great neighborhood, lots of kids, and the town is great for young couples like us. We go in for Sunday dinner once a month and it's fun and the kids love it, but we're happy here," she said.

"And what about you, my wayward son?" asked AnnMarie.

"Heading back out west when school's out, New Mexico or somewhere around four corners. Get a job using my army and college training. No more teaching or coaching."

"Good for you, Will. Really, good for you. I'm sorry to fade so early, boys, but Mama has got to hit the hay. You're staying over, William, don't even think about missing Pat and the kids' New Year's Eve day breakfast."

I said, "Me too, I think. Patrick, you done good. After all is said and done, I am so proud of you. I really am. Well done! Good night all."

I woke up with Billy curled around me in the spare bed, little boy smells filling the room.

CHAPTER FIFTEEN

New Year's Eve

The restaurant was beautifully lit and decorated low-key, a jazz quartet playing tunes from times gone by, many well before our time. It was nice, romantic, and grown-up.

Once we were seated, Mr. Andolini had made a big fuss over Ray. "Ah, Signorina Ramona, you have grown into such a beautiful woman! Bellisima!" And rightfully so. He gushed, "She looka like a movie stah," and opened and poured our Crystal, on the house. We toasted the New Year. "Let's not talk about the Gaels tonight, waddaya say?"

"Works for me, Willie."

"I got something to say, have had for a long time. I'm serious, so listen. I've been dreading this moment for six years, so I guess I needed the atmosphere to get some courage. It's killin' me to say this, Ramona, but I never stopped thinkin' about you all these years. Never. All through the army and through college. And we were never really that far from each other, y'know? But I couldn't call or come, Ramona. I just couldn't do it.

77

You broke my heart, Ramona. You broke my heart. I never thought I'd have the whatever to say that to your face. Was it just a high school kid thing? I mean, I never felt it was. What happened to us?"

I could see her Russian was rising. Maybe this was bad timing by me.

"I broke *your* heart? I broke *your* f—— heart? Excuse me, but you ran away to the army, and I never saw you again until you were living at Mama's six years later. We haven't spoken to each other since I told you I wasn't going to the prom. You froze me out. You ran away, Willie. You left me, you bastard!. You never even said goodbye."

"Now hold on, lady. You blew me off for the prom. The *prom*. To go to the beach with your dipshit, stupid girlfriends? You chose them over me? No explanation, nothing. 'Oh, by the way, Willie, I'm going to Seaside with the girls instead of the prom, but you can still go.' Yeah, like I would do that. I loved you, Ramona. I loved you all my life. Who the hell else would I even want to take to the prom? We never even spoke a word to each other after that weekend you went to the shore. What was left to say?"

Ray had started to cry, as had I. I felt like a jerk, but I also felt like two tons had been lifted off my shoulders. Maybe I'd ruined our evening. Mr. A was casting worried looks our way, but we didn't seem to be bothering any of his other guests, most of whom were our parents' age.

"I'm going to the ladies."

"Okay," I said, standing, not knowing if she was coming back. Mr. A looked over with a WTF expression, and I shrugged and went palms up.

I stood up and held Ray's chair as she approached the table. I'm Jersey, not Arkansas, alright? She said, "Wow, didn't expect that tonight, Willie. Been holdin' that in a long time, eh?"

"Not the right time or place. Look, Ramona, I'm sorry. It was stupid, it's in the past, and I should have just let it lie."

"Nah, yah done the right thing, Will. I coulda called you or come to DC, but I was convinced it was on you. I got your phone number from your folks. Now I'm not so sure. Let me ax you something, as we used to say. Why'd you ask me to help you coach?"

"'Cause you know more basketball than I do. Why'd you accept?" I answered.

"And…and…? Jeez, Willie, do I have to drag it out of you?"

"All right, damnit. It was an excuse to see you, even if you didn't want to or couldn't do the coaching. Those last two years I was at school we were about twenty minutes from each other."

"I know. I saw you a coupla times," she said.

"Are you shitting me? Why didn't you—"

"Oh, Willie, you're such a goober. I have been so mad at you for so long, but I was so happy when you called," she admitted. "It felt so good to see you again."

"Me too, Ramona. Y'know what? Let's not do this again, okay?"

She smiled and lit up her side of the table and reached for my hand. "We have the whole night, Willie. Let's just talk and get to know each other again, okay? Maybe we'll pass on the party, waddayatheen?"

"Ah am theenking ju haf wery goot idea, missus lady. But can we must plis order food now. I am hearing dey haff nahza blinis."

"Vat, ju dun lahk mah blinis no maw?"

"Ramonooshka, you have very fine blinis, I am being polite to cooks in dess fine place is allis."

"Mah blinis, dey not goot enuff no maw for you, meester big stuff? You tink you da tsar of Vallington?"

"Please, stop, so we can stop laughing and order. Please, I'm begging you." I waved a waiter over. Eventually, we had appetizers. I gave Mr. A a hand signal, which he repeated to the sax player. The next tune began with a piano riff leading to a soft, velvety alto voice singing,

The long and winding road
That leads to your door,
Will never disappear
I've seen that road before…

Ray's eyes flew open. "You didn't."

"I did. You vill dense? Vit me iz vhat iyam teenking?"

"Are you essking?"

"Dah."

"Zen dah."

We got up and danced.

Wow! All these memories came boiling up to the surface as we danced, it seemed, all night. Mostly we talked.

"Do you remember that New Year's Eve at your house?" she said. "We were in fourth or fifth grade, I think, and your sister baby sat for us and let us stay up? She was in high school then, right?"

"Yeah, and she let a bunch of her friends in and they were drinkin' beer and smokin' weed…"

"And you and I split a can of Schaefers and we both got sick…"

"And you wanted to try a joint but the big kids wouldn't let you. Jeez, Ramona, you were outa control even then." I laughed.

"Y'know, it's a good thing we did get sick that night, Willie," she said. "Maybe kept us from bein' stupid. Think about all the booze and drugs in the class of '76. My god, what a wasteland. We both got out of it. A lot of them didn't."

"It was easy to get stuff right across the river. I know, some of guys were buyin' in Speer Village," I added, "even when we were juniors, as soon as they got cars. Some of those fools just had too much money. And the buyin' led to dealin'. Remember when the cops and the State Police brought the dogs in? Middle of third period, locked down the classrooms, busted about twenty kids, maybe more. Cops found some heroin and some cocain, honest to God."

"Then all those parties that summer after senior year at what's-his-name's lake house," said Ray, "you were already gone, but I went to one and that was enough for me. It was disgusting, Willie, really.

It's too bad, I think sometimes, we had to grow up. I loved bein' a kid, and I loved walkin' to school every day with you," Ray said, changing the subject. "Holding hands, talking to Mrs. Politikovich, the crossing guard, who always looked out for us."

"I loved that lady. Think she still works there? I should go see," I said.

"Remember when your dad got us that beat-up old basketball? That was about fifth grade 'cause we were already at Union School then, right?" she asked.

"Yeah, boy we wore that out pretty fast," I said, "then we both got new ones for Christmas, and they lasted a long time. I thought about that Christmas a lot. It was the best. Remember?"'

"I do. We were in sixth grade, and we used to go over and play with the older kids when they didn't have enough to make teams," she said. "We got our asses kicked, but we learned a lot and we had a lot of fun, didn't we?"

"We did," I said, "and we got a lot of respect, too."

"We had a lot of time just to hang out by ourselves, listen to music, watch all the Christmas movies and cartoons, pretend make out," she said.

"I wasn't pretending," I said.

"We didn't know what we were doing, Will," she said.

"Nah, I guess not," I conceded.

"But we thought we were such hot shit, didn't we?" she asked.

"Maybe you, never me," I said as I dodged a shove.

"Yeah, right," she said as the music stopped, and we returned to our table.

She said, "I think I spent half my childhood at the court at Washington School. Just to get away from them fighting. There and to your house."

"You miss playin' as much as I do?" I asked her.

"I do, Willie," she said. "It was such a living part of who I was for so long. Almost like a drug. I mean, the coaching partly makes up for it, but there's just an ache there where basketball used to be."

"I'm so sorry now I never got to see you play in college," I told her. "There were a coupla times I coulda gone when you had games close to here, but I was too angry, or proud, to go."

"Pride's a killer, Willie, ain't it?" she asked. "Look what it's cost us. You ever gonna call me Ray again?"

"I'm thinkin' about it, Ray. I'll get back to you on that." We both laughed. She got me.

Sitting at the table, I held both her hands and asked her, "What are we doing here, All State?"

"You tell me, Willie Boy," she said.

"I lived six years without you," I said, "didn't like it so much. I love it when you're around now, and I can see you. You light me up. I love to hear your voice. I wish I could touch you, just to put my hands on your face."

"Go ahead. Touch my face now," she said. "And then kiss me. Remember how you used to do that?"

I remembered.

Eet vas goot naht?

Dah!

CHAPTER SIXTEEN

January 5, 1983

Back to school. Vacation over.

The first morning, I got up early and got into school and asked Jane Farrell, almost always the first one in, if she would cover my first-period class. "You'll be rewarding me for this at some future time, charmin' Billy," she said.

"No doubt, m'lady. And I'll be lookin' forward to repayin' that obligation in full, I will," I responded.

I drove over to Rutherford to Mrs. Politikovich's corner, not expecting to see her after almost twenty years, but there she was, in her usual place waiting for the little ones, who started school later than we did. I parked the car and walked up behind her, as if I wanted to cross the street. She looked at me strangely then her face lit up and she shouted, "Billy Edwards! My goodness! Goin' back to school?" and reached out to give me a big hug.

"It's so good to see you! What brings you here? Did you move back into the old neighborhood?" she asked.

"You won't believe this, Mrs. P, but Ray and I are coaching basketball over at St. Ethel's, and we were talking about you the other night and—"

"Oh my god, are you back together?" she blurted out. "No, don't tell me. I can't stand it."

"How do you know about any of it anyway?"

"Come on, Billy, it's my job! I keep the mommies up to date. Everybody knew about it when you broke up senior year. Some of them could even quote your speech in the cafeteria. Jeez, Billy, that's the Dark Ages. This is Rutherford. Then you disappeared."

"Why didn't you say something? I always had a crush on you. You weren't that much older than me. I woulda axed you out," I said. "Just kidding."

"So you're a teacher now? I didn't see that comin'," she said.

"Just for this year, then I'm headin' west, maybe New Mexico. I was out that way in the Army and I loved it. You can come if you're free."

"Little late for that. But it's so kind of you to stop by, made my day.. You watch yourself with Ramona. Really. Be careful, okay."

"*Hua!*"

"Is that stupid army talk?"

"Gimme another hug, Mrs. P. You look terrific, as always. You're still the best!"

"You be careful now. Look both ways." And she laughed.

I hurried back and made it to first period with twenty-five minutes left, bowing humbly to Ms. Farrell. Actually, I hated to miss first period, as it was my favorite class of the day, a seventh-grade math class. That's all, no asterisk, no honors, just seventh-grade math. Average kids. The stars, like Luddie, were tracked as much as possible into Maureen Traynor's class, seventh-grade math*. Our task was to trudge through fractions, long division, Venn diagrams, and on and on...

84

So every once in a while, we had a slightly out of curriculum experience, if I knew I wasn't going to be observed or evaluated.

"Sorry I was late," I said to the class, "but we'll still have fun because we know that…" holding my right hand up and cupping my right ear and leaning toward the class, I wheedled, "Come on. Let me hear it…Oh man, that is so weak! One more time or… wait, wait for it…I hear that decimal train a'comin', it's rollin'—"

"*MATH ROCKS!*"

"Better. Okay, what's a digit?" I asked. "Ellen?"

Ellen said, "It can be a number or a finger."

"Smart kid," I answered.

"How many digits?" I asked.

Louise, who seldom has anything to say, blurted out, "Ten, like ten fingers."

Teacher responded, "And young Louise has, yes, hit one out of the park and answered one question with two answers. Good job, Looie!"

Big blush and smile.

"Another question," I declared. "Is there, I say is there, any relationship between the number of fingers and the number of digits? Raise hands. Ruth Ann."

"Ten deegits 'cause are ten feengehrs," she proudly said in her German accent.

"Excellent, Ruth Ann." I smiled.

I wrote 23 on the board."Is this a digit?"

"NOOO!"

"Why not?"

"It's *two* digits!"

Now it might take a while to get to this point.

85

"Can anyone explain what happens when a number gets bigger than one digit? How do we write it?" Looking for placeholder here or zero.

Anyway, this eventually took us to "What if horses had numbers? How many digits? One for each front hoof, right? No fingers. What would our numbers be? How would horses count?"

One and zero... It might take us a while to get to this conclusion and several visual aides. Remember, I sucked as a math minor at Monkey State.

"Okay, then, what's our first horse number? Jessica?"

"One."

"Right."

"Nicole, what's the second horse number?"

"Two."

I pretended to faint and implored her. "Now, just hold on there a minute, lady."

I wrote 2 on the board. "This isn't a horse number!" I crossed it out.

Adriana, a new girl who just moved into the parish from Spain, raised her hand. I called on her. "Yes, Adriana."

She stood and said, "Diez—I mean ten."

"Almost," I said. "Can you say it another way?"

Silence.

"Say the digits!" Waving my arms and shouting until someone in the back said,

"One...zero..." from the back of the class.

A Marv Albert "Yessssss! And it counts."

And I rushed to my desk, grabbed a special piece of yellow chalk, drew a gold star, and with a white piece of chalk, wrote

Magdalena Novak on the board. Cheers from the class. Magda stood, as per Edwards seventh-grade math traditions, and accepted her accolades, came up, and received her Tootsie Pop.

"Well done."

"All right, math warriors, your mission, should you choose to accept it, is to write the next fourteen horse numbers for homework, ready for inspection at zero eight hundred hours next time we convene. You can start now." Sometimes teachers speak in caps.

And we have entered the world of binary. A universe frought with peril for young Will Edwards in somewhat over his head.

* * *

Later that day, our first game of 1983, with our newly elected captains Rafferty and Dooney (I sensed ethnic block voting, perhaps some arm-twisting), was against St. Henrietta, down on the western edge of Newark by the old Pabst brewery, pretty much the hood. A uniformed security guard met us at the curb and escorted us through a metal detector. The Gaels, even SJ and Eddie, turned a whiter shade of pale. Walking through the gym to the locker room, we were the only whites in sight and were hooted at and mocked by the crowd. Down twenty and the game hadn't even started! No sign of the Henrietta coach.

In the locker room before the game, after they were dressed in their unis: "You're kiddin' me, right? You're sittin' here like little babies, almost cryin' because you have to go out and play the big tough city kids? Is that why we do all this work, so you can wimp out? You're scared? You're *scared*? You oughta be ashamed of yourselves! If you're too scared to play, get changed and I'll meet you on the bus. Coaches"—Ray had joined us again—"I'll be out on the bench. You bring them out. Or bring 'em to the bus."

Ray and Sister got them fired up, mostly mad at me, as that was the first anger they had seen from me, and they came out looking like themselves. The coaches had decided over the break we would close each pregame, after Steph sang the "Ave," with the Lord's Prayer led by Sister Mary. Then "Gaels on three! One, two, three, Gaels!" But I could see they were wired. So was I.

To no avail. Henrietta won the tap, made a quick layup, pressed us, SJ threw the ball to one of their players, and we were four down six seconds into the game. SJ got the ball in to Trudy at the top of the key. She pivoted around and passed downcourt to Raffy for a hoop, and we were off life support. Henrietta's girls were very aggressive and mouthy, and we had two homers carrying whistles who didn't seem to notice or care about the chippiness of the home team. Add to this the race factor, and the game was heading for catastrophe.

We were down five at the quarter, but Doons and Eddie each had two fouls. Ginna, with her new glasses, and Greet held down the fort subbing for them. We had to stay in a 2-3 zone as they were too quick, so we packed it in and dared them to shoot over us. Remember, no three-point shot yet. But there was pushing and shoving, and elbows were flying. Doons begged me to put her back in. "Not till the third quarter," I told her. Can't have that third foul in the first half, even I know that.

I put Mary Pat and Cat in for a minute for Ginna and Raff, fearing that Raff's big mouth and short fuse would cause us grief. Just before the half, Eddie stole a pass and broke away for a layup, missed it, and was clearly hammered by one of Henrietta's players. Eddie bounced right up and got in the girl's face. The girl yelled at Eddie, "Step back, bitch!" as the officials separated them. I'm up and on the court yelling, "Where's the foul? Where's the T on that kid?"

"Sit down, Coach" was the response. The crowd is yelling and hooting. I debated taking Eddie out right then, but she only had one foul, and I didn't want to give in to them. Their ball, they missed a shot, Anna rebounded out to Eddie, same play; Eddie was fearless and made the layup as the buzzer sounded for the half. Down two. I high-fived everyone as they trotted off the court and into the locker room. Made eye contact with their coach, an attractive young black woman, who didn't seem to have a clue.

Sister Mary, Ray, and I spoke quietly outside the door to the locker room. I said, "Waddaya think? We got a shot, right?"

Not looking all that confident, Ray answered, "Playing five against seven, Coach."

Very calmly, Sister Mary counseled, "Here's what we need to do. Go back to pressure, but move the back line up so Trudy is at the top of the key, and Mary Alice (Raff) and Mary Grace (Doons) move up to the foul line extended just outside the lanes. We'll put some more pressure on them. And put Trudy at the Rover spot."

I concluded, "Okay, sounds good. We'll give it a shot. Let's show the kids what we want."

God, I was so lucky to have these two. Inside the locker room, I told the kids, "Great job hanging in there with them and getting back into the game. We are so proud of you. Okay, now, Gaels, what did you learn?"

Raff yelled, unabashed, "That we can beat them!"

All joined in, "Yeah!"

SJ added, enthusiastically, "Yeah, we'll kick their ass."

I jumped in, "Easy with the mouth, SJ. This ain't the street. Okay, here's what we're gonna do..."

Trudy stole a cross court pass and hit SJ breaking for a layup, tie game. I saw a sizeable group of Ethel fans had arrived, including both SJ's and Eddie's fathers, Mr Johnson in his police sergeant's uniform, Mr. Monroe, a high school teacher, in his jacket and tie. The Gaels clearly saw them as well. When the girl who mouthed off to Eddie went up for a shot at the other end, she was sandwiched by Raffy and Doons, a reverse oreo. Foul, thank you Jesus, on Raff. Doons mouthed something to her, and she drew iron on both free throws. For the next five minutes, we controlled both backboards and ran off ten straight. They called time. Our kids were all over the place. "Sit down and be still!" I yelled. "You think this game is over?"

Luckily, for me, there was a wall behind us, no bleachers full of parents. "Two deep breaths. You're playing hard and you're playing smart."

Ray asked, "Doons, what did you say to that kid?"

She asked, "Can I say it? It was a bad word."

Eddie said, "She said, "Step back, bitch!"" Looking at Sister Mary, she pleaded, "Sorry, Sister." We all laughed.

89

I pulled them in and yelled, "Okay, now go out there and show us you know how to finish this team. Gaels on three! One, two, three, Gaels!"

Got all the starters out for a breather late third and early fourth quarter: Anna for Raff, Ginna for Eddie, Cat for SJ, and Mary Pat for Doons. Trudy never came out unless injured, gassed, or in foul trouble. She had shown the most progress of all the girls and, with her height and athletic ability, would likely be a successful high school player. With two minutes left, we were up by twelve, all our starters back on the floor, and the game getting ugly.

I called time and spoke to the officials about it and got the usual blank stares. They went man, we held the ball in our rover by setting down screens. They didn't seem to know how to foul, so they let the clock run out. The shake hands line was closely monitored by Sister, Ray, and me, and I think I heard a few "Step back, bitches," but I let them go. The last kid in our line, Liz Milak, said sweetly to the last kid in their line, "See you at St. Ethel, honey," and blew her a kiss.

And it almost started all over again. Never mind that. The frightened little girls who entered the gym had gathered themselves, found their courage, and had risen to the occasion. And Liz Milak? Never take a kid for granted, I thought.

In the locker room after the game, adrenaline still running high, I sat them down and said, "Okay, listen up. Think about yourselves sittin' in here before the game started. You were scared, weren't you? And I saw it and I got mad at you for bein' scared. Was I wrong?"

"Yeah!" in unison.

"Okay, I was wrong. So if you weren't scared and you went out and beat them by thirteen, then I'd say you were...Oh, what's the word? Coaches?"

Teagan blurted out, "We were brave! We were brave!"

Then they all joined in and chanted until I called for quiet. "What are the Gaels?"

"WE ARE BRAVE!"

Sometimes, I have read and heard, moments like this define a season. Good job, Teags!

All the kids had rides home with their parents or someone else's, so I had a long bus ride home, traffic on the Parkway. I asked Ray if she wanted to grab a beer and burger at Sullivans, but she said she was busy. And Sister was getting in Monsignor's town car as I left the building.

St. Ethel, 49
St. Hyacinth, 36
Won, 4; Lost, 1

Rafferty came running out, stopped when she saw me, and said, "I forgot my books, Coach."

"Hop to, Mary Alice, the Rafferty bus is leaving," shouted Pat, her father, in the driver's seat across the street. "Whatareya doin' there, Coach? Yer lookin' alone and forlorn? Ya hungry?"

"Why, yes I am, I am indeed," I replied. "What's the plan, Patrick?"

"Why, we'll be celebrating another Ethel victory, of course. Whyntcha jine us?"

"I'll follow you, how's that? Where we goin'?" I asked.

"Now, that's a foolish question, Coach, don'tcha know?" said Pat.

"Right you are," I answered.

"Can we ride with Coach?" yelled Mary Alice. "Yeah. Can we? Can we?" some sibling voices joined in.

Pat looked at me hopefully.

"Why not? Hop in," I said.

So now I had four Raffertys in the bus—oldest, Mary Alice, in front and Patrick, Jr., Annie, and Moira in the seats behind her.

"Waddaya wanna listen to? Never mind." I pulled a Creedence Clearwater Revival tape and turned it way up and the kids went nuts. The bus had an old tape deck, but it worked.

91

The kids were fun. We turned CCR off and played twenty questions. The little ones struggled a little; there was some sibling rivalry, and Mary Alice lording it over the younger ones, but we laughed a lot. We were all starved by the time we got to Mikey's. Table for seven. Three medium pies, three beers, four Cokes. I was stunned at how well the kids quieted down and behaved at the table.

"Season's goin' pretty good so far, eh, Will?" asked Pat.

"No complaints here, folks," I said. "They work hard, they're quick learners, they get better each week. I hope you can see that from the stands."

"Oh my god, Will. This one never stops talkin' about it," said Peggy, mother of the brood, causing "Raffy" to turn crimson and moan, "Mohommmm." "Yes, we see them playing more smoothly, more confidently. I expect that will continue?"

"What's important at this point is that they're willing to listen, learn, do the work," I said. "They're not afraid, especially the two captains. Got ourselves two real leaders."

Annie, sitting next to me, leaned over, mouth full of pizza, and piped up with, "Mary Alice has a crush on you."

Luckily, Annie was out of reach. Raffie again turned crimson, threatened to reign pain and suffering upon her little sister for whom I would pray tonight.

We finished without more incidents. The Raffertys are a lovely family, and I told Pat and Peggy that and asked them to tell Mary Alice not to worry. It would go no further, and I would not mention it again. I gave Patrick twenty for my share, and of course, he protested. He gave in after I threatened to give it to Annie.

CHAPTER SEVENTEEN

January 6, 1983

Next day was Epiphany, so we didn't practice. I stayed in my classroom, enjoying the rare quiet of an empty school, and corrected papers, prepared lesson plans, and Bob Dylan's *Blonde on Blonde* on my cheap boom box, loud enough to bring Luddie to my door, just as Bob was "singing" "Sad-Eyed Lady of the Lowlands." I think she stayed in school as long as she could. I'll have to look into that. She said, "Coach, you're not going to believe this. I got a letter from Larry."

"You know my buddy Larry Fumunda from Noowik?"

"Don't tease, Coach, you know who."

"No kidding? What'd he say?"

"He was happy to have such a loyal fan, but his name really is Larry. I guess I believe him. He sounded so nice. But listen to this. He's leaving four tickets for me when the Celtics play the Knicks at the Garden next month on Sunday afternoon, February 6. Good seats, too! Can we go, Coach? Can we, please?"

I was dumbfounded, speechless, completely at a loss. Here's this bigger-than-life superstar, known everywhere on the planet, and he takes the time to pay attention to this little seventh-grade math wizard who can tell you Jojo White's career scoring average. I said, "You should ask your parents to go, Luddie. Don't you think they'd like to go to the big city?"

"They hate New York, and they hate basketball. And anyway, they work at Marcal on Sundays. They don't really care what I do so much."

"Well, I'd have to talk to them anyway. Are they home now? Can I call them on the phone? How about I drive you home?"

Luddie looked panicked and said, "No, that's all right, I'll take care of it, Coach."

"Doesn't work that way, Luds. I have to hear it from them."

"Coach, they hardly understand English."

"Don't worry, we'll figure something out. Who else do you want to take?"

"Coach Ray and Sister?"

"No one on your staff or on the team?"

"They all think I'm a freak, Coach. I didn't even get invited to the sleepover at Mary Margaret's."

Sleepover? Whoa! "They don't think you're a freak, Luddie. Think about asking some of them. If not, we'll see about Coach Ray and Sister."

Oh, boy! Revelation upon revelation. I called the Guidance office to see if Jane Farrell or Sister Regis were still around. Jane Farrell answered, and trying to sound adult, grown up, and professional, I said, "Ms. Farrell, this is Mr. Edwards, can I come down and talk to you about a student for a few minutes, or are you on your way out?"

"Ah, Billy boy," she said, laughing, "such a grown-up now, are we? Truth be told, this Irish lass is on her way out the door, but if you'll stand for a pint, I'll gab for hours. Maybe a Jameson as well, it's been a long day. Meet me at Sullivan's in twenty minutes. I know yer still young and innocent, so let me give ya directions to Sullivans. Ya are of legal age now, aren'tcha, Charmin' Billy?" She laughed. "I'll be the winsome lass at the corner booth. Be sure to bring your ID."

Man, talk about not seeing that coming. Jane was an attractive redhead in her thirties, and we had met for coffee a few times. She was a great source of gossip and has probably held her own with the guys at the Legion, but…just friends, no spark. Well, that's just not true at all, but to this point, we had stayed in our own lanes. "Gotta go talk to Ms. Farrell, Luds. I'll get back to you soon. Don' worry, we'll work it out."

I went up to the bar and ordered two pints and two Jamesons up, and one of the Sullivans carried them to the table where Jane waited, big grin across her Irish face. "So, Billy, you've come to make the Monsignor's dreams of basketball Valhalla come true?"

"Why, yes, Jane, that's exactly what I plan to accomplish here in this Gaelic backwater, along with bringing civilized behavior and culture to all you lace curtain wannabes. Now that yez are acclimated to indoor plumbing."

We both laughed and knocked back our whiskeys. I knew better than to try to outlast Ms. Farrell. "What brings us here, William of Rutherford, other than the grace of each other's presence?"

"Ludmilla Woijahowicz," I answered. "Know her?"

"I do indeed. She is a math savant, your statistician, and would run away to Boston to marry Larry were he not already wed."

"Oh, Red, you are good."

"Yes, this is true," she came back, "but yer still buyin,' you silver-tongued devil. What about her? Just assume we're in my office and the confidentiality lamp is lit and rules are in place."

I told her about Luddie's reluctance to go home after school, which she knew about, since Luddie spent some of that time with her or in the library. And now with me. I told her about the basketball tickets, but not about my part in their delivery. "What's going on at home?"

She replied, "I've had the parents in. Had to have a translator. They brought in Clara Bilotskivic to help. I think her daughter is on your team."

"Like you don't know the name of every kid on the team. And their mamas and papas and aunties."

"You are *too* kind, sir. Anyway, they are having a rough time. They are older, you know? Came here to the Golden Door in 1973 when Luddie was three, though how they managed that, getting out of Poland, is a mystery they do *not* want to discuss, but Holy Mother Church was involved. Work all kinds of shifts at Marcal up on Rte. 80 and have to leave Luddie alone a lot.

"She doesn't like it…I think she's afraid to be left alone, hence the attraction of Mother Ethel. There have been some break-ins where they live, over by the warehouse section. Clara told me later that she believes Caz wants to go back to Poland. Or at least East Germany. God, can you imagine? He is not happy here.

"We'll have her take that Fordham Battery in the spring. Once the big boys ID her, she'll be grand, Billy boy. There's a four-week summer program at Felician College and maybe a shot at a scholarship to Holy Angels. And she'll be on the radar and will likely be able to go to college for free. Of course, none of this is to be shared, but Sister Mary is already in the loop. My god, is there nothing that old woman doesn't know?"

"Why, Ms. Jane, you are an exceptionally competent colleen."

"And you, Coach Willie, are a unusually perceptive knave for one just out of his teens." Later, as we were leaving, we spotted FitzGerald and McDonald getting soused at the bar. After glaring at me as I mouthed f—— you to them, they gave Jane big smiles. "Hello, Ms. Farrell, you have a good evening now," said Mac as Fitz glared at me.

"Some excess testosterone in the air, William?" she asked, smiling, as we parted. "We did enjoy putting on the flirt though, didn't we?"

"We could always go back in and start again, m'lady," I suggested.

"Ahh, your reach might be exceeding your grasp, charmin' Billy," she countered. "Sleep well."

"And you as well, Your Grace."

"You're not the kind of lad to forget a debt now—in truth, two debts—are ya, Billy?"

CHAPTER EIGHTEEN

January 7, 1983

Speaking of colleens, a bunch of them showed up the next day as the Academy of St. Elizabeth arrived; their disdain for our homey little gym apparent in their wrinkled noses and sneers. In two months hence, after spending the winter "rounding out their résumés," it would be back to tennis lessons, horseback riding, Irish dancing, and etiquette classes. They were followed by their Pendelton and L. L. Bean–clad parents making sure that their future debutantes didn't touch any surfaces or come into any unnecessary contact with the great unwashed. Okay, that's cold, but what if they travel to St. Henrietta? Rubber gloves and surgical masks?

Our kids showed no letdown from Wednesday's comeback at Henrietta. Although St. E's had looked tall and athletic in the pregame, once the game began, our scramble confused them. Their coach, a young woman named Addie Lou Collins, a recent grad of the College of St. Elizabeth, adjacent to the academy, didn't seem to know, or care that much, how to fix it. It was 16-2 at the quarter. Their parents group looked like they were ready for their second martinis when they hadn't yet had their first. Oh

99

wait, maybe they were having them now. More than a few high-end thermoses in their midst.

Second unit—Ginna, Cat, Anna, Mary Pat, and Reenie—played the last five minutes of the second quarter.

Starters for first two minutes of third then the shockers: Liz, Teagen, Stephanie, Patsy, and Mary Margaret. All our seventh graders. I kept hearing an old man's voice yelling at our girls. "Get over there!" "Shoot the ball!" "No! Catch the ball!"

It was coming from the stage, but I couldn't see a face. The voice was really one of those irritating ones that carries and goes right through your head. He kept on the whole game, especially when the shockers were in.

Not a pretty sight. Addie Lou left her starters in. The two squads were now evenly matched. We were in a 2-3 zone, didn't get a shot for two minutes, then Teagen stole the ball and made a layup. Our bench went crazy. The kids loved Teagen. A minute later, Liz made a bucket, same response from the bench. Just before the buzzer, Mary Margaret grabbed an offensive rebound and put it back in the basket. I jumped off the bench. "Good play, Em Em!" The kids' enthusiasm was much more subdued. Hmm...I'll have to look into that. Score: 33-13. Addie Lou finally put in her scrubs. I put the second unit back in for three minutes. The third unit finished out the game. Final: 46-17.

St. Ethel, 46
St. Elizabeth, 17
Won, 5; lost, 1

After the kids left the court, I asked Addie Lou, who seemed like a nice young woman, if she wanted to get a coffee from the kitchen, so we sat and chatted. She had grown up in Morristown, gone to Immaculate Conception K-6, St. E's all the rest of the way. I sensed a restless soul. She said, "I think I'm ready to move on, but certainly not in any way with basketball. Looking to get in a masters and doctoral program in biology and statistics combinations. Why am I telling you all this?"

I answered, "I have a kind face. Don't worry. Your secret is safe. Will your folks pay for grad school? Man, bio and stat is a killer combo. You are so employable!"

Addie said, "My folks have the money. I have already applied to Boston College, Notre Dame, Fairfield, and Loyola in Chicago."

"Wow!" I enthused, "That's serious business. Leavin' town, right? You go, girl. Good for you!"

With that, her princesses began coming out of their locker room. On her way out, she turned and said, "Thanks for listening, Coach. And for the coffee, and for not rolling up the score. See you next month."

Catching up later with Ray, I asked her, "Did you know one of the kids had a sleepover?"

"No, I didn't, Will," she replied. "Shall I look into it?"

"Carefully," I said. "That would be grand, Coach, and while I have your attention, did you notice the drop in bench enthusiasm for Mary Margaret's basket compared to the other two?"

Ray scoffed, "Oh, Willie, she's such a bitch and all the girls except Patsy know it and stay away from the two of them. Oh, by the way, I had a phone message today at school from a Mr. Fox. When I called the number, I got the Turtleback Zoo. Know anything about that, William?"

Straight-faced in my best lying mode, I answered, "No."

"You're a lying sack of shit, Willie."

"Am not!"

"Are too!"

And we both dissolved into laughter, and I ran away before she could land a punch.

But she caught me, and before she could haul off and belt me, I enveloped her in what appeared to anyone looking to be a hug. Just then, thank God, the Gaels came out, and we were able to retain our identities as authentic adult authority figures. Just barely.

"Childish epithets hold no svay in the court of Veelyum, you fool!" Thinking to myself, *This is childish and it has to stop.* Two grown-ups, I hesitate to use the word *adults*, chasing each other in the parking lot to deliver punches and noogies. Says it all, don't you think?

101

CHAPTER NINETEEN

January 10–12, 1983

The following Monday, we travelled to St. Hyacinth, a Polish parish school serving the small industrial towns where all the good Polish and Hungarian and Slovak restaurants and beer halls and delis were. By this time, seats on the bus were basically reserved with lowly seventh graders in the back. In a role reversal, in high school, they would find seats in the back always went to seniors. Ramona and Sister sat behind me and their captaincies across the aisle from them. On this particular trip, Ray and I passed the time singing some Beatle tunes. I had a pretty good voice and had fronted a garage band sophomore year, which Ray tried to put a stop to that summer. You couldn't use Ray and "carry a tune" in the same sentence. Anyway, I was soloing on one she didn't know, "Ob-La-Di, Ob-La-Da," when Dooney butted in and asked, "Coach, who sings that?"

Falling for one as old as Mama, I answered, "The Beatles." Pause. "Let's keep it that way!" The entire bus yelled back, clearly prepped and waiting for the kill, then erupted in peals of laughter. Even Sister and Ray! I wanted to give them a dozen gassers, but rules are rules. They got me.

Back to business. Not much going on in hoopland for the Lady Petals. No, I'm not making it up. No celebrating that night for St. Hyacinth; we rolled over them, and again, everyone played. We saw some real improvement in the second unit, and we left them in for the entire second quarter: Ginna, Cat, Reenie, Greet, and Mary Pat. Again, the loudmouth. "Get outa there." "Move outa the lane." "Don't miss the ball." All game. I leaned over to Sister and asked, "Sister, do you know who that loudmouth is? He was at our last home game too."

St. Ethel, 45
St. Hyacinth, 17
Won, 6; Lost, 1

An Irish feast that night was prepared by Margaret Rafferty, Peggy Dooney, Pat Delaney, Maureen McDonald, Nancy Flanagan, Annie McGuire, and Siobhan FitzGerald. With some of Celia Norman's pasties contributed as well: shepherd's pies, Irish stew, soda bread, sausage links, fish and chips, and sliced corned beef and cabbage. I couldn't stop eating. And none of the non-Irish kids made so much as a peep, and they attacked the food with enthusiasm. As did one Monsignor McAntee. Scowls from Fitz and Mac directed at me, big smile, mouthing two words, one the began with F, the second with Y, back from me. Neither mouthing seen by Himself. Wasn't life grand?

January 11, 1983

After practice, I drove over to the Gulf Station in town, owned by my buddy from Rutherford High, class of '76, Angelo Lastina. More accurately, Angelo Salvatore LaSpina. He was the only mechanic I knew who wore a white shirt and tie to work. "I'm a businessman, not a grease monkey. Businessmen wear ties," he always said. Put coveralls on over it.

You could eat off the floors in his station, three bays. He sold Gulf products, tires, and rented U-Hauls. Anything he didn't stock, he could get by end of business that day. Solid as a rock and loyal to the end. Always giving me stock tips, like I ever had a ten spot left over. Eh, it was a choice, right? He played Vivaldi, Pucchini, Verdi, and the like through JBL speakers in his station and switched to Golden Oldies when the high school work/study kids came on in the afternoon. "Oldies okay, not that heavy metal shit they call music!"

Closed the garage at six, trusted the kids to pump gas and lock up; opened half-days on Saturdays, always training kids to take over. Almost ready to buy his station down the hill in Little Ferry.

We were just sitting in his office, almost closing time. "How's Arlene? Shouldn't you have two or three bambinos by now?"

Hands over his heart, "Cara mia," he said. "Love of my life."

I never knew anyone more thoroughly Italian than Angelo. *Nevah!*

He had gone nights to Fairleigh Dickinson in Rutherford, but he was a gear head to the core. Drove a '55 Crown Vic, fire-engine red, in high school, which was now investment, car show quality and never saw the road. Now he owned the Gulf station and had a BA in business administration. We had met in Union School in fifth grade and had been friends since. I was 6'2", he was 5'9". I didn't know a socket wrench from a carburetor; he didn't know a downscreen from an offensive foul.

Tony Andolini was the third member of the group, though he didn't come along until high school, being from the other, more affluent side of town. In junior year, when kids started turning seventeen and getting cars, Angelo dubbed himself *The Golden Guinea.* He was discreet enough not to paint it in gold metal flake on the side of the Crown Vic. Then he decided Tony was The Silver Guinea. They each bought the appropriate ties, Angelo's silver, Tony's gold, to wear on Friday's with their letter sweaters. Angelo played soccer, which Tony and I insisted was not a real sport; Tony, of course, was an all-state pitcher. One Friday night on the way home from an emergency run to Rutt's for onion rings, in Tony's '74 Monte Carlo (birthday present), I said, "What about a nickname for me, you dumbass guineas?"

Angelo said, "Don't worry. We been workin' on it! How do you like the Green Guinea, 'cause you're like Irish, y'know?"

"Yer f——n' kiddin', right?" I squawked.

"I *told* ya that sucked," said Tony.

"You got somethin' better, I suppose," Angelo parried. The two of them were like two little old ladies, back and forth at each other for hours. It drove me nuts.

"I do," Tony countered. "First, he's not Italian, remember? He's adopted. Second, the closest metal color to his hair is bronze, right? So he's the Adopted Bronze Guinea! Brilliant work, Tony! Good job." They both looked at me expectantly.

I extended my arm over the front seat, made a fist, started to turn it thumb down, then slowly reversed, and gave them a thumbs-up! "Hail, my fellow Guineas!"

January 12, 1983

Development game! Even the Bidwells would have gotten into tonight, which would also, hopefully, have the effect of attracting girls to enroll at St. Ethel. A "development" game is a fundraiser (Imagine that, a fundraiser at a Catholic school!) But this wasn't for the bishop's fund, the diocese, orphans, or pagan babies, this was for St. Ethel. Maybe hoops might get new unis! So raffles, fifty-fifties, shooting contests, the whole deal.

We played a team from northwest New Jersey, Reverend Brown, and fed them after the game on takeout pizzas from Mikey's. We used Our Lady of Sorrows High School gym (it had high bleachers on one wall!) and, as Monsignor Dan, the principal, had been in the Jesuit seminary in the Bronx with the monsignor, we got a good deal. The place was packed even though people had to pony up $5 for an adult ticket. A wee bit of clerical pressure was exerted on the parish families to exchange the four tickets they were given for twenty dollars.

And Reverend Brown brought a fair sized-group of parents, who resembled the St. E's moms and dads more than the blue-collar folks we see down here. Three Irish lasses were on the court at all times. We won going away. Everyone played, so we didn't run up the score. As I observed the goings-on and the smiles at the postgame feast, I was thinking that girls play basketball for different reasons than boys. In the early eighties, there were not women playing hoops on TV.

But then, there were. A five-foot, four-inch blonde named Kim Mulkey had led Louisiana Tech to two consecutive NCAA Division I Championships Titles. Before that, without the national TV audience, Montclair State had ridden Sharpshooter Carol's jumpshot to the final four. Not long after that, the NCAA gained control of the women's tournament and small schools like MSC would never see the big time again.

St. Ethel, 49
Rev. Brown, 30
Won, 7; Lost, 1

Ray and I had spoken many times to the girls about playing for yourselves, for each other, and for now. There was the affirmation that came from belonging, sharing experiences both elating and heartbreaking, and carving a notch on the identity belt. We are brave! They liked the athletic competition. There was the joy of being a kid and belonging to something that mattered. I could feel this watching them at the team dinner, fooling around and yapping like girls do, but doing these things with kids they wouldn't have even known if not for basketball.

But damned if that loudmouthed old man wasn't there again, now adding numbers to his commands: "Gettouta there, fifteen." "Bad shot, twenty-two."

CHAPTER TWENTY

January 14, 1983

We had a fairly long bus ride north, up Rte.17 to Blessed Kateri. Blessed Kateri was a seventeenth-century Mohawk Indian woman who gave her life to Christ and died at age twenty-four. She was beatified a few years back and was on the road to sainthood. I think it was a forward-looking parish, maybe a bit charismatic. Okay, that's enough, I'm already in too deep, but seeing the church and the K to 8 school, it looked like an affluent area. Not a place likely home to working men and women. No three-deckers, two families or row homes.

Their coach was a young Jesuit priest who was a beast on the sidelines, yelling in a Midwestern drawl at his girls the whole game. Not an accent heard that often in North Jersey. I'm thinking that these Kateri kids were fortunate they weren't born back when Ignatius Loyola was running the Jesuits; the good father wouldn't just be yelling at them. I think the officials were his cousins or brothers-in-law. Rafferty had two fouls and a T by the middle of the second quarter. I was more pissed at her than the officials, but I alternated Mary Pat and Reenie on offense and defense as much as I could, and Mary Pat hit for six points.

But in truth, Trudy was unstoppable. She could now put a few dribbles down and execute a jump shot. The first time she did it in a game, the bench went wild. "In the zone," as the saying goes. We were twenty-five points better than them on our court, but not here. We had to grind it out and won by six. Their kids were sullen on the shake hands line and the coach said, "Coach, your team was lucky today. Maybe not so much next time."

St. Ethel, 35
Blessed Kateri, 29
Won, 8; lost, 1

"Thank you, Father," thinking, *We will so kick your ass at our place, you arrogant fool.* Long ride home in commuter traffic, so no team meal. Sister was tired, so we took her home. Ray and I went to Sully's for shepherd's pie and a pint. Comfortable in a booth at Sullivans, I asked Ray, "Find out anything?"

Ray answered, "Not yet. A bunch of the mothers are going out for lunch tomorrow. They invited me along. Sister is busy. They're more vicious when she's not around. I think she knows that."

"Hey, All State, did you know Carol growing up or in high school?" I asked.

She answered, "Well, I knew who she was in high school. She was two years ahead of me, and she lived in Cranford, y'know? Never saw them in the States, different groups. I played against her in some summer leagues at Montclair, and we hung out one summer when we were both in college. She was goin' into senior year. I was goin' into sophmore. Damn, she could shoot! Never saw anyone who could shoot like that. Not just that though, she knew how to get her shot, use screens, and set up her teammates. Sure, she had an attitude, but she was really nice when you got to know her.

"Actually, we were pretty tight that one year and one summer, and I would stop by Nutley or Montclair State whenever I came home from Bloom. Catch a game if I could. Y'know, I understand the attitude, everybody, guys especially, wants to take her on and can't believe it when she whips them."

"So she was kinda like this girl I know, this Ray," I said.

"Not even close. She's way outa my league, Will. Anyway, she lives in Nutley with her family now. She's trying to play pro, but the leagues haven't had much luck," Ray said.

Will: "Ya think she'd come over and talk to the kids? Do a clinic?"

Ray: "You gonna pay her?"

Will: "I thought yez were buddies? What am I gonna pay her with?"

Ray: "Wake up, William. She's a professional athlete now. Let me give her a call, maybe she's doing something for the diocese. Or for Monkey State. I'll give it a shot."

Will: "Whoever said you were uncooperative was full of..." I danced away from a right hook. Taking a deep breath, I changed the subject. Subtle as an eighteen-wheeler...Trying to sound offhand, as though she couldn't read every move and thought I had, I said, "You wanna do something tomorrow night?"

"Can't, Willie. Going with the girls to see Pat Benetar at Brendan Byrne. Why don't you come over for brunch Sunday about noon?"

"What should I bring, your Ramonaship?"

Ray quipped, "Being a smart-ass doesn't become you, William...Smirnoff, celery, Bloody Mary mix, and horse radish."

"Ugh, you're gonna be hungover, aren't you?"

Ray deadpanned: "And if I am, what of it?"

"There's the fine lass I've grown to know and love. Hit me with your best shot, sweet thing."

As a glove flew by my right ear and hit the back of the booth behind me, I knew she missed on purpose.

Donald Schlenger

112

CHAPTER TWENTY-ONE

January 15–16, 1983

Saturday night there was a jazz concert at William Paterson University, name changed from Paterson State College, and located a safe distance from the ethnic hodgepodge and urban decay problems of downtown Paterson. They had a good jazz program and the concert was cheap. I was going to call up Jane Farrell but chickened out and went by myself. Sat next to some aficionados who knew the musicians, so it was a good night. When we discovered most of us were vets, they asked me out for coffee, and we talked for a couple of hours at a coffee house on campus. I didn't know much about jazz past the big names, but it was an interesting evening. Exchanged phone numbers and said we'd meet at the next jazz night. Ray would probably hate it.

Next day, staples in a ShopRite bag, I drove up to Leonia where Ray had a nice apartment. I knocked on the door, I heard the lock turn, and I heard Ray gasp, "Aaarrrggghhh!"

Went to the kitchen, made two Bloodies, turned to Ray, and called out, "Haira the dog, Ramona!"

113

Giving me the finger, she swallowed half the drink in one gulp. I had brought some cassettes from our high school days, mix tapes, started out with the Stones "Gimme Shelter," "Witchy Woman" by the Eagles loud, "Born to Run" by the Boss louder... Until she yelled, "Turn that crap off. It's givin' me a headache!"

I turned up the volume to "Call the Landlord" when Derek and the Dominoes came on with "Layla" and ran out of the room. "Go take a shower. You're disgusting! I'll be back in an an hour."

Exited rapidly. Then ran back in and sang with Clapton, "Raaaaayla, got me on my knees, Rayla, beggin' darlin' please... "I had dressed warmly and went for a run, listening to "Kinda Blue" on my Walkman. What a great invention! Not that I got Miles Davis, but there was something compelling about the music. They could play so fast, and I listened to it a lot. Anyway, it made me feel cool. Always an important consideration in Jersey.

I reappeared at Ray's door, knocked, and hair still wet, she let me in. Unsmiling, she barked, "So what the hell were you doin' at Sullivans with that slut Farrell?"

I barked back, "As though it were any of yer damn business, you forgot to mention."

Ray bellowed, "Get the hell out of here!"

I responded saccharinely, "Well then, *Coach*, I hope to see you at practice tomorrow. Or maybe not. Have a wonderful day." Big fake smile.

"Oh, don't be a jackass. Sit down."

"So how's *your* day goin' so far, sweetheart?" was my comeback, and we both broke out laughing. She got up and brought us in some coffee and bagels. "Wait," I said, "Farrell's really a slut? Really? Damn!"

I got smacked again. "You know, someday I'm gonna hit you back. And that'll be the end of it."

"Oh, really?"

"Yeah, really."

I lunged over and covered her completely, planting a sloppy wet kiss on her cheek. "Eet vas nasza, you arra lahking dees kees?"

"Get off me, you big slob! Ugh, you're digusting!"

But we both laughed.

Time to change the subject. I asked her, "So the intelligence network is pretty fast here. McDonald and FitzGerald saw Jane and me at the bar and must have made sure that word got to you. I wonder why they would do that? And how?"

Ray answered, "Whisper, whisper, giggle, anonymous phone message on my machine. Man's voice."

"That's their second or third shot across the bow, Ray," I said. "It'd be worse if the monsignor hadn't told him to lay off when we had the parents in."

"Look, Willie," Ray declared, "we can always tell them to go f—— themselves, right? It's not like we're highly sought after professionals or coaches desperate for that job."

"Okay, you're right. I need to spend some time thinking about next year. If the monsignor pulls the plug, or it's pulled for him, I'm probably history. But for the sake of the kids, I'd like to get through the season. So how was the girls' day out? Who was there? Where'd you go?"

Ray answered, "Now here's where it gets interesting. Mavis and LaShonda, Mary Masaryk, Francis Plutarski, Betty Milak, Janet Hdawonicz, and Clara Bilotskovic. Celia Norman begged off, saying she had some work to finish, but dishin' with the girls isn't her kinda thing, I don't think...We went to an Olive Garden, nobody drank, cheap enough, at Paramus Park Mall. Guess whose names weren't on the list?"

"None of the Gaelic mommies. What did your group have to say about the sleepover? Who went anyway?" I asked.

"Well, all of the seventh graders: that's Liz, Teagan, Stephanie, Patsy, and it was at Mary Margaret's. The others either weren't invited or refused to go because a friend wasn't invited. Nick and Celia wouldn't let Ginna go, but she wasn't going anyway, and neither was Cat, because SJ and Eddie weren't invited," Ray reported. "Rafferty, Doons, and Flanagan for the same reason. And the rest weren't invited. They must have asked who was."

I posited, "I guess these kids have the chutzpah…that means 'balls.'"

"I know what it means, Will."

"Nah, ya dunt. Ya tink ya know, ya dun know nuttin'. They have the balls to ask, 'Who's going?' So it was a flop. Fitz and McDonald will likely see my hand in this."

Ray said, "Only the seventh graders attended. Peggy Rafferty called me later and told me a real bombshell. McDonald wanted your job, with Fitz as his assistant, but the Monsignor turned them down. She said there might be a retaliatory sleepover. God, I can't believe we're talking about this crap! Mavis and LaShonda are definitely opposed, they just want to get their kids out of Ethel safely and happily. The others are fitty-fitty."

"We have to stay out of this, Ray, but that's good work gettin' that tidbit from Peggy. Explains a lot," I said.

"We had crap like this when I was a kid, too," Ray said. "It's junior-high-age girls, y'know? Egged on by parents. They have to work it out for themselves. We have to let it go unless it turns into bullying. That's not likely with this crew. No wusses here." Pause. "Among the players anyway."

She lunged away before I could pounce. A suitable metaphor for the story of Ramona and Bill, all things considered.

"Wanna watch some videos?" I asked. "I got some good ones and some crappy chick flicks."

"Lemme see." She leaned over me and grabbed the plastic bag. "Oh I love *Grease*. Kenicki reminds me of you."

"C'mere, Rizzo," I said. "There's admission to *Grease*." I pulled her up, sat her on my lap, and looked straight into her eyes.

"Yeah?"

"Yeah. And somethin' else. I'm serious. And you'd better listen. We like to tease and bust chops, right? It comes with the territory. But this haulin' back and sockin' me has just got to stop. I mean, for Chrissake, Ray, we're twenty-four years old. It looks ridiculous. Knock it off already! And don't go poutin' 'cause you don't like what I said. It's time to knock it off. I mean it."

She didn't say a word.

Donald Schlenger

CHAPTER TWENTY-TWO

January 17, 1983

A lot of running and review at Monday's practice, and some coolness from the eighth to the seventh graders. All told, their hearts weren't in it. I had considered letting them scrimmage, seventh against eighth, and letting Raff and Dooney have a go at Patsy and Mary Margaret, but I gave them over to Sister and Ray and went to my classroom to sit and think about what we should, or what I, should do.

When I got back, we spent ten minutes on what's called "time and possession," which we had been doing about once a week from the beginning but would now do every other practice. Luddy would get out the clock and light up the board. We would set it, for example, at thirty seconds, Ethel up 1, their ball. No time-outs. Get the kids to play in the moment. Then change it to us down, clock at :05, their ball. Then have to teach them how to foul. Lots of stuff to learn, not a lot of time to learn it. But it was very tedious, so we never worked on it more than nine or ten minutes at a time.

No point in bringing Monsignor in on the other stuff. But I sure as hell wasn't going out of my way to pretend with Fitz and McDonald. As Ray said, we had nothing to lose. But I'll bet Ray had them scrimmage. She's a little more of a sadistic type than I am. Four years of being beat up in college hoops'll do that to you.

119

January 18, 1983

We headed east to St. Anne on Tuesday; another Polish enclave, this one with a German population as well, with great views of the Manhattan skyline."They were usually pretty good," Sister said, a sly smile creasing her ancient face.

"What?" I asked, to no avail.

We came out of the locker room into a gym not as small as ours with a running track around the upper wall like in the old YMCAs, but old school, with a pretty good crowd. As we went into two-lines-layups, a blare of Wagnerian music announced the entrance of the St. Anne's Eagles, twice circling the gym, in step and calling cadence. Forming three lines, they began calisthentics. I had to yell at our kids, standing there staring open-mouthed, to remember what they were doing. Then, at another crescendo, their coach made a theatrical entrance. We shook hands, and when the music died down, he told me his name was Ernst Reidelbacher. He was a Vietnam vet, still a major in the reserves, and volunteered his services to the parish where he was also a deacon.

"You got a nice little club there, Coach," he offered. "We saw your game at Henrietta. Oh yeah, some of the fathers scout all our opponents. We have a whole support system in place. I been doin' this since I came back from Southeast Asia in '75. I know we don't play you again, so maybe I can give you some advice and make some suggestions after the game."

I answered, "Uh, yeah, that'd be great, Ernie—"

"It's Ernst, Bill."

"That'd be great, Ernst. Really. I would appreciate it. I'm kinda new at this," I said, trying to look and sound sincere. They let this pompous ass alone with their daughters? Maybe his uncle was the bishop. Or Heinrich Himmler?

At that, the buzzer sounded. I turned to see Sister and Ray suppressing giggles and sternly warned them, hissing, "You vill not laff at zeh Majah, dumkopfs. I awdah you to stop zis at vonce! You sink zis is funny?" Even Sister burst out laughing.

I'm sure the girls, jogging back to the bench, wondered what their coaches were doing, but as good Catholic girls, let it go. Except Rafferty, of course, who tilted her head and looked at us all crosseyed and sang a few notes from Wagner. Their starters were taller than ours, and good athletes, but very wooden and regimented. Though I hesitate to mention this, they reminded me, both in stature and hairstyle, of the old black-and-white films I had seen in school of Hitler Youth frolicking in the Alps. They had a lot of trouble with pressure, and SJ and Eddie had great first quarters; Ethel up by seven at the end. Ginna entered at the quarter but was turned back when Reidelbacher complained about her "illegal" eyewear. "You're kidding, right?" I asked angrily.

"Eyewear must be attached to the head," recited one of the officials. They both resembled, ahh, never mind. Oh, what the hell, the little guy in *Casablanca* who kept saying "Oooh, Rick..." I think he was in *The Maltese Falcon,* too.

Luddie to the rescue. She had charge of the first aid kit and had made sure Ethel was ready for anything short of a natural disaster. "I got this, Coach!" she yelled and pulled the elastic what-ever-ya-call-them out of the kit. Ginna entered the game, high-fiving Luddie on the way.

"Good job, Luds! Yeah!" I exclaimed and got a big smile.

While this was going on, Trudy was whispering to Ray, her eyes tearing up. I looked over to Ray when the girls went back on the court, shrugging, palms up. She mouthed, "Later."

I called Greet over and told her to go in for Trudy. As she hustled on to the court, I called to Trudy to sit down next to me. "Tell me what they're doing. Or saying."

Visibly upset, she shook her head in quick, little jerks. "Okay," I told her, "go sit by Coach Ray and Sister. Can't play when you're crying like that."

We played the pressure beginning at midcourt, unrelenting, rotated the rest of the second team in and out during the second quarter. Ray leaned over and said, "She's ready."

"Are they hitting or playing dirty?" I asked Ray.

"Just language, she said," Ray answered.

I called Trudy over, "Be a player!" I told her.

Oh, and she surely was. Finished with nineteen points and twelve boards.

I wasn't letting up on this guy. Up thirteen at the half.

All our parents had arrived, and again, their noise blunted the now deflated home fans. I was pumped! Sister and Ray stopped me outside the locker room. "You have to calm down, William," said Sister. "This is not about you and this little Nazi. Take a breath now before we talk to the girls."

"Sister's right, Coach," added Ray.

"Good job, coaches. You're right, as usual. Now, Ray, what was Trudy upset about?"

"Lotta racial stuff going on out there that the refs aren't hearing. Or pretending not to. N-word to all our kids, not just SJ and Eddie. What'd you say to her?"

"Told her to be a player."

Sister said, "This is my department, I'll take care of it right after we talk to the girls."

Neither Ray nor I had a clue what she was up to but knew better than try to dissuade her.

The girls were just finishing their orange quarters, supplied every game by mothers in turn, when we came in. "What's with that cracker, their coach?" demanded SJ.

"Must think he's in Mississippi, SJ," said Ray.

"Yeah, well he's a little creep!" added Dooney.

"We do not need to be disrespectful when speaking of adults, Ms. Dooney," said Sister in her seldom heard anymore official nun voice. Used only in dire situations. A deathly quiet filled the room.

I let it sink in then said, "Hey, remember me?" breaking the spell.

"Great first half, Gaels! Now let's go out and finish it. Keep doin' what you're doin'. Don't bother with what they're sayin,' all right? Can you do that? Keep your mouths shut? Yeah, keep your mouths shut. This ain't the street. Beat them with the basketball and your brains. Starters back in. Same D, Trudy is Rover.

Gaels on three! one, two, three, GAELS!"

I stepped into the group and said, "Remember what you are, Gaels! Captains?"

Dooney and Rafferty in unison led them, "We are brave! We are brave!"While the teams were warming up before the second half started, I spoke to "Ernie," "Wanna tell me what all this name-calling and racist shit is all about, Coach?"

"No idea what you're talking about," he said and turned his back on me.

"Gonna catch up with you and your storm troopers," I said. "And we're gonna kick your Aryan asses today."

Here's all I remember about the rest of the game: Three minutes left in the third quarter, 43–22. Dooney steals a pass, outlets to SJ breaking, layup, two points. The second before our crowd erupts, a beefy, redfaced Bavarian type yells out:

"*SOMEBODY GUARD THAT SPOOK!*"

Nothing moves, not a sound. Then bedlam. Angry fathers yelling at each other, red-faced mothers employing language they would smack their daughters for using. Players starting to square off, our bigs, led by Dooney and Flanagan, ready to take 'em all on. I ran on to the court to ask an official for time. He gave me a technical foul for being on the court. Clock has stopped. Ray has pulled most of our kids, who were frightened by the threat of adult violence, off the court and gathered most of them in a huddle for self-protection. Meanwhile, Sister has yanked Mary Grace and Mary Pat, fists clenched and rarin' to go, back to our bench by the ear. Old nun's trick.

I started across the floor to the loudmouth when John Johnson, laying a strong hand on my arm, shook his head and said, "Let the priests handle this, Coach. You don't need to be engaging this Nazi peckerwood."

I turned in the other direction toward Reidelbacher and yelled, "What kind of—?" when JJ grabbed me again and escorted me to our bench. "Big mistake, Coach." The kids, with Ray and Sister on the bench, took this adult drama with wide eyes. I was more than a little embarrassed.

I would have punched the little shit in the mouth. Not a good idea.

I saw the monsignor and Father Perlowsky heading quickly toward the St. Anne bleachers, across from their bench, followed by two really large rental cops, likely former altar boys here. "Walter, come down here and come with us, please. Don't embarrass yourself or this parish any further," demanded Father Perlowsky.

And damned if that wasn't just what Stanley did, looking ashamed and smelling like he might have had a few on the way from work.

A semblance of order was restored and play continued. We played hard and fast, not concerned about protecting our lead, but St. Anne's was really just dispirited. I felt bad for their kids. But not that bad. When the game ended, we had won by 38, and I herded the girls into the locker room, ignoring Major Reidelbacher and his storm troopers. I stopped, looked at Reidelbacher, but the military brain kicked in, and I just said, "This is on you, Major. Shame on you. I think I'll pass on any tips you might have for me. Here's a tip for you. Give up coaching." I turned and walked away with my team.

St. Ethel, 59
St. Anne, 21
Won, 9; Lost, 1

Once inside, Trudy and Anna broke down crying, comforted by Reenie and Rafferty. "Coach, it was terrible the things those girls were saying to SJ and Eddie. And to the rest of us too. We felt so bad," said Greet.

"I was ready to punch that one's lights out!" exclaimed Dooney.

"I never heard anyone talk like that," said Mary Catherine, many heads nodding in agreement.

"I don't need any y'all to fight my battles or feel sorry for me. Y'all got no clue about what it's like!" SJ was rigid with rage.

Official nun voice: "You'll just please put that anger and mouth away, Ms. Johnson, and realize these girls are your friends and that they love you."

SJ started to protest, arms crossed, but her lower lip quivered then the tears came, and she ran and buried herself in Sister's habit, soon joined by Eddie, then Ginna and Cat— the four amigas. Then the rest piled on around Ray. Last to join were, tentatively, Patsy and Mary Margaret. Never see this with boys, this roller coaster of emotions. That wasn't a complaint. God bless them.

Sister let them cry it out then she and I went out, and she told Ray to stay in the locker room. Ray talking to them softly, telling stories from her time. I told Sister about my brief incident with Reidelbacher at halftime and asked her what had happened with her and Father Perlowski. "I told him we knew about the race-baiting taking place on the court, and if it continued in the second half, I would speak to Father about it. Don't know if it did any good, but I told the monsignor anyway. This is going to the bishop, William. I won't stand for it, and I'm old enough that they can't do anything to me. They're all afraid of me anyway," and she chuckled. "There is a wonderful Navajo proverb for this. Maybe, with prayer, I'll remember it."

The Johnsons and Monroes were waiting for their daughters and asked if they could take the girls home. I said sure. But when they came out, SJ and Eddie protested and said they wanted to ride with the team. Just then, a subdued Stanley, followed by Father Perlowski, approached the three Johnsons. SJ turned her back to him. He pleaded, "I'm sorry for what I said. I embarrassed myself, my daughter, and my church. I hope you can forgive me. I'm not like that." LaShonda started to say something, but John held up his hand, gesturing her to silence.

As he turned to go, Sgt. Johnson, absolutely dead-eyed and stone-faced, stuck out his hand and said, "We're good," and nodded to Father Perlowski that it was over, saying, "Thank you for your kindness, Father." Stanley was not up to any eye contact with Sgt. Johnson, however.

And they shook hands. Situation defused by a priest and a cop out of range of the cameras, no one even knew it happened. Wow! Lessons learned. Then I looked at the sergeant and realized it must have taken every ounce of self control not to beat Stanley to a pulp. I knew absolutely nothing about what kind of stength that took. Hope I never learn the hard way, but I got up close and personal to the real thing that day.

On the bus ride home, I told Ray, "You were really great with the girls today, assistant coach Voytek. I mean that. I couldna done that."

"Second that from me, honey. Lovely to see your soft side, Ramona. God bless you," said Sister Mary.

As the kids were getting up to get off the bus, Dooney yelled, "Coach was gonna kick some ass!" And they all yelled, "You go, Coach!"

"Ah, that's gonna cost ya some gassers, you little darlin' girls," I said, laughing.

"Not fair," they all yelled.

"And what good and loyal teammates you have that will be j'inin' ya." I laughed.

Thankfully, we had decided ahead of time to pass on a meal at school and everyone went home to recover and lick their wounds. I checked in by phone with the kids most involved, just to let them know their coach was thinking about them.

Mama had a meal waiting for Ray and me, as Sister had a function to attend with the Monsignor. We had cabbage rolls with old country rye bread from the Strucko's Polish bakery, very satisfying. As Ray and I were both beat, I just walked her out to her car and said, "I am vanting to kiss you, Ramonushka."

"So, vhat's keeping you, Villyum? Need to freshen up?" she challenged."Come ovah heah, you silly boy."

So ve had long nahza kees good night. Very nahza kees it vaz. Teengs vaz beginying to change.

Donald Schlenger

CHAPTER TWENTY-THREE

January 19, 1983

We delayed the start of practice on Wednesday to let any girls who wanted talk to Ms. Farrell or Sister Regina in Guidance or Sister Mary or Ray in a one-on-one and about half took advantage of it. I didn't think they were up for, or mature enough for, any group stuff. Have to ask Jane about that. Ran them hard the last fifteen minutes, which we called the Mary Grace Dooney Track Meet, and called it a day. Ray had to leave a little early anyway. Ran Mary Grace a little more. Had to, she would have been disappointed had I not. Another short lecture about actions and consequences, but I gave it a Navajo twist. Really, I did. Sister wasn't in the gym, so I made stuff up about evil spirits, ghosts, haunted kitchens, and magic dodge balls, which I just happened to have. Then some more running.

As the girls were filing out, Eddie Monroe stepped into the gym, approached me, and said, "Bill, you gotta listen to this! Last Saturday, the four amigas had a sleepover at our house. I swear to God, I know the kids had been angling for it, but I never thought their parents would go for it. They all had sleeping bags, yapped all night, did each other's hair. That was an education for all! Slept till noon. Made pancakes and eggs for breakfast. It was like a miracle! I know I'm making too much of it, but man! They're having one at Norman's this weekend. Are you fu—oops. Sorry."

"Wow! God, we've been hoping something like that would happen. They're inseparable at school. We were just hoping the parents would go along, y'know?"

"Yes, I do, Coach. Yes, I do. Listen, man, I know it ain't easy, doin' what you're doin'. But Mavis and I and the Johnsons got your back, brother. I know it ain't the real world, but I love this stuff, man. And I'll deny I ever said that."

"Thanks, Eddie. I'll deny I ever heard it." And we man-hugged. "Listen, Eddie, on second thought, do you and John have some time tonight for a beer and some talk? You can pick the place."

"I can't believe you just said that, Will. Yeah, we do. We're takin' the wives up to this little blues and jazz club in South Hackensack. It's called Oliver's. Y'know it?" he asked.

"Yeah, in fact I do," I said.

"Okay. Meet us there about 8:00. The girls are at Kat's, bein' amigas. Get somethin' to eat first," he said.

"Got it. Seeya there."

Oh, boy.

So I drove the twenty or so minutes up to South Hackensack and walked into Oliver's at 8:15, hoping they would be there and I wouldn't be the only white guy in the place. I wasn't. They called me over to their table, smiles all around, John ordered me a beer.

"So what are you doin' at Ethel, Willie boy?" asked LaShonda.

"Don't waste any time gettin' to the point, baby!" exclaimed her husband. "Give the boy a break."

"Nah, that's all right," I said. "I'll tell you my story, but then you'll have to tell me yours."

They all agreed.

I told my parents' tale and added my army and college chapters. "Not too sure about next year. I mean I like the coaching though I don't see it long range. I like what I did in the army. I loved the Southwest and the travel. I think I need to go back to school."

"What about you and Ramona?" asked LaShonda.

"Work in progress at this point," I answered. "Lifelong friends from age four. Then boyfriend girlfiend in high school. Breakup in senior year. Nothing for six and a half years till this past November. Lotta drama. I'm workin' on it. Now one of you."

"I grew up in Englewood," offered John. "Had a nice growin' up. It's a nice town. Played football and basketball, enlisted in the Marines after graduation in '62, did my tour in Vietnam, Paterson State Class of '69, joined the cops in Paterson. At some point found myself on leave in Charleston and met this beautiful young thing who swept me off my feet, married her on the spot, and brought her home to Jersey. In a nutshell."

"John was doin' the town with a bunch a loud, rude black boys in uniforms," said LaShonda, "and me and my friends just figgered they was Yankees who didn't know no better. But this one guy was kinda cute."

"She means me," John interjected.

"I certainly do not," insisted his wife. "It was that light-skinned boy named—what was his name, JJ?"

"Doan have no idea what you be talkin' 'bout, woman," John insisted.

"Okay, folks, that'll be enough of that," said Eddie. "Willie here won't be able to understand a word we're sayin' you keep that up."

Everyone laughed.

"Will, you said you wanted to talk to John and me tonight," said Eddie, "about what happened at the game?"

"Yeah, I guess," I answered. "I never saw anything like that. I mean, I read about it in books, sure, or seen it in movies, but right there with kids? Has that happened to your kids before? Has it happened to all of you, bein' called names? I know I sound naive, but…Now I'm embarrassed."

"Well, William," said Mavis, "this is not a subject we normally share with our white friends. In fact, I don't remember anyone ever asking before." Shaking of heads in agreement. "Yes, we have heard worse words than that hundreds of times in our lives, more in South Carolina where LaShonda and I are from, more as children for sure."

"Ever use any of them words, Willie?" asked John.

"Heard 'em a lot. Still do. Lots of working-class people see no problem with it. Same as guinea, spic, chink, kike, y'know, like it's all the same. No point even arguin' with that, is there? We all grew up with that around here."

"We'd beg to disagree with you on that. And you know better. You have to speak up, even though they don't like it." Mavis was agitated.

"Okay," I said. "Please don't take offense, but explain to me how it's different."

"You have friends you call 'guinea' or 'chink' to their face?" asked Mavis.

"Well, yeah, sometimes, foolin' around, and they'll call me 'mick' or 'donkey,' no harm, no foul," I said, a little defensively. I should have seen what was coming.

"Any friends you call 'nigger'?" she asked.

"I...uh...hmm...," I stuttered.

"I didn't think so," she said. "Why do you think that is, Willie?"

"Because you can joke around about those other words," I said. "They're epithets, but among friends, they can be used as humor. But 'nigger' is a bad word. It's a really bad word. And everybody knows that. It's a weapon."

"And why is it a bad word, Willie?" asked JJ. "Do you know?"

"Three hundred years of slavery, murder, rape, lynching, Jim Crow, cross burning, segregation, just the look of hatred in the eyes of ignorant crackers," I said. "You're better than them. You been born with white skin he, explains...Bob Dylan song."

"You been sneakin' into my history class, Willieboy?" asked Eddie.

"You know 'Strange Fruit' by Billie?" asked LaShonda.

"I do," I said. "Don't know all the words though. 'Mississippi Goddam' by Nina Simone?"

"This boy knows Ms. Nina's stuff," said Mavis. "Must have one a dem Negroes inna wood pahl fo shuha."

"Now you give that poor boy a break, woman," said Eddie, and we all laughed.

"Truthfully, I haven't said 'nigger,' not since I learned better, and that was in fifth grade in Rutherford. Ray and I made friends with two new kids in our class, they were—okay to say black?—and some of the other kids started calling us…y'know—"

"Nigger lovers?" said Eddie.

"Yeah," I said. "We were at the big school then, Union School, in fifth grade, and this bunch of sixth graders surrounded us and started in…All of a sudden, it got real quiet. Ray and I stood up and she said, 'What'd you say, you asshole?'

"I stepped up into his face and said, 'Well?' He pushed me and a huge fight started. Ray, me, DeWayne, and Charlie Jo against about eight or nine of them. We did okay. Ray always had a mouth, still does, and never backed down. Teacher had to pull her off the one kid. We all got suspended."

"What'd your parents say?" they asked.

"All four parents are European, had their own views of American race problems. Not big fans our black brothers and sisters, so we'd been hearing this stuff all our lives," said Ray.

"From our fathers, anyway," I added.

John said, "What you saw with that guy when he came to apologize? You wanted me to knock him silly, didn't you? I could feel it. That woulda been my badge, gun, and pension, Will. All of us have heard that shit every day of our lives and almost always have to learn to ignore it. You know why? 'Cause it'll get you killed. Most every black parent gives his or her kids the 'talk,' about words like 'nigger,' and I'm sorry to say, the police, right?" Looking around for agreement. "You know what else? He said,

'I'm not like that.' Well, shit, man, of course he's like that. Most white people are..."

"And any black man or woman who tells you different is shinin' you on or never lived with white people," said Mavis. "You save up a lot of anger over a lifetime. And that can kill you too if you let it. But we have ways of not lettin' it, don't we? Now you get up here and show me if white boys can dance, Willie."

Hoots and cheers as I turned beet red and the band played something up tempo. "You just saved the night, Mavis."

"Black women have lots of practice savin' things, Coach," she said.

"Would you rather be in Charleston, Mavis? Is it easier?"

"Maybe when the kids are on their way. Life's easier in the south, but there's more opportunity here," she said, "Hey, you dance real good for a—"

"Don't say it! And anyway, I'm a white boy from *Jersey*, and that makes all the difference, lady!"

We both laughed as I spun her around, and we shimmied and twisted, me following her lead. We returned to the table to a round of applause from some of the customers.

"That was all Mavis," I said as I bowed toward her.

"Why, thank you, William." She smiled.

"How abour your stories, girls?" I asked.

LaShonda said, "Oh, Mavis and I grew up next door to each other in one of the black sections of Charleston by the naval base. We went to black schools, no chance of college."

"We both got jobs in restaurant kitchens and worked our way up," added Mavis. "Didn't have much to do with white folks. Church-goin' girls with big families who like to socialize and dance and eat. It was a good life. Very different from here."

"You must miss it," I said. "Any family here in Jersey?"

"Sometimes, especially in the winter. Goodness, it's jess so ugly here!" said LaShonda.

"We all have brothers and sisters around in north Jersey, so it's nice for us and the kids," said Mavis, "cousins, aunts, and uncles, big Sunday dinners and cookouts."

"I have another question," I said.

"Oh no," they seemed to say in unison. "No more questions."

"No, really. Not about today, about the sleepovers. Do you all think they're a good idea?" I asked.

Mavis answered, "We've talked about this a lot, Will. We decided the girls need to learn how to live with white people and to succeed in the white world, like their daddies have. Mamas too. It's been a strain on them sometimes..."

"SJ kinda cracked after the game," I said, "All the kids were cryin.' They'd never heard anything like the abuse the Hitler Youth was layin' on our kids. What a terrible thing to have kids that age doing, assuming that's what it was. Credit to our girls not to start swingin'. Especially your two and Dooney and Rafferty."

"Our girls know better, but they're still only kids. They can only take so much," said LaShonda. "But to the point, they need to know that there are white folks who they can trust, and they have to learn how to read the signals. We talk a lot about that."

"So do we," said Eddie. "Talked a lot about the white boy coach, too. But you passed all the tests. So did Ray. You picked the leaders and were hardest on them, just like in the Marines."

"Army too," I said.

"Now don't go comparin' those doofuses with Marines, doggie," said JJ.

Everybody laughed.

"It seemed like the parents were pleased with the sleepovers," I ventured.

"The four amigas were a riot. They really were. None of them

135

had been up that close and personal with the white-black thing before. It was great," said Eddie.

"I know it's not the real world. It's like they're in a bubble, but it plants a seed, doesn't it, for later in life?" asked LaShonda.

Mavis added, "We weren't allowed to play with white kids once school started. Remember, we went to segregated schools. Yeah, yeah, I know, *Brown v. Board of Ed* in the '50s, right? Took a long time to travel to South Carolina, Will."

"God, I hate to hear that," I said. "But Ray and I hoped that the mixing would work and good things would happen."

"Hell," said JJ, "you gonna hafta teach this white boy some propa gramma, Mistah Monroe. He be talkin' lahk a homey. Ah doan unnastan' a word he sayed."

"You leave that poor boy alone. He be getting ready to escort Mama LaShonda around the dance floor, ain'tcha, sweet boy?" LaShonda crooned.

"What's up with this? You ain't even dance witchyoah date yet?" complained JJ, and everyone cracked up at the reference from *Animal House*.

When we returned, the conversation turned to music. "You like this kinda music, Will?" asked Eddie.

"I do. I like blues if it's simple, like twelve bar blues that I can follow anyway," I said.

"Listen to the musician," said Eddie. "Jazz too?"

"Don't understand it, but I like Miles Davis and Coltrane and Brubeck," I said. "To listen to when I run anyway. Don't know much else."

"Do you play?" asked Mavis.

"Used to be in a band, played a guitar," I said. "Haven't played in a while."

"Well, we may have to investigate this," said LaShonda and looked around the table.

"Why would we do that?" I asked.

They all looked at each other and smiled. "We'll let you know."

"Speakin' of which, how about Eddie's story?" I asked.

"Grew up in South Jersey, way down by Millville, tomato country, met Johnny at Parris Island. We were buddies all the way through to the Mekong. Saved each other's lives more than once and that's all I'll have to say about that. Came home, went to Stockton State, got a teaching degree in history, then a masters at Seton Hall once I started teaching up here in Hackensack. Go Comets! Went to Charleston with my buddy John and found the love of my life. And by god, I'm gonna dance with her tonight! Waddaya say, sugah?"

"Them teachahs shuh can talk, ain't that the truth?" asked JJ.

"That's 'cause they really smart and words keep spillin' outa they heads," I said.

"Aintchoo a teachah, son?" asked LaShonda, and she laughed and laughed.

We called it a night at 10:30. I can't remember when I laughed so much. Antidote to anger indeed. I learned a lot and felt very lucky to have spent an evening with these open and insightful people. And funny. I had known black guys in the army, especially at Huachuca, but they had always seemed kind of distant and careful. Maybe it was me. Have to think about that.

CHAPTER TWENTY-FOUR

January 21, 1983

Another road game Friday at St. Cecelia's, a mostly Italian Parish and co-ed K to 8 school. Knew nothing about them going in. Their coach, Sister John Damian, welcomed us warmly at the door and had a kid show the girls to the locker room and the coaches to our bench where she and Sister Mary had some serious catching up to do. She was dark but not Latin, short and stocky, with dark, lively eyes and an infectious smile over what looked to be a stern demeanor when necessary. The two old friends were laughing, eyes wide, gossiping, hands on each other's arms, hands over mouths saying, "No!" "Really?" "She didn't!" And so on. Clearly enjoying each other's company as religious women who had known each other and worked together for decades. It was something special to behold. That they were very fond of each other was evident. Ray saw it too and squeezed my hand. Sister had told us she and Sister John Damian had been in college together for a while and then run into each other over the years at conferences and retreats.

We got the girls charged up and ready to play. "We are brave! Gaels on three! One, two, three, Gaels!" And let them out onto the court, regulation-sized. Good-sized crowd already. Ray nudged and pointed her chin over to Mac and Fitz, who had just walked in and sat down by themselves or, as Ray would say, with all their friends. Ray headed straight over to them. Told me later what happened.

As she approached, I could see them beginning to look uncomfortably at each other, not making eye contact with her. She climbed up to where they were sitting, extended her hand, and said, "Mr. McDonald and Mr. Fitzgerald, right? Patsy and Mary Margaret's dads? I'm Ramona Voytek, Bill's assistant coach. Just thought I'd come over and say hello."

"Er, uh, hello, Ms. Voytek," said Pat.

"Nice to meet you," said Mike.

"Y'know, I can't tell from your voices which one of you chickenshit assholes left a message on my machine, but if it happens again, it'll go to the monsignor. I'm pretty sure he can tell which of you it was. And he'll take it from there. Am I makin' myself clear, lads? Well… am I? So glad we had this talk." She turned and came back to the bench, leaving them sputtering and lovely shades of pink.

Sister John Damian turned into a tiger on the sidelines once the game began—Cecelia's full court pressing, us breaking the press, not letting them score, rebounding and outletting for easy hoops. Cecelia called time with the score 16-4. Their girls were bigger than our kids, more mature, looked older, more worldly… Jeez, I wondered what the *public* school kids here looked like. They slowed the game down, tried to drive gaps, pass across, to little avail. Our break got stifled, but we had no trouble getting the ball to Trudy at the rover and good screens from Doons, Raff, and Greet. Second unit finished the half with Ethel up 18.

I had the sense that Sister John Damian was not the type to throw in an early towel and asked Sister Mary about it. "Oh most certainly not. She is not above changing the whole game plan around, especially if she thinks you've gotten over confident."

Turning to the girls, she gave them a predatory smile, which none of us even knew she was capable of, and said, "Now get out there, and don't let them off the floor!" Must be some ancient Navajo archetype thing called upon only rarely. Wow!

They ran out yelling, "Ethel, Ethel, Ethel," like a war cry.

Sister turned to us and said, "Whadja thinka that, hey? I'll never hear the end of it we let them back in this game."

Cecelia made five straight hoops to open the half. I called the second unit together, told them what I wanted, for them to be aggressive, don't give ground, do what you practice, and do it hard! Gaels on three. Whistle blew. Five out, five in. Dean Smith does this all the time. Let's see what happens here.

Ginna stole a dribble and made a layup and the free throw, her whole face lighting up and Nick and Celia, in one of their few appearances, are out of their minds. Reenie grabbed a rebound, pivoted and cleared, hit Cat on the run—another layup. Ginna and Cat trapped a dribbler who commited a travel violation. Our ball. Mary Pat inbounded under our basket to Anna, two points and made a free throw. Reenie stole a pass and converted a layup, lefthanded, both hands in the air as she dashed back up court grinning and yelling, "Awful Awful!" at a cheering Ethel bench. Ten points in thirty seconds, back up 18. All the parents and the bench were celebrating. Cecelia called time. The girls were too excited for anything I said to sink in: "Deep breaths, pressure D, Mary Pat's the Rover...play hard. Any of you wanna come out? No, really. Greet looks tired."

They looked at me like I should be led away to the nearby medical center.

But damn, they kept it up, and even the shockers got in the last three minutes. It was a happy bus ride home, chanting for Mikey's, singing Queen. Sister Mary was staying overnight for special prayers and meditations with Sister John Damian, the monsignor would pick her up tomorrow.

And the old man was at it again. Dooney and Rafferty said something about him to me. I looked at Sister like "What gives?" She just shrugged.

I told the kids we would get to it. Next home game, I would stop it.

As the girls were getting off the bus, I asked Ray, "Hey, Coach, just off the top of my head, did we ever find out anything else about Smutsy? From Grandma's story? Like what happened to him? Remember? From the story?"

"SMUTSY!!" yelled Reenie, just passing my driver's seat at that time. "How do you know my uncle Smutsy?"

St. Ethel, 53
St. Cecelia, 35
Won, 10; Lost, 1

CHAPTER TWENTY-FIVE

January 22–23, 1983

Saturday afternoon, Ray called me and said, "Guess what, William?"

"You go first, Raymoaana."

"You know I hate that!"

"Yes, I believe you've mentioned that before. On the other hand, my list of 'Things Ramona Hates' has now filled up two notebooks, so I apologize for losing track."

"Okay, wiseass, I'll tell you anyway. I called Carol this morning, and she was glad to hear from me. Waddaya think a that, small time? We're meeting for coffee tomorrow morning. You can't come."

"I'm duly impressed. Are double-head shot glossies available?"

"Not for punks like you. But Carol is giving a clinic for middle schools at Montclair State next Saturday, that's the 29, and Montclair has a game in the afternoon. We can make a day of it, lunch included, ten bucks a head. Waddaya theen, snooky?"

"Oh man, you're the best! Well, let me qualify that...No, really, that's great, the kids'll love it. We'll tell them on Monday. No, make that—you'll tell them. Vatcher doon today?"

"Chillin'. You?"

"I'm goin' to the big liberry at Monkey State to look at careers and grad school catalogues. Gonna be three or four hours doin' research. Especially looking at careers and grad schools out west. Interested? Wanna come? Maybe shoot over to Tierney's for a couple of pints after?"

"Ugh, that place is a dump full of drunken, smelly old harps and f——n' dirtbags."

Now that just really pissed me off. She could have said, "Okay, I'll come to the library with you," but not Ramona. "Yeah, Ray, right. Good reason to not go to the library. Waste of time. What was I thinkin'? What a stupid idea. See ya Monday at practice. Have a nice weekend. I'll be out all day today and tomorrow."

I hung up. The phone rang, kept ringing, I didn't answer it. I mean Tierney's was Montclair State history, fer God's sake! Get your ID, grab a beer at Tierney's. A rite of passage. The hell with her!

Very worthwhile afternoon, however. Buried my nose in career guides, grad school catalogues, and military career opportunities. The world opened before my eyes, and it extended far beyond north Jersey. But mostly, I concluded that I didn't want to coach or teach. And couldn't find any reason to remain in Bergen County, New Jersey. That was for certain. The military thing, with my army intelligence experience, was really intriguing. Didn't leave the library until six but had no one to share my discoveries with. Passed on Tierneys and ended up at Sullivans, downin' beers with the lads.

The next day, Sunday, I got up early and met some guys from school for a big diner breakfast at West's on Rte. 46, an old hangout down the mountain from Montclair State. Our bellies full, we drove up to a park in Montclair and played basketball and then touch football until it began to snow. Lot of laughing and ball busting, some flying elbows and facedowns, but otherwise, a day well spent. I was dirty and sweaty when I got back to Mama's, saw that Ray's car was there, and drove on. Didn't want to put up with her bullshit today. So

I drove to the Central in East Rutherford for a beer and a calzone and ate it at the bar.

Ray's car was still there when I got back. I rushed through saying, "I'm dirty. I need a shower," and ran upstairs. When I came back down, Mama had gone to bed, and Ray was watching TV. I got a glass of milk and said, "What's on?"

"Where've you been?" she asked. "I tried to call you all day yesterday and today, no answer."

"What does that tell you, Ray? I specifically told you on the phone I was gonna be out all day, didn't I?"

"I forgot, but so what? Y'know what, hot shit, maybe you need to coach by yourself for a while."

"I'll tell the girls you said goodbye."

Getting up off the couch, she said, "You f——n' suck, Willie!"

Door slammed. I felt like shit.

About an hour later, I drove up to her place, knocked on the door every ten minutes for an hour until she answered. "All right," I said, "I'm an asshole. I don't know where that came from. It won't happen again. I'm sorry. Really, I am sorry."

The door opened a few minutes later, her face in the opening. "Is this all because I wouldn't go to Tierney's?"

"Damn it. It wasn't just one thing, and you know it. I had a lot to talk about and—"

"If you had ever picked up the phone—"

"Goddammit! I told you on the phone I wasn't gonna be home Saturday or Sunday!"

"So get over it, Sunny Jim—"

"Did that five minutes ago. Sorry."

And we laughed…and I drove home.

Knowing I shoulda said something. I also knew when, not if, this happened again, I wouldn't cave so easily.

CHAPTER TWENTY-SIX

January 25, 1983

At Monday's practice, we had told the kids about Saturday's trip to Montclair State and got the paperwork started. We had gotten the monsignor to cover the ten-dollar-a-head price. Some of them had heard of Carol, who was only five or so years out of college. We worked a lot on pressure, both on offense and defense.

Driving east on Tuesday to Our Lady of the Harbor, beginning our second round of the schedule. I'm not sure what town the school was in, but it was a lovely, ancient church with a more modern school a few blocks from the river, maybe Weehawken or Hoboken, I can never tell down here. We had spent some of Monday's practice going over notes Sister had made after the game and felt ready.

Not so fast. Coach Suzanne—her same unpleasant, combative self—and her Vikings shut us down pretty quickly in the first quarter, and we never recovered. Outcome never in doubt, but the kids kept grinding. But gracious in victory? Nah, not even close. "Told ya so," she quipped.

I turned to Luddie. "Luds, get me that gift bag in the medical box, please."

147

"Gracious in victory, just as I would expect, Suzanne. You're my vote for coach of the year. And Miss Congeniality as well," I jabbed. "By the way, do you have a place by the river?"

"No, I don't. Why do people always ask me that?" she asked me.

"Anyway, Coach, I gotcha a little gift to celebrate your victory," I said, handing her the little bag.

Looking at me suspiciously, she thanked me and opened the bag, "Chinese herbal tea and two navel oranges?"

Our Lady of the Harbor, 47
St. Ethel, 30
Won, 10; Lost, 2

Driving home in the westbound commuter traffic from Manhattan, we knew we would get stuck and had cancelled team dinner. Didn't get home until past seven. I just went to Mama's, had some pirogies, and crashed. Don't know where Ray went, she kinda just vanished. Tonight, okay by me.

Losing does, indeed, suck. I hoped the kids weren't going to get used to it.

January 28, 1983

Two hard practices to help make sure they didn't. We travelled west on Friday to Convent Station and the Academy of St. Elizabeth and a different world. Convent, college, and academy all in a beaufiful, bucolic setting. Would like to see it in the spring. "Jeez," said Ray, after Sister and the kids got off the bus, "a lotta bucks went into this place."

"Lotta bucks to keep it goin'," I responded. "No po' folks here, ah' spect. Addie Lou spent ten years here in school. Now she's a teacher and coach here!"

"And you know that how?" the green-eyed monster demanded.

"We met for drinks a few times," I said innocently. "Just friends."

"Oh yeah? When was this?" Ray was getting hostile now.

"I don't know. Last month? Over Christmas break? She called me on the phone."

"She *what*?"

I pantomimed holding a fishing pole and reeling in the big one while breathing out "Psyyyyyyyyych."

"Ooooh, I'll f——n' kill you," she said and jumped me in the driver's seat, but I was laughing so hard that she broke her full nelson and began laughing too. The security guy looked into the bus. "Everything all right in there, folks?"

We straightened out and got up, embarrassed. "Yes, sir, sure is."

I turned back to Ray. "Gotcha!"

Ray growled, "I'll get you for this, you bozo!"

I sat her down, and I sat down across from her, "No, you won't 'get' me for this, Ray. This part of our lives is ovah, remember?"

I gave her a peck on the cheek and walked away.

Our journey to maturity was indeed a long and winding road.

Addie Lou's plight had not improved. The St. E's parents looked like they had stopped for a few at Rod's, the famous eatery just outside the convent property. Some of the dads took a long, long look at Ray as we entered the gym. She turned around and winked at me. I waved my fingers toward the moms and got some nice smiles back.

In the locker room, I was brief. "The game after a blowout always tells a lot about a team. You still got it?"

"Yeah!"

"Well, that's what we want to see today. Sister?"

"No mercy!" She cupped her hands behind her ears, looked at each of them, until they shouted in unison, "*NO MERCY!!*"

Everyone played, almost everyone scored, and we won a blowout.

St. Ethel, 52
St. Elizabeth, 23
Won, 11; Lost, 2

Addie Lou, Ray, Sister, and I sat and chatted over cups of tea for a while waiting for the girls to change.

"It's a real struggle you have here, isn't it, dear?" asked Sister. "No help?"

"Mother Superior didn't want any parental interference. I guess last year's season ended in a debacle and the coach quit in the middle. I really don't know much about basketball. I played at the Academy. I read some books over the summer, but you can see…Well, you can see…," Addie Lou lamented.

"Will says you're going to grad school next year. Good for you," said Ray.

"Yes, knock on wood. Only another month of this," Addie Lou replied.

The mighty Gaels strolled into the gym. We each gave Addie Lou a hug and wished her well. Nice girl. Back to Ethel for Mikey's. I yelled to the girls, "Ready to go on the bus at 8:30 tomorrow morning. Good work today, Gaels!"

Hollowed-eyed stares to Pat and Mike, on to Mama's for pirogies and kielbasy.

I leaned over to Ray and whispered, "I got three phone numbers. How'd you do?" and jogged to the bus.

CHAPTER TWENTY-SEVEN

January 29, 1983

The eighth graders showed up in bunches: the Amigas from Delaneys; Rafferty, Dooney, and the no longer shy Trudy from Raffertys, and Mary Pat, Reenie, and "Greet" from Hdawonicz. Sleepovers all, but at least changed out of their pj's. Teagen, Liz, and Stephanie rounded out the group. Sister Mary begged off. Her spot filled by Luddie. Two seventh graders didn't show. The kids mostly slept on the half hour ride up to campus. Ray took them into the gym as I parked the bus.

Walking into the gym, I didn't see anyone I knew, so I figured it was all public schools. Girls yapping, animated, high drama, ponytails whipping, sitting cross-legged by teams at the various baskets, Carol chatting with Ray, Gael mouths open in awe of Ray. Nine other teams sitting knees crossed then dead quiet on the whistle. Two ball dribbling, two ball alternate dribbling. Layups, reverse layups, jumpshots, elbow to elbow slide jump shots (Ray rebounding), round the horn…This is all Carol showing how it's done. "Thanks to my friend Ramona Voytek, who could play some mean basketball out at Bloomsburg State in Pennsylvania. Give it up for Coach Ray." Big round of applause, whistles, and hoots from the Gaels.

"Okay, now this is what you do, every day. *Every day!* If you want to be a good shooter."

She lay flat on her back, right hand under the ball, flipped it up, caught it. Did this fifty times. "Okay, I'll stop at fifty. Same thing, opposite hand." Fifty times, left-handed.

Teagen leaned over and whispered, "Carolina drills, right, Coach?"[2]

"Right, Teags," I said, smiling. We do that almost every day, but not fifty times.

"Okay," said Carol, getting up and going to one of the ten hoops set up in the gym. She stood just in front of the basket, hand under the ball, elbow straight, and flipped a ball through hoop. One step back. Same thing. Repeat all the way back to beyond the top of the key. Repeated it with her left hand. "Okay, if you miss, you have to try again before you can step back. This is called..."

"Range finder drill," said Liz.

"Range finder takes a lot of practice and time to master. If you don't have a hoop, you can do it against a wall without moving back too far," said Carol.

Then she stood on a block, shot a layup, caught it coming through the net while sliding to the opposite block, shot a layup, repeated, and continued till she had made twenty, now building up a glimmer. Mrs. Flanagan told me that girls don't sweat, they glimmer. "What's this drill called?" she asked the crowd.

"Mikans!" the girls yelled back. I know Luddie was hoping she would ask who George Mikan was, but no question from Carol. Maybe Carol didn't know who he was.

---

2   . Carol attended Montclair State College from 1974–1978, scoring 3,199 points before the three-point line was introduced. She averaged 38.6 PPG in her senior year and led the Indians to the NAIA Final Four, losing to UCLA in the semifinals. Within two years, the NCAA took control of the Women's College Basketball Tournament. Carol made the 1980 United States Women's Olympic Basketball Team, which did not compete due to the American boycott of the Moscow Olympics. In 1994, she was inducted into the Naismith Basketball Hall of Fame in Springfield, Massachusetts.

"Okay, girls," shouted Carol, "each team grab four balls and head to one of the ten baskets. St. Ethel, you come with me." I *love* this woman.

Ray introduced us and told Carol what a great coach I was, embarrassing the hell out of me, certainly her intent. "Saw you play a few times in college, Carol. All I can say is wow," I mumbled.

"He's kind of shy and tongue-tied, even for a guy," said Ray.

"Just the way we like 'em, right?" snapped Carol.

"Always happy to be a punch line," I came back. "Ray will be scouting in upstate New York on Tuesday, snow or no snow."

"Well, see, he does have some chutzpah," said Carol then glanced at Ray and said, out of the kids' hearing, "that means..."

"I know what it means, Carol," she said sharply.

I stopped laughing long enough to say, "It was in her *Word of the Day Book* last week," and quickly turned toward Ray with a warning look and waved my finger at her.

Carol laughed at the both of us, "Time's a wastin'."

"Okay, four girls, four balls, up here on the floor." Carol made sure all coaches were following.

To her surprise, almost all our girls could do the Carolina drill, and range finder and the Mikans. "They're well coached, Carol. What can we say?" Ray explained.

When all the girls had completed all the drills, Carol directed, "Okay, we're gonna play sudden victory, two games at a time, coaches not playing will officiate. Jump ball, first basket wins, no subs, no time-outs. Winner stays on. Got it?"

This is a favorite camp game, and it's loud and very exciting with kids cheering and screaming. We won our first three games. Trudy won the taps, to SJ or Eddie breaking, two points, game over. Got scouted, got beaten. Alternated fives after that. Kids had a ball. Had a five-minute water break. Then Carol directed each team to line up straight back from the foul line at the basket it used for the earlier drills, first two kids had basketballs.

Knockout!

You have to make a foul shot. If you miss, you must grab the rebound and put in a layup before the next shooter makes a foul shot. If not, you're out. If you make it, get the ball. Give it to the next shooter. Go to the end of the line. The more shots you make, the longer the game. The longer the game, the more running. Coaches love this.

Carol let the kids play two games. Lots of cheering and screaming, lots of fun. Trudy and SJ won our games. One more game, the real game this time. Because now, coaches were only in one line. Ray and I looked at each other. "Ten bucks," she said.

"Your're goin' down, lady!"

"Not in this lifetime, humpty," she said.

Then Carol snuck in behind Ray. "What're we playing for?"

"Ten."

Knockout against the best woman shooter on the planet. Other coaches jumped in, eager to take a shot at Carol even if the cost for losing was ten bucks. All of them went down, leaving Ray, Carol, and me.

Then Ray missed a foul shot, muttered f——, knowing she was toast. I made mine. Carol hit the rim, ball rolled in, shooter's bounce. I made one, but I decided I'd miss the next one, but... Carol missed. Then so did I!

She made her layup and drained the foul shot. The crowd erupted. Well, all but the Gaels.

Carol high-fived all the kids on their way out. We each gave her a ten. I wished her well in her career and meant it. She said to me, "Ray says you really have the touch with kids, and you know your stuff. I wish you had brought Sister Mary. There's a story to be told. I'd love to meet her."

"Well, give Ray a call. Sister would be thrilled to meet the Carol. She was kind of a pioneer for *her* time, too. She talks about you all the time. Really. And she tells great stories. Hey, Carol, thanks for a great morning. And good luck with your career."

With that, we gathered up the girls and walked around the old part of the campus, with the red-tiled roofs and white stucco walls, for a while. It was my favorite part of the school, which I love to this day. If I ever make a lot of money, I'll give a nice donation to good ole Monkey State. Ray took them through a womens' dorm just to see what it was like. Then we walked up to the Student Union, a newer building, with our meal tickets, and had a long, yappy lunch. Mostly, the kids couldn't stop talking about how Coach Will beat Coach Ray in Knockout. Ray took it all in stride on the outside. On the inside, she was plotting revenge. Russian blood is a harsh mistress. I stayed silent. For now.

After lunch, we voted and took a pass on the Montclair State-William Stockton game. Kids were beat, so were the coaches. On the bus, I asked, "Remind me, who won the coaches' Knockout?"

Ray yelled, "Silence! Or many gassers on Monday. We all know it was a fluke, right, Gaels?"

"Right! Girls rule!" they all yelled.

"Wait!" I said, standing up next to the driver's seat. "I have a better idea. Let's sing. You all like to sing, right? Here's a great new song, 'O What a Beautiful Day. In knockout, I beat coach Ray. It was a wonder to see. That Coach Ray couldn't beat me!' Everybody sing." And I waved my arm to lead the chorus. Then I started laughing and couldn't stop.

No response.

"Feminine treachery once again. Seventeen against one! That was a great song! Not fair!"

"Booooo!" was their response. Because we were early, we dropped the kids off at home, if there were people home, or called from the gym and waited if there weren't. I didn't have much of a problem spending the monsignor's gas money. When all the chickadees were in their nests, I went to Mama's and crashed. Ray was going shopping, she said. I suspected she was going to an outdoor court in Leonia and shooting foul shots.

CHAPTER TWENTY-EIGHT

January 31 to February 1, 1983

We ran the girls pretty hard in practice yesterday and didn't have to explain why. Didn't even mention who we were playing tomorrow (Henrietta). I couldn't wait, and I know Dooney and Rafferty were almost foaming at the mouth; SJ and Eddie, more quietly, also. The seventh graders were getting an education for sure and didn't seem that eager to join the fray. We finished one-on-one tournaments at each end, really a grinder. Trudy won, of course; good confidence builder for her. Then the "Knockout" chant began. Ray and I obliged. Eddie knocked me out to cheers. Stephanie, jumping up and down like a jack-in-the-box, knocked out Ray. Cat won. "Gaels on three, one, two, three."

"Gaels!"

Ray yelled, "What?"

"GAELS!"

The next day, Henrietta's girls, led by their coach, an attractive young black woman named Shayna Goldberg, NBA-shuffled into our gym, sneering at all in sight. Luddie, fearless as ever, led them

157

to the locker room while Ms. Goldberg and I grabbed a cup of coffee in the kitchen. "How you guys been doin'?" I asked her.

"You probably think this is a tough bunch. But they're not tough kids, Will. They're really not," she said. "Most of them are honor students from good homes, but they put on this tough girl shell going up against the white girls. Every time, no matter how many times I get on 'em about it. But I'm from the hood, too, so I guess it's part of the ritual. Y'just hope they'll outgrow it, y'know?"

"Wow, Coach, I never thought about it like that before," I said. "Just saw the two by fours on the shoulders and thought, 'Man, we didn't do anything to deserve this,' but you make it pretty clear what *they* see. They all from West Side of Newark?"

"Yeah, not exactly a garden spot," she answered. "A lot of them get aid from the diocese and the convent. It's really a miracle. They have no idea how lucky they are."

"Did you go there?"

"C'mon, Will. I'm Jewish." And she pulled out the Star of David on her gold chain. And laughed. As did I.

"L'chaim, Shayna." I said, "Only Hebrew I know."

"You too, Will. It'll do." And she smiled and turned to the Henrietta locker room.

Ray caught up with me going across the gym. "Nice girl," I said. "You believe she's Jewish?"

"She told you that?"

"Yeah. We're goin' out for a beer later. Wanna come?" I said in a voice that meant I didn't want her to come.

Green-eyed monster lurking, smoke rising, "Nah, my college boyfriend showed up. We're goin' into the city, see some friends. I took a personal day tomorrow, might miss practice."

Oh, man, she hit that one out of the park. Well played, lady.

The game started out as a battle. Trudy jump shot. They scored off a rebound. SJ breakaway layup. They scored a three-point play. Another Trudy jump shot and one. Raff stole a pass, hit Eddie breaking, two for us. Then we broke down and they had a run of six. I let them play, put Anna in for Dooney, who walked off right past me, down to the end of the bench pouting and looking pissed at me. I told Sister to take over and went and sat down next to Mary Grace Dooney. "Are you injured, Mary Grace?"

"No, I'm fine," she said, elbows on knees, hands clasped, and staring at the floor.

"Well, since you walked off, I thought you must be hurt."

"I forgot."

"Sure, you did. Like, when you're down here at the end of the bench, by yourself, I'll forget to put you back in the game."

"Do what you gotta do, Coach," she said.

Stifling a laugh, I said, "Gee, Doons, I know you're a tough kid and all, but that was not the right thing to say at this moment," and patted her shoulder.

"Get her back in there, you jerk." Everyone heard that one. I looked up at Monsignor with a "What gives?" expression.

I got up and travelled back to my spot. Showing up the coach when he or she takes you out of the game... Well, that's bad business. And the kids had been drilled on this. Behavior, as my psych prof used to say, to be extinguished. Immediately. And then to top it off with, "Do what you gotta do, Coach." Now *there's* your chutzpah.

Gaels back in the game, down two at the quarter. Pulled Eddie for Ginna. Good to go.

Second quarter was all Gaels. We stole the ball, we got offensive rebounds, they dribbled off their feet. Shayna *called* two time-outs, to no avail, and was grateful for the halftime buzzer. Our second unit finished the half; Dooney hanging tough in no man's land. Gaels up by ten.

First unit, Mary Pat, and Cat started the half. Henrietta was more aggressive now, more chippy, but the officials clamped right down on them. Eye-rolling by their kids of no help. Lots of Ethel mouthing, "Step back, bitch." It had to be killing Doons to be watching this. I looked down. No, she wasn't watching. She was looking at Liam, who was glaring back at her. Then Reenie and one of their bigs faced off. Reenie! Yessss! Our ball inbounds, SJ to Trudy, Trudy to Reenie, Reenie for two. Ethel erupted. Third quarter ended, up thirteen. "Get outa there!"

Rafferty came over and told me Dooney was crying. Sister Mary went down to sit with her. Starters and Ginna started the fourth quarter. I looked down the bench. Sister gave me a little head shake, "Not now." We ran off eight straight, Henrietta called time, and we're down 21. Second unit in for us with Teagen in place of Ginna. "Come on, start playin' right!" Starters looked at me like, "Well?"

Sister and Mary Grace came down and sat on either side of me with Sister nearest to the team. Doons leaned in and said, "I was wrong what I did. I was mad that you took me out. I'm sorry, Coach. It won't happen again. And I'm sorry I wised off to you."

"Go slap hands with everyone on the bench so they know it's over then go in for Anna."

I feared for any Henriettas who got in Dooney's way or chose to take her on. Cheers for Dooney when she reentered.

Ethel by 24. No problems on shake hands line. Rafferty calls everyone together in a huddle, coaches included. "Mary Grace has something to say to us."

While I'm not sure that Mary Grace knew ahead of time that she had something to say, but a Dooney to the core, she rose to the occasion. "I acted like a jerk. I embarrassed myself, and I hurt my team. It was stupid. If any of you ever do that, I'll kick your ass. Sorry, Sister."

Group hug and laughter. Sister's magic touch came through once more.

When the girls went into the locker room, Liam Dooney made a beeline for me. "All settled, Coach?" he asked, hopefully."Girl's got a head of stone, she does."

"She acted like a kid, recovered like a grown up. Well done. You can be proud of her, Liam," I said. "Also, great job by Sister Mary."

"Listen, Will, we're goin' over t'the Legion later. Wanta jine us?"

"Best idea I've heard all day."

"Okay, then. We will seeya later."

St. Ethel, 53
St. Henrietta, 29
Won, 12; Lost, 2

"What'd Liam want?" asked Ray.

"Invited me to the Legion for a few when we get back," I answered.

"I thought you were goin' out with that other coach," she said.

"Oh god, Ramona, gimme a break," I said.

"Well, *I* wasn't kidding," she declared.

"Y'know, just great, Ray. That's just somethin' special." I turned and got busy cleaning up the gym.

She turned as if to say something then continued toward the door.

"Ray?" I said in a softer tone so she would stop and turn around, "You know what else? Aahh…never mind." She hesitated for a breath but kept going.

I got to the Legion a little after the fathers arrived, and they had a Schaefer and a shot of Jameson waiting on the bar. "To Coach Willie!" toasted Pat Rafferty. "Coach Willie!" they all repeated.

"Liam," Charlie Delaney said, "I'm not so sure Mary Grace would be happy to see her Da hoistin' one to Hardass Willie."

Laughter all around. Liam said, "Shyte, lads, the last time I made her cry she was six, by god! And that made *me* cry, damn it! Willie the Hammer got there in two months without even tryin'."

161

"So where's the beautiful Ramona?" asked Kevin Flanagan. "She's the only reason we came. Sure as hell not to see your mediocre mug...or physique."

"Had other plans," I said, keeping a straight face.

Just then, Eddie Monroe and Johnnie Johnson came in. "Ahh... still on southern people's time I see, boys. This here's Warrant Officer Monroe and Sgt. Johnson, formerly of the Mekong Delta, currently of the Hackensack VFW. Please welcome our less fortunate brothers in arms." This was all Liam.

"If there's any dogface privates in the room, shouldn't they be buying the Marines a beer?" asked JJ. "Isn't that the rules?'

I'm thinkin' JJ and Eddie must really be comfortable with these guys. Have to ask them about it in view of our conversation at the jazz club. By now, everybody was laughing, high-fiving, fist-bumping, slugging down beers and shots. Feeling the military brotherhood seep back into our blood. "Corporal Rafferty," said Liam, "would you be a good lad and see that all the doors are locked. We have some serious business, so put a cap on the booze for a bit.

We have a problem. Word from the diocese has the bishop takin' sick leave as of Sunday. In the interim, some Monsignor from Paterson is standing in for him and his first act of office will be to 'retire' Monsignor Terrence at some point much earlier than he wishes to. Can't tell yez the source, but it's pretty high up, and he's never been wrong before. Not sure we can do a damn thing about it."

"Why should we care?" I asked naively.

"Well, sonny," said Pat Rafferty, "the new acting bishop is a cousin of one Patrick Fitzgerald, who has been nosing around the diocese lobbying to get his favorite priest appointed here at Ethel. Which would indicate that one Coach Willie Edwards, known to all of us here as 'The Hammer,' would be summarily fired."

"Do we have a way to stop this?" asked Eddie.

"Don't know how far we're willing to go," opined Rafferty.

"Hey," I said, "I just want to get through the end of the season and finish what I started. If you're bargaining, that's your counter."

"Yez know, this lad thinks like an Irishmen and that we're goin' up against the fookin' Brits down in the Pariliament—oops—the diocese," said Charley Delaney.

"We need a show of support for the monsignor, a big show, at the diocese, with news and TV coverage, don't yez think?" asked one of the guys.

"I'll get the girls goin' on that. It'll be grand. Get ta see our mugs on TV, right?" said Liam.

"Careful now there, lads," said Kevin McGuire. "The hats always get their way. Or get even, if they don't. They play the long game now, don't they? Cemetery plots, Christenings, weddings, all of it. All I'm saying is be careful. There's a lot at stake here, lads."

"Excellent points there, Kevin," said Liam. "We will not act in haste, and we will consult with himself."

"One small point," said John Johnson, JJ to all here, "what's your leverage?"

"Ah, now we got some grand leverage on one Mr. Michael McDonald, don'tcha know there, JJ," said Liam. "It'll haveta stay under seal for a while yet, but we're golden."

"And it's not US Army under seal, lads," said Delaney, "it's IRA under seal. No wives. No coaches. No girlfriends." All eyes on me.

"All in?"

"All in!"

I was waiting for "Up the republic!"

CHAPTER TWENTY-NINE

February 2–3, 1983

Wednesday was a snow day. A blessing for all, but teachers more than students I hate to admit. I shoveled off Mama's walk, sprinkled salt and sand, went down to the bakery to get some kolachie for us, and we sat and made a list for me to take to the Shoprite. Mama usually does the shopping, especially for meat and produce because "What does a child like you know about these things?"

Not today, too much chance of falling. But sometimes, in the nice weather, we'd drive up to Corrado's, the mega store of all kinds of meats and produce for all ethnic groups in Paterson, and she'd wander around in some pattern indecipherable to most mortals and meet me at a prearranged time and place with two carts full of produce, sausage, meats, and other stuff I never asked her about. Old country magic. On nice days, I'd take a book and head up to Garrett Mountain or to the Falls. I loved those days.

Today, I was on my own for basics. By now, probably all the milk and bread were gone, but we were good, just a few items for dinner. After I got back, I took a shower then a long nap. I woke up and wondered what to do about Ramona. Damage done? This was bad. Really bad.

Mama made paprikash that night, so I went and got Sister. We had a few beers, devoured all the dinner, and watched *My Blue Heaven*, a fifties technicolor movie with Dan Dailey and Betty Grable on TV. The two old women loved it, had probably first seen it a dozen times, singing along with the gang. I knew the song from "Fats" Domino, so I sang along as well.

They wanted to know where Ray was, and I told them she'd gone to Manhattan with her old boyfriend. Overnight. They were outraged and troubled and could see I was a wreck. Did I want to talk about it? Maybe another time. Not tonight.

* * *

First thing Thursday morning was an assembly for eighth graders. A Franciscan brother from the Monastery in Sussex County, sent by the diocese, aptly named Christian Messenger, spoke to the girls about chastity. I asked Sister Mary later what he had to say, and she admonished me, "Why, shame on you, William. Those are secrets known only among the fair sex," smiling all the while. This was so far over my head. Okay, a celibate male, instructing young teenage girls about protecting their virginity? A promise they made to the Virgin Mary. What's wrong with this picture? But he was handsome and charismatic and had the lasses in the palm of his hand. I bowed reluctantly to the wisdom of the Holy Mother Church.

I intercepted him as he left the stage and invited him for coffee, as I had some time before classes began. "Sure, sounds good," he said.

We sat in the kitchen. Turns out Chris was a Jersey boy also; he attended college in New England and served in the Peace Corps. He found his way to God in a remote village in southern Ethiopia where he was the only American. A Franciscan monastery was nearby, and Chris, a lifelong atheist, was moved by the Franciscan teachings and perhaps more by the primeval ceremonies in the local Ethiopian Orthodox Church, dating from the fifth century in the Christian era. At any rate, the experience changed the arc of his life.

"Can I ask you why you went into the Peace Corps, Brother? Where did you go?" I asked him.

"I had a good college education, I really did," he answered. "But I felt like I was missing something. I wanted to live in the world. I wanted to serve, y'know? Make a difference, see what living in the world was like? Not be a tourist, not that. You know what, I didn't want to wake up when I'm sixty and think, 'I played it safe my whole life.' So I applied, got accepted, went to Utah and New Mexico for training, and got sent to Ethiopia. Lived there from '66 to '68.

"And honestly, Will, between the Franciscan monastery and the mystery of the Coptic Ethiopian church, I became a believer. Never had a moment's doubt. Believe me, that was not the plan. I had even applied to grad schools and was ready to go, but then I knew the right thing for me was to surrender and give my life to Christ.

And what about you, Will?" he asked.

I said, "Well, two years in the army out of high school then college then here. The monsignor gave me a math job and hired me as basketball coach. But I think I'll be heading west after the school year. I had training for army intelligence and was stationed in Ft. Huachuca for a while and saw a lot of the west. And the world. I loved it. Looking for something to make use of my sociology degree and analytical skills."

"Are you a believer?" he asked.

"Cradle Catholic," I answered. "Attend Mass here at St. Ethel. I love the monsignor and Sister Mary. They have been very good to me. And Sister is the brains of our basketball defense.

Can I ask you something else? Where were you in New Mexico?"

"Our Peace Corps training group," he said, "about seventy of us were in Ship Rock on the Navajo Reservation. We lived in the BIA boarding school and taught Navajo kids in summer school."

"Oh, man, I gotta go get Sister Mary! Excuse me, Brother Chris. One of our nuns here, one who helps me with the basketball, is a Navajo from Ship Rock. Let me go see if I can find her. You got time?"

"For Sister Mary Begay, I have time."

"What?! You know her?" I yelled.

"Well, I know who she is." He laughed. "Everyone who's been in the Netahni Nez knows who she is, Will."

"Be right back," I said and ran up to the office to have Sister Mary paged, but she was next door talking to Jane. "Sister, you gotta come down the caf and talk to Brother Christian. Really, come with me."

"Well, all right, William, I think I can oblige you and the good brother," she answered, a little amused.

Brother Christian stood up as we entered the kitchen, and I said, "Brother Christian, this is Sister Mary Begay of Ship Rock, Navajo Nation, New Mexico. Sister, Brother Christian trained for his Peace Corps service in Ship Rock in 1966. He's familiar with the—what'd you call it? The netnee somethin'?"

Brother Christian stood up and they shook hands and greeted each other in Navajo, I guess it was, "Ya ta hey," just as the bell rang for first period, signaling that I had to leave.

"Listen, that's my call to class. Brother Chris, thanks for your time. Do you have a card? Great. Thanks. Hope to see you again. Thanks, Sister. See you later. Bye."

We shook hands and wished each other well. Interesting guy, interesting life. Felt like he knew a lot more about me than he let on. Franciscans were pretty sharp, too. Probably went to that New England college I thought I wanted to attend.

I hurried off to meet my seventh-grade math warriors.

Practice began without Ray. We had Blessed Kateri, with the mad Jesuit, tomorrow at our place. The team we were "lucky" to beat at their place. I was looking forward to a rematch. We worked a lot on aggressive defense and did a lot of five on five, subbing the seventh graders in and out for whoever screwed up. It got pretty nasty on the floor. I blew the whistle a lot. It wasn't a fun practice. I must have been channeling Bob Knight, thinking about tomorrow. No O-U-T or knockout after practice. A few extra gassers. Steam was coming out of my ears by the end, not at the girls.

"Take a knee," I said. Before they asked, I snapped, "No, I don't know where she is. Listen, remember when we played this team, up in the boonies? Their coach, the priest, told me after the game that we were lucky to win. I'm still annoyed, a month later, thinking about it. Take that home with you tonight. You guys had a *great* practice today. I know it didn't feel like it from where you were, but you did. Really great. Gaels on three!"

"GAELS!"

Just then, Ramona, hair flying, came running into the gym. The kids went wild. Some guy came in behind her. I turned and got the basketball cart, put the balls and pinnies away, and started getting the chairs and tables out from under the stage. The girls helped me finish. Ray stood by the door, talking to the guy, who then left. Guess he didn't want to meet the "new" old boyfriend. I sat on the stage waiting until all the kids got picked up. Then I got Luddie, passed Ray and asked her to step outside so I could lock the gym, and took Luddie home.

Ray was sitting on Mama's stoop when I arrived. She said, "I'm sorry, Willie. Listen, we need to talk—"

"Oh, yeah, Ray?" I said. "Whata we need to talk about? Y'know what, Ray? Go the f——k home. I don't need to talk to you. You got the f——n' gall to shack up with some guy and throw it in my face? What the f——k is wrong with you?

"That's not what hap—," she began.

"Get out of here—"

"Damn you, Edwards, shut the hell up and listen for once! I didn't go to New York! I didn't shack up with him!" She was sobbing now. "He's my roommate's brother. Their mother died, and he took me back to PA for the funeral. Are ya happy now?"

I looked at her, my mouth and eyes wide open, not knowing whether to laugh or cry. "Oh my god, Ray, I'm so sorry. I'm such an asshole. This is all my fault."

"We're both to blame, Willie. Becky was my best friend the last two years at Bloom, and I loved her mom. She made me feel like part of the family, like a niece. Used to hang out there in Berwyck on weekends and holidays when I didn't wanna make the drive home. Home was Buffalo then anyway.

It was a very sad time at the funeral. Becky's mom was so young, still worked as a high school science teacher. Such a loss for them. Me too, really. So come here, let us calm each other down.

"Becky used to love to come back to Jersey with me. We would stay at Mama's. She loved to go to the shore and to the city. Broadway, the Village, Yankee games. We even took the cruise around Manhattan once. Real small-town girl. She played field hockey at Bloom, not on a ride, just loved the game. Took her five years, but she made it. She's a chemical engineer now in Scranton. Way smart."

We were quiet for a long while. "I shouldna said that about Shayna, it was stupid," I said, now crying myself. "But she's a nice girl, you'd like her.

Well, that's part of it. I'm not interested in anyone else, Ray. Never was. Had six years of opportunites though, didn't I? So did you. Yet here we are, right back in Washington School playground stomping puddles and trying to beat each other in races."

"That's the thing, William. Sometimes, it's hard to reach back to that time and get past the six years apart. I think we have to be careful there. Like with this, I took the bait, as usual, didn't I?"

"Dees vas zo much eezy vhen ve vas ten, eez true, dah?" I asked.

"Dah," she answered, "but ve havto be beeg peoples now. Dah!"

"I love you, Ramona," I said, putting my arms around her.

"I love you, too, Will," she said, holding me.

We sat quietly, holding each other on Mama's stoop, for a long time, listening to each other breathe until…

"You feex?" asked Mama, sticking her head out the kitchen door.

CHAPTER THIRTY

February 4, 1983

I woke up this morning feeling beat up, exhausted, but relieved.

Two big surprises that afternoon. Ray sat with Sister Mary's arm around her in a corner of the kitchen softly crying, and I got a smile from Sister that signified "It's all right."

Back in the gym, in marched the Blessed Kateri troops led by a smiling Jesuit, who bore some resemblance to the warrior we battled last month. He shook my hand, smiled, and said, "Hi, Will. Call me Tim. Tim O'Neill. Can we talk for a bit?"

As Luddie led the girls to the locker room, Father Tim and I got a seat in the bleachers. Father Tim was in his midtwenties, dark Irish, black hair, brown eyes with a sense of humor and mischief seemingly held at bay by his Jesuit forbearers. Reminded me of some of our Irish guys who attended regular convocations at Sullivans. Absent the Irish lilt they cultivated and the north Jersey accent. He spoke with a flat, southern Indiana farm boy drawl.

"First," he said, "let me apologize for being a complete horse's ass the first time we met. Really, I mean it. I'm a Hoosier born and raised, southern Indiana farm boy, and all I know about coaching basketball I learned from watching Bobby Knight on TV. That tell you all you need to know?"

"Wow," I said, "there's a story to be told. Road to Damascus?"

"Good one! No," he said, "more like, road to the diocese of Paterson, in Father Kane's car, and a dressing down by the monsignor in charge of athletics."

"How'd you feel about that?" I asked.

"Like a weight taken off my shoulders," he answered.

"Enjoying it more now then?"

"Well...," he hesitated.

"I know," I said, "doesn't feel like a life's work, does it?"

"Exactly!"

"Did you ever hoop, Father Tim?" I asked.

"In a little Catholic high school about twenty miles from the farm. Named Bayley-Ellard. My dad's a farmer with his brothers mostly, but he teaches English and coaches baseball at Bayley. But there were only 180 kids in school, so we only had baseball and basketball and band, Went to a small Catholic college in Indiana, St. Mary of the Woods, then the seminary for a while. Going to Fordham next year. Can't wait!"

"Well," I said, "your kids are well coached, so they know what they're doing. Keep 'em workin' till the end, Father. You'll be fine. I've seen a couple of the younger coaches kind of throw in the towel already. Not good for the girls to have that happen. Bad lesson for all, big hypocrisy." This is me, with two months of junior high coaching experience, dispensing wisdom to a future soldier of Jesus.

"Thanks, Will. And you've done a great job with your girls. They're feisty. What're you up to next year?"

"Headin' west, I hope," I said. "Spent time there when I was in the army. Loved it. I grew up about two miles from here, had never seen anything like all that open space, the mountains, the quiet. Wow! I fell in love with it!"

"Good for you, Will," he said.

With some home cooking from the officials, and given that our girls had gotten so much better, it was no contest. Once again, everybody played. Had we been playing against the Father Tim we had met in December, the damage would have been far worse.

St. Ethel, 47
Blessed Kateri, 25
Won, 13; Lost, 2

I caught Father Tim on his way out the door. "Father, I really enjoyed talking to you. If you want to get together some night and have a beer, give me a call. Here's my number. I live two blocks from the school. It was really a pleasure. Good luck to you."

"Thank you, Will. I hope I can take you up on your offer. My time isn't my own though. God bless you." And we shook hands goodbye.

The gym was empty. Luddie had gotten a ride. Sister was waiting for the monsignor to go to dinner. She walked over to where I sat in the kitchen, nursing a cup of tea.

Sister whispered to me, "William, you did good."

"I did, Sister, but it was all Ray. Where is she by the way?"

"She went home," said Sister Mary. "She's waiting for you there if you want to come over, she said."

Monsignor had stuck his head in the door, and Sister Mary said good night.

When I got to Ray's, she was in her pajamas, her cotton pajamas with little kittens on them. "Let's not talk or do anything. Just come to bed and hold me till we fall asleep. We can talk in the morning, okay?"

"That's what *I* was gonna say." I laughed.

Your basic Jersey, "Yeah, right," was her reply.

But after all the drama and rage and terror of the past few days, it felt like heaven just to snuggle and decompress.

CHAPTER THIRTY-ONE

February 5, 1983

We slept in on Saturday, not caring when we got up. Ray suggested we go out for breakfast. "On you, right?" I asked.

"Such a gallant partner," she said. "Okay, on me, just this once, since I'm makin' the big public school bucks."

"Long shower?" I queried.

"You might not be up for it, Villiyum," she teased.

"You veesh."

"No, ah dunt, you dunce," she said laughing.

Long enough, indeed.

Swiss cheese omelet with mushrooms! To die for! At Howie's Fifties Café in Ridgefield Park. Ray had poached eggs and salmon.

"How 'bout Mama the other night?" I laughed over coffee.

"She has no shame," replied Ray, "Ees my house, dah?' Hey, no harm, no foul. Ve feex, right?"

"Let's have a nice day today 'cause I'll be gone all day tomorrow takin' Luddie to the Garden. Waddayawanna do, any ideas?"

"I thought *I* was goin'," she said. "What happened? You were pissed when I was going to New York and you gave my ticket to—"

"The monsignor," I said. "But I'll call him and tell him you changed your your mind and that you decided to go."

"Sure you will," she said skeptically. "Let's go back to my place right now, and you can call him."

"On it. Let me get the check." And I called for the waitress, paid the check, even though it was her treat, left a good tip, and we headed back to Leonia.

"Well done, Snookie."

Back at Ray's, I dialed the Rectory, blocking Ray's sight of the phone, and pressing down on the buttons so it was a dead line. I faked the whole conversation so that Monsignor happily gave up his ticket. I hung up and smiled at Ray.

"Nice try, dollink." And she broke out laughing.

"Waddaya mean?" I complained, trying to keep a straight face. "He said you could use his ticket."

"Feeling guilty, are we? Making up untruths to your own true love. Shame, shame on you, Willieboy," she said with a big smile. "I admit I deserved to lose the ticket, but you have to make it up to me today. Rockefeller Center, St. Patrick's, nice dinner. But you must confess, you fool!"

"I can't stand it. I did it. I'm guilty. I deserve to be punished." And threw myself at her feet.

She placed one foot on my back and proclaimed, "Queen Ramona reigns triumphant again!" before I pulled her down, and we both dissolved into laughter. We were there for a while.

We drove to Rutherford to catch the train to Penn Station and then walked up to St. Patrick's. Ray lit a candle for Becky's mother, and we sat and kneeled in a pew for about twenty minutes. Kinda noisy with all the tourists in and out, so we walked over to Rockefeller Center.

Ray decided we should go ice-skating, which I hadn't done since high school, but apparently she had kept up with in PA. She was pretty deft, but it took me a while to get my balance back. Anyway, it was fun, and I enjoyed watching Ray really enjoy herself and lose herself in the skating. Thank God there were too many other skaters on the ice or she would have wanted to race.

We had a nice dinner in the restaurant there and took the train back to Station Square, yapping all the way like we would have if it had been a first date, and we were still kids. Never once talked about the troubles we had been going through, the fighting, the hurt, or the years we lost. A day in Manhattan. One to remember.

We took my car back to Ray's and spent the night talking basketball, past and present. "What's gonna happen tomorrow?" she asked.

"I really don't know," I said. "We have seats behind the Celtic bench, so we're right there. Beyond that, I don't know. I hope Bird will say hello to Luddie, that would make her day. It shouldn't be that big a deal."

"What about that crazy Jesuit coach from Kateri? What was his story?"

"Well," I said, "he must have undergone an exorcism. Country boy from southern Indiana, calmed down, no trace of the lunatic from December. I guess he got called in and read the riot act. Goin' to Fordham to the seminary next year. I liked him. He had that gleam in his eye, y'know? Very quick, very smart, but has that flat farm boy drawl. Doesn't miss much, I think."

Back at Ray's, we continued to work on our plan for world peace.

CHAPTER THIRTY-TWO

February 6, 1983

We lucked out and the expected snow turned right, out into the Atlantic, and south Jersey got buried. Celtic luck, not our problem. Monsignor himself drove the town car through the Lincoln Tunnel into Manhattan, insisting that Luddie sit up front with him and pointing out all the notable sights as we descended the helix. Not many really, as we went right into a parking deck for the Garden on 8th Avenue and 38th St. To my utter disbelief, the guy working the parking lot said, "Howarya, Monsignor? Goin' t'the game t'day? Celts in town, tough ticket, I'll say."

"Ah, Jimmy boy, it's all grand. How's the missus and the little ones?" he said, slipping Jimmy a twenty and exiting the car.

"We're all good, Monsignor, thank God. Moved up to Riverdale last month, a grand apartment. Thanks for the tip, Monsignor. Enjoy the game. You too, little one."

"Now, listen," said the monsignor, "We're gonna have lunch at my favorite pub over on 36th St, as I told you. And since you provided the tickets, Luddie, lunch is on me. Will that be okay with you, lass? We'll have plenty of time to walk around at the Garden."

"Yes, Monsignor, that would be great." Luddie was growing in confidence by the minute.

The monsignor's pub was the Molly Wee, a little Irish hole in the wall just off 8th Avenue. You would have thought the Holy Father himself had just walked in. The monsignor schmoozed for a while and bought a round for everyone at the bar. It was like old home week. Only Irish Need Apply. When he joined us at our booth, he said, by way of explanation, "Goes back to when I played at Fordham. We used to play at the Old Garden, up on 48th Street."

Luddie and I ordered shepherd's pie, Sister and Monsignor had fish and chips. As Luddie was about to launch out of her seat in her excitement, we finished quickly and walked down to the Garden, Luddie's mouth a perfect O as we found our seats three rows behind the Celtic bench. We had learned that our tickets allowed us to stay after the game ended and see if the players would talk to us, well, us being Luddie. The players were on their backs at midcourt, being stretched. When they came off, Larry walked by us and said, "Hi, Luddie." I thought she would stop breathing. She looked at me, eyes like saucers, "How'd he know who I was?"

The world through a child's eyes…Sister's and mine as well. Warmups, player intros, and the game began slowly, picked up pace. You know what you don't realize when you watch the NBA on TV? How big these guys are and how hard they smack each other around. I would have never survived at this level. I mean, we were right there. We could hear and feel the contact and the violence. The Celtics were so good. Luddie was ecstatic, but Sister was in a dream state, likely never having even imagined anything like this, I'm sure. Halftime came. Luddie started to get up, but the monsignor put his hand on her arm and said, "Just a minute, Luddie, we might be having a surprise here any minute."

When the court cleared, the Garden public address announcer came to center court, miked from that cool mike that drops from the ceiling, and spoke:

"Ladies and gentlemen, if I could have your attention please. On behalf of Madison Square Garden, the New York Knickerbockers, the Roman Catholic Archdiocese of New York, and the Archdiocese of Paterson, we would like to honor two of the great figures of basketball of the New York Metropolitan area. They have both played and coached in this area for decades, she at Caldwell College in New Jersey, he a Hall of Fame coach at St. Peter's Prep."

Sister's mouth dropped open. She covered it with her right hand, and she stared at Monsignor, who pretended to be listening earnestly to the announcer.

"She is a sister of the Dominican order, where she has served God for many decades. He is a Fordham Ram and in the Fordham Hall of Fame, a Jesuit brother, and now Monsignor. Ladies and gentlemen, please give a Madison Square Garden welcome for retired Sister Mary Begay, formerly of the Navajo Nation in Ship Rock, New Mexico, now of the Dominican Sisterhood in New Jersey and Monsignor Terrence McEntee of the Jesuit Brotherhood."

Hard to keep order of what happened then. Monsignor arose and helped Sister out of her seat. She reached over for Luddie and the three of them walked out to the center of the court, brightly lit in the powerful Garden spotlight. Thunderous applause. Everyone on their feet. Sister Mary's knees visibly wobble. The two are shaking hands with Knick and New York City and New Jersey officials. Oh... my...god. Literally. Monsignor must have called in some favors for this one. His eminence had died the year before or Monsignor would have had him here as well. But there were some big diocesan wheels to be seen.

I have read often of beatific smiles, but I have never come close to seeing one until today. God bless the monsignor. What a thing to do! And what a wonderful thing for Sister Mary Begay, child of the Navajo Nation.

And we hadn't yet met Bird and the Celtics!

When they got back to their seats, Monsignor was silent about the wheeling and dealing he went through to accomplish this for Sister Mary. Himself being included might have been a surprise. An unseen hand? I was sorry Ray had to miss this.

One of the Celtics' locker room guys came over and said, "Hey, Luddie? Larry'll be back out in a few minutes, so stay right here. Congratulations, Sister, Monsignor."

Then another amazing thing happened. Coach Brown, now the Knicks' coach, led some of his players toward us: the great Bernard King, Bill Cartwright, Paul Westphal, Rory Sparrow, and Louis Orr. They asked to shake Sister's hand and to receive her and Monsignor's blessings. Some brought their young children and wives with them. I had tears in my eyes by the time the last one left.

Then Bird and the Celtics came out. Bird called out to her, "Hey, Luddie, come down on the court and meet the boys."

"*Can* I, Coach?"

"Go on, Luds. That's why we came."

Chief, McHale, Archibald, Ainge, and Buckner came out and sat on the bench with Luddie and Bird, talking hoops and stats and strategy, Luddie keeping right up with them. Then Chief got a ball, put Luddie on his shoulders, and told her, "When you get home, you tell all your friends you dunked one at the Garden, okay?"Luddie jammed it through, then jumped off his shoulders and ran out to the foul line, bent down, and looked closely at the midpoint of the foul line. Then looked up at me and yelled, "It's here, Coach!"

She ran back to the Celtics and told them the story I had told the Gaels, and they gave me a thumbs-up. They had enjoyed calling Bird "Ptak" during their halftime with Luddie, and she got a big kick out of it as well.

Each of them came up and spoke with Sister and the monsignor as the Knicks had.

We were all tearing up. I looked at Bird. He asked, "Was it you?'

I shrugged and smiled.

"What a great kid! Keep me posted. Maybe we can do something for her."

"She's a genius, Larry. Really. Thank you for your kindness today. Really, you're *not* Polish?"

"I know, right? My pleasure, Will. Have a good rest of the season."

I thumped my chest and said, "Go Green!"

Then Luddie shook hands with all of them but saved a big hug for Larry Ptak.

But it wasn't the Celtics' year. The Sixers were to be NBA champs, led by Coach Billy Cunningham, Moses Malone, the Great Dr. J, Andrew Toney, Bobby Jones, Mo Cheeks, and Darryl Dawkins.

Then just before the Celts left the court, Coach Brown came back out, got our attention, and the three of us huddled right behind Marv Albert, the voice of the Knicks. They wanted me to send them her grades and any other info, if she was having troubles, family stuff. They had big plans, and they wanted to make sure she stayed on track. They had both been taken in by her. But not a word of this to her. Gave me their cards, and we were ready for the second half. Which passed in a blur. Celtics by fourteen.

As the crowd began to head for the exits, Monsignor leaned over and asked me, "Will, can you find your way to the parking deck and bring the car around to the 8th Avenue entrance? We'll be waitin' for you. Tell Jimmy it's the monsignor's car. Give him this twenty. And take your time. Sister and I have some old friends to catch up with, and we'll take Luddie along to see the sights. Give us at least half an hour. Got that, Billy boy?"

Luddie broke out laughing, but a stern look from himself cut her off.

Just then, Chief came running out with a Celtic gym bag. "Hey, Luddie, we forgot your loot."

"Wow, you're kidding, right, Chief?"

"No joke, Luds. All yours. From the guys."

"Oh man. Thank everyone for me, please?"

"You got it, girl. Be strong."

I looked at her incredulously. "Luds? Chief?"

"Listen, Coach. I'm finally cool, okay? Deal with it."

And she broke out in a smile and a beautiful laugh I had not seen or heard before. And gave me the bag to carry to the car. No fool, our Ludmilla. That was my cue to take off for the parking lot and, about an hour later, pick up my passengers at the designated spot on 8th Avenue.

"Will," said, "go up 8th Avenue and turn left on 44th Street. Can ya do that, boyo?"

"Sure thing, sir," I said.

"Luddie, this part of New York, where we are now, is Manhattan. When you get to school tomorrow, go to the library and ask Mrs. Harris to show it to you on a map. This part of Manhattan is called Midtown. When Coach turns left up here, he's turning into a section that used to be called Hell's Kitchen, still is by old-timers like me.

Will, can ya turn left up here now, this is 44th. Coach is a Jersey driver, Luddie, ya gotta tell'm everything twice."

He and Luddy got a big kick out of this.

"Coach, can ya pull up over here on the right, in front of Owney's? There's a good lad. Luddie, I was born up on the third floor above the bar and lived there till I went away to school. Now waddaya thinka that?"

"Were all these bars and restaurants on the street then?" Luddie asked.

"What a good question. Luddie!" exclaimed Monsignor. "No, all these buildings were tenements, kind of run-down apartment buildings. Almost everyone on all the streets around here, in Hell's Kitchen, was Irish. Thousands and thousands. Now remember, this was over sixty years ago in the 1920s. Now it's called Clinton, and it's a lot of fancy restaurants, apartments, and shops. Maybe you'll live here someday. Got it? Will, let's go up Riverside Drive to the Bridge, can ya do that, lad?"

"Is the monsignor—ooops."

"Good save," said my new friend Terrence. As if.

From the back seat now, acting as tour guide, he pointed out various landmarks or places he had been. The whole panorama opened up, and Luddie's eyes were wide open, more so when we crossed the George Washington Bridge, the skyline, lit up in the dark now, to our left.

When we got to Luddie's, Monsignor got out of the car with Luddie as Mrs. Woijahowicz came rushing out of the building to kiss his ring, Papa following close behind. They began a warm conversation in Polish, laughing as though they had known each other for years. Maybe they had. Monsignor blessed them and then led them each to a corner behind a wall and heard their confessions. The peace and tranquility on Mrs. Woijahowicz's face was astounding. I had seen that look of serenity twice now today. I got out of the car as she approached. She took both my hands in hers and said, "Meester Coach, tank you zo much for your kindness to Ludmilla. You have made her like a different girl."

And she kissed my hands. And Papa gruffly shook my hand, "Yes, tank you, sir."

"She is a wonderful girl, very, very smart. We are very proud of her," I said, wishing I could speak Polish. I was overcome really. My little Luddy.

I nodded, finally overwhelmed by the whole day, motioned to Luddie to come over. "So, how was it?"

"Eh, it was okay I guess." And jumped into my arms. "Hey, I told the Celtics your story about the dot in the center of the foul line. They loved it and they all laughed. You're the best, Coach!" Again the laugh. Then she stepped back and, serious now, said, "What were you and Coach Brown and Larry talking about?"

"Just chattin' and catchin' up about the league," I said. "We'll talk next week in school. Promise. It's all good, Luddie. Hey, I didn't know the monsignor spoke Polish."

"Oh, yeah, he came to Poland to help us and a bunch of other people come to America. With a bunch of cardinals. When I was little. I thought everybody knew that," Luddy said matter-of-factly.

I started to speak but was cut off.

Monsignor came by, looking exhausted, said, "Let's get in the car." And we took off home.

I thought to ask the monsignor about how and where he learned Polish, but he looked like he was in another world. And not to be trifled with as he sat in the back with Sister Mary. It occurred to me that, other than his name, I knew nothing about him. Best not bring up what Luddie told me. Oh, he liked basketball. And he was Irish. And now the Hell's Kitchen story.

When we got back to drop off Sister Mary, before getting out of the Lincoln to let Sister out, he leaned forward from the back seat and said softly, "I don't know how one so young pulled this off, William Edwards, but it shows great political potential. How'd ya get past the Jesuits, boyo?"

Without turning around, I said, "In all modesty, Monsignor, I'd say I learned at the hand of the master."

After a rollicking laugh, he leaned back and said, "This is one we've got to keep our eyes on, Mary."

Throwing caution to the wind, just to see what he would say, "One question, sir. Where and when did you learn Polish?"

"Excellent question, William, but asked at the wrong time. Timing is always key, wouldn't you agree, Mary?" he asked. She smiled and nodded.

I was speechless. He didn't want to tell me. Even after all that about Hell's Kitchen, he still kept his secrets.

* * *

For three years in the 1930s, Terry McEntee, the Fordham Ram center, was the college basketball star of the New York metropolitan area, an otherwise dark time in the city. At six feet four inches, he was among the tallest players in the area, and his fearless aggressiveness and deft shooting touch made him a difficult opponent to defend. In those days, play was stopped after each field goal and the referee tossed the ball up and the teams jumped center. Fordham basketball, during his years there, was very successful and along with Manhattan College St. John's, and City College of NY garnered a lot of attention during the winter months. Terrence's number was retired, and he was elected to the Ram Hall of Fame.

And while Terrence loved playing basketball, it didn't deter nor distract him from his life's goal of ordination into the Jesuit brotherhood. He had tasted good and evil growing up in Hell's Kitchen as the "nephew" of a certified gangster, whom he loved dearly nevertheless. But Owny Madden had seen to it that Terrence was educated properly and, to the extent it was possible, was insulated from his uncle's world.

Upon his ordination, Terrence was assigned to assist the pastor at St. Stanislaus Roman Catholic Church and to teach Latin and coach basketball in St. Stanislaus Catholic High School in Brooklyn in the fall of 1940. The parish was almost exclusively Polish, a language Terrence did not speak. This was an emergency for the diocese and a favor called in by Monsignor Hinefski of St. Stanislaus and was not to be permanent. The Jesuits had other plans for Terrence, who, eager to begin his new assignment, travelled to the heavily Polish Greenpoint section of Brooklyn where St. Stan's was a neighborhood landmark. He had never been to Brooklyn in his life. Not even to a Dodger game.

After meeting with the monsignor and getting his room and board settled, with two weeks remaining until the fall term began, he went to St. Stan's HS, next door, found the headmaster's office and introduced himself. Father Kazimir Rovinski was a talker, and after an hour, Terrence got his class assignments, the names of some Polish tutors, and a list of boys returing from last year's St. Stan's Basketball team, which had suffered through a two and twelve season.

"Have to put an end to that," he thought.

CHAPTER THIRTY-THREE

February 7, 1983

All the next day, Monday, staff at the school was buzzing about the archbishop being moved out for health reasons, some calling it a coup, and a temporary replacement in his seat until the Vatican decided what to do. Big-time politics at work here? Or just an old man's frailties? Monsignor next to go? And soon? The Peggys, Dooney and Rafferty, were working the phones today to notify all the basketball parents of a meeting tonight at 5:30 after practice. Loving the drama, I'm thinking.

Ray came into the gym for practice, and I walked over to her and whispered, "Lotta drama goin' on today. Big politics in the diocese. Parents meeting after practice, so let's let the girls show off at the end of practice. Got it, Coach?"

"Dah."

Practice was spirited and physical, as it always was when there were fathers around. We knew nothing about Mother Seton, who we had tomorrow at home, other than what Shayna had

189

told us, that Henrietta had beaten them by three at Henrietta. Likely a physical game, and I felt the girls were up for that. Fast break drills. Knockout, escape from practice. Ray was all over everyone's back.

New drill. Layup shooting game. Two teams, one on each block. Dooney, Rafferty, and the seventh graders on left block, rest of team on right block. Fifteen wins. Shoot, get your own rebound, give it to next girl, go to end of your line. I keep left block score, Ray keeps right block score. Begin on whistle. Lots of yelling and screaming. I love this drill. We'll fiddle around with this for the rest of the season. Dooney's team lost by one. "I know, captains, not fair!" I commiserated.

We had a lot of contact, competitive drills, and grinding. "Bring 'em in, captains,"

"Gaels on three! One, two, three, GAELS!"

They helped me set up the tables and benches while Ray gabbed with some of the mothers, and the parents drifted in. Smell of coffee, sight of pastries, and Ramona decided to hang around a while.

Liam rose: "Parliamentary rules. I'll take the chair."

Fitz: "Says who?"

Liam: "All in favor? Ayes have it. Chair recognizes Kevin Flanagan."

Kevin: "It's clear the archbishop will not be coming back and that a replacement, temporary or not, will soon be in place. From what we hear, this fella will not be a friend of St. Ethel or the monsignor."

Fitz: "Now, just a minute. You have no cause—"

Liam: "Sit down and be still. You have not been recognized by the chair, Fitz. Roberts Rules, y'know."

Fitz: "That's just bullsh—"

Eddie Monroe, sergeant-at-arms, in his official high school teacher voice: "He said, 'Sit down.'"

Fitz sitting down.

Roger: "Motion in support of Monsignor McEntee maintaining his position as pastor of St. Ethel."

Many seconds.

Liam: "Discussion?"

Eddie: "Call the question."

Liam: "Ayes have it. St. Ethel Basketball Parents Organization sends official letter in support of Monsignor to Diocese."

"Thank yez all fer comin'."

It was like watching the great Tip O'Neill.

Not exactly Robert's Rules of Order, but it got the job done.

People settled into smaller groups and caught up on the gossip, some of the women left, hauling Gaels along with them. Liam and Pat Rafferty went over and sat with Fitz and Mike in their corner. Pat pulled out a pint of Jameson and poured a dollop in everyone's cup. They chatted for about ten minutes then Mike's face got coronary red. He shook his head violently and almost shouted, "It's out of my hands, now, Liam, damnit. It's bein' made in Washington or New York by the hats. I think Terrence spent all his capital yesterday at the Garden. Did you hear what he pulled off? My god, he's out of his mind!"

So the old man's plan had fooled them all. As he had told Liam and me last night, he'd retire officially on April 1, two months earlier than demanded by the diocese. He'd pack his bags and head home to County Meath, north of Dublin, where his younger sister had a home among the ancient ruins of Ireland's past. Nobody the wiser.

On the way out, I said to Liam, "Academy Awards to you and himself."

"Why, the missus always says, 'Liam, that young Willie, nothin' gets by him, does it now. And he's such a boy still.'"

"So," I speculated, "he set up this whole scenario, misdirected us all including the hats, so he could go out quietly on his own terms. Am I getting this right, Liam?"

"Pretty much, Will. A few minor details here and there."

"What about Mrs. O'Toole?"

"What about her? Now, listen up here, sonny. Recall we took this oath at the Legion, and we wasn't playing cops and robbers. So here's the thing, Will. Let it be. Hmmmm…Good name for a tune. 'When I find myself in times of trouble, Mother Mary comes to me, speaking words…'"I joined him, singing tenor, "'Words of wisdom, let it be. And in my hour…'"

"Damn if we don't sound like Paul and John," said Liam.

"Nice Irish tenor your got there, lad," I said.

"Okay, message received, loud and clear," I acknowledged. "Thanks for this, Chairman Dooney. You're a dear and good friend."

"Once in, never out," he whispered.

"Up the Republic," I whispered back.

Liam's eyes flew open, and he spoke in alarm, "Now dontcha go sayin' that IRA shyte in anyone's hearin', ya damn fool! It's nothin' to be jokin' about, boyo! These IRA lads are hard men, and they see nothin' funny about their business. And ya never know who's listenin'. Do ya get may meanin', Willie? Do ya now?"

Shaken, I just nodded. He wasn't kidding.

* * *

After the gym was cleaned up and everyone gone, I explained to Ray what was going on. "They think there's a faction in the diocese that backed moving the bishop out. He's old and infirm. This faction wants their guy in, but they have to get him by the Council of Bishops and then the higher-ups above them. Anyway, he will make life difficult for the monsignor, who will then retire, and then they will replace me. Short version."

"We know we can walk on these coaching jobs, right?"

"But I don't want to leave the girls in the lurch, do you?" I asked.

"No, of course not," she said.

"Okay, we will look for guidance from Liam, the monsignor, and Sister Mary. Between them, they know everything. Agreed?"

"Dah."

"No one's around. C'mere and gimme a kiss, you fool," I said.

"Vhat eff ah dun vant to?"

"Of course you vant to!"

"Dah."

"See you tomorrow."

Donald Schlenger

CHAPTER THIRTY-FOUR

February 8, 1983

I saw the clock hit every hour. Felt scared, like my life was at a turning point and I was going make a terrible mistake I could never take back. I was kind of out of it all day, like a crazy professor in a TV sitcom: Knicks, Celtics, Monsignor's deceptions, Ramona, Navajo nuns, ancient Ireland, beautiful African American Jewish girls, Polish math savants, Addie Lou, brilliant clerics, archbishops…Never really got close to what was at the bottom of it all. Duh. At every turn was Ramona, waiting for me to fix it, to do the right thing, to open my heart and let her explain.

I woke up in a sweat, sheets all over the bed in a twist. Whoa! Don't need this dream no more. We feex? Da. But still shaky when I got to school.

The kids in my classes got a dose of hard-ass Willie. Bell to bell, pop quizzes, no smiles.

School finally ended, and I sat in the kitchen with Sister and a pot of tea. "William," she said, "I'm so happy for you and Ramona. Did you have some time together over the weekend?"

"We did, Sister," I said. "We spent Saturday at Rockefeller Center being tourists. It was like we went on a date when we were kids without all the baggage. Went to St. Pat's, skated at Rockefeller Center, had dinner. Great day all around. It was as if we reached back six years ago but we weren't kids. Am I makin' sense?"

"Yes, you are. And why do you think that is, Will?" asked Sister.

"Y'know, Sister," I said, "we had a crisis, and I went back to loss of faith and trust. And rage. Ray brought us back, Sister. She made me shut up and listen. I couldna done it, I was off the cliff."

"Well," she said, "it might surprise you to know that she never once gave up on you."

Just then, Ramona came through the door, followed by a stocky, fair-haired guy leading a group of girls who looked like a junior high school basketball team. Sister Mary smiled as I got up and said "Oh, William, we can continue this another time. Will that be all right?"

"That would be great, Sister. By the way, have you recovered from Sunday? Were you surprised?"

"Oh, William! It was the most wonderful day. Thanks to you and Terrence. God bless you."

Terrence? Mary?

"Sister, God has blessed me many times over bringing you into my life," I said truthfully.

My heart was full, really, for the moment, anyway…Ramona saw us together and smiled. Right at that moment, I remembered a plan I had made a few weeks ago before everything fell apart. It was like getting hit by lightning, and I had to catch my breath. I could do it today if the timing worked out. Oh yeah! Hadn't seen that in a while. I smiled back. Watch out, Will and Ray are back. I introduced myself to their coach as Luddie, in her green satin Celtic jacket, came over and led the girls to their locker room.

"How about some coffee or a soda?" I asked Coach Butch Majeski.

"Coke's good if ya got any," he said.

"How you guys doin'?" I asked.

"I dunno if we played anyadduh same teams. You guys played that black school, didn't ya?"

"Twice," I replied.

"Howjuzdo?"

"Beat 'em both times."

"Yeah, we kicked the shit outa 'em at their place. Youda thought black kids could play betta…"

"Hey, Butch, I gotta go check on my kids. Nice talkin' to you. Have a good game."

Shayla had told me Henrietta had beaten them by four at home. But this guy, man, God help us, freshmen football maybe, but junior high girls? In a Catholic school?

I walked over to the locker room. Ray was waiting outside. "What were you and Sister talking about?"

"The Knicks game." Half-true answer.

"Ready? Are you brave?" I yelled.

"We are brave!" the team responded.

"Gaels on three!" This was the four Amigas. "One, two, three, Gaels!"

Mother Seton Academy, grades K-12, was located in one of the four Oranges, didn't know which, but probably not South Orange. Mixed bag ethnically. Gaels out first to cheers, then Mother Seton, trying to look urban cool, tough, somehow not pulling it off. One in a hijab, one looked like Urkel's sister, one white girl with a spectacular red-haired Angela Davis Afro.

Mother Seton kicked the crap out of us for the first six minutes. "Get outa here!" We had six fouls already, and I had to take out Raffy and SJ and put in Greet and Ginna. Well, damned if that didn't turn out right. Ginna and Eddie were like flies buzzing around bothering the ball handlers and seemed almost telepathic. Trudy made two jumpers and a put back. "Pass the ball!" They called time-out, and I got Cat in for Eddie and Flanagan in for Dooney. "Gaels, we're goin' full speed both ends. Trudes, huddle them up out there and make sure they know what we're doing."

She did it then called "Gaels on three! One, two, three, GAELS!"

The second unit, with Trudy, played until three minutes left in second quarter and didn't give an inch. "What's the matter with you!?" With their mouths watering, I put the starters back in with Greet, Ethel up eleven. They finished the half up fifteen.

I had finally had enough. I told Sister and Ray to take the girls in, I'd be a minute. "Watch your temper, William," cautioned Sister.

Monsignor caught my eye and shook his head, but I charged up onto the stage ready to rip this old fool a new one. He was sitting next to Fitzgerald's wife, whose first name failed me. "Hi, Coach," she said. "Daddy, this is Mary Margaret's coach, Will Edwards. Coach, say hello to my father, Tommy McNamara. Daddy, shake Coach's hand."

We shook hands. "It was nice of you to come up and say hello, Coach. Daddy loves to come to the games. You've probably heard him." She leaned over and spoke in a near whisper, "Will, my father has some dementia and Tourette's syndrome. He gets excited at the games, but he means no harm."

"Okay, Mrs. Fitzgerald, just had to check. I glad you can bring him. Nice thing to do. See you later." I turned to go and the monsignor and the two car dealers were right on my heels.

I ignored them all and rushed back to the locker room. I looked at Fitz and shook my head.

"Great work, both units," I told them all. "Great effort, great teamwork, even when you weren't playing with your regular group."

Ray called me over to a corner where the kids couldn't hear us. "Why'd you take those kids out in the first quarter?" Then, "I think Reenie's caught up with Rafferty and you should be..."

"They were playing like bumper cars in Asbury Park, fer Chrissakes," I said.

"You coulda just called a time-out and talked to them," she countered.

"That's what you woulda done, call a time-out?" I asked.

"Yeah, why not?" she asked.

"And you'd start Reenie over Rafferty?" I asked.

"Yeah, I woulda. Why not?" she said.

There were answers to all these questions, but not now, and I sure as hell wasn't getting into it with her. Enough of this. "Okay, Gaels, bring it in. Great stuff this half, both units. Got us back in the game, got us back in the lead."

I looked over at Ray and told the girls, "Coach Ray's gonna take over the second half for the rest of the game. Tell you who's starting who's in, who's out, make the calls. Do we have 100 percent confidence?"

Dooney started, "Coach Ray! Coach Ray! Coach Ray!"

Mary Pat called, "Bring it in. Gaels on Three! One, two, three, GAELS!"

And like a herd of colts, they galloped out the door.

Ray turned to me and smiled. "About time, Willieboy."

Sister walked in at that moment, and we could tell she had heard every word. We both looked at her and laughed. "How we doin', Sister Mary?" asked Ray.

Anyway, Ray done good, even though she chickened out of starting Reenie over Rafferty.

St. Ethel, 44
Mother Seton, 28
Won, 14; Lost, 2

Sister asked, "Talked to Tommy, did you?"

"You or himself coulda told me," I answered sharply, causing her to smile.

"You think it's funny, you explain it to the kids…Sister," I said. I think she knew I was pissed.

After the game, the girls gave Ray a big cheer. I shook her hand and said, "You done good, Snooky."

CHAPTER THIRTY-FIVE

This was a mystery trip for dinner, instead of dinner back at Ethel, so we went the back way, throughout southern Bergen County, to disguise our destination. Through the Heights, WoodRidge, south on Rte. 17, across Union Avenue, then through the warren of towns along the Passaic River. All through this trip, the girls had been calling out the names of restaurants we were approaching or thought we were. Then I would turn off the route or pass them. Or slow down as the bus approached a known restaurant then speed up at the last minute. The parents had reserved a room and were waiting for us. Somewhere in Lodi, I put on the turn signal, pulled the bus over and stopped, got out of my seat, and started screaming at the girls. They looked frightened as I began:

"WHAT IS THE MATTER WITH YOU PEOPLE? HAVE YOU NO DECENCY? HAVE YOU NO MORALITY? IT IS ABSOLUTELY FORBIDDEN AND AGAINST CHRIST'S TEACHINGS TO GAMBLE ON A ROMAN CATHOLIC SCHOOL BUS AS THE SEASON OF LENT APPROACHES. YOU ARE ACTING LIKE HEATHENS! DO YOU HEAR ME, HEATHENS? LAY DOWN YOUR SINFUL WAYS IMMEDIATELY! YOU ARE SINNERS IN THE HANDS OF AN ANGRY GOD! AND YEZ WILL BE PUNISHED, AHH, YEZ'LL BURN IN HELL FOR ALL ETERNITY AND SATAN WILL DELIGHT IN YER SUFFERIN'."

By the time I finished, red-faced and out of breath, there were giggles.

Yes, I know that last part was from Cotton Mather, who up till senior English I always thought was a Texas quarterback. Reverend Mather was not a Catholic, but his fire and brimstone worked in this harangue, I thought. I also knew that Dooney had set up a pool so the Gaels could put money down on a local restaurant, like a Super Bowl pool, betting on our destination. Luddy had kept the records and held the money. Like their working-class Das and Papas, gambling was ingrained in their lives. Football, basketball, and of course, the track.

Sullivans used to run the numbers back in the days before the state of NJ took over gambling and created the lottery, and then the state reduced the payoff that the mob gave out. When the Gaels began booing and throwing their smelly socks at me, I went back to driving the bus, singing in an off-key baritone,

"SINNERS! HEAR WHAT I'M SAYIN'. SINNERS! YOU'VE BEEN GAMBLING, NOT PRAYING!"

A chorus of less than angelic adolescent voices exploded into the "Hallelujah Chorus," and I knew I was beaten.

On northbound Rte. 17, I spied a run-down *Goody's*, pulled into the lot, parked the bus, and killed the engine. "Okay, here we are. Everybody out." I opened the door and said, "I loved *Goody's* burgers when I was your age. C'mon, great fries, too. And shakes. What's betternat!"

Several voices behind me: "Oh man, this place is a dump." "Come on, Coach, you gotta be kiddin'." "No way I'm goin' in this flea trap."

I waited by the *Goody's* entrance as they slowly and suspiciously left the bus and approached me. "Who had *Goody's* in the pool?"

"Nobody," said Luddie before Dooney could yell, "What pool?"

"Nobody had *Goody's*? It's a good deal then 'cause the dinner's not here. Psyyyyych! Loserrss!" And I ran around the parking lot, chased by Rafferty and the bigs, yelling, "Who's the man? Come on, Rafferty. Admit it and we'll go to dinner. Let's hear the Gaels yell, 'Coach Will rocks on three.' Then we'll go to dinner."

Then, out of nowhere, Mary Catherine yelled, "'Coach Will's a dork!' on three," and they yelled it over and over. "Coach Will's a dork!" "Coach Will's a dork!"

"I give, I give. I submit to your feminine treachery!" I pointed them back on the bus, and we continued our magical mytery tour.

Thank God Sister had driven over with Monsignor, but Ramona was crying she was laughing so hard. I yelled for quiet, finally got it, and called for Stephanie to sing anything she wanted. She stood by her seat, as she always did:

> *Yesterday, all my troubles seemed so far away.*
> *Now it looks as though they're here to stay.*
> *Oh, I believe in yesterday...*

And she, and a chorus (Reenie, Teagen, Liz, and Anna) stood behind her, replacing the strings, beautifully navigated the Lennon-McCartney masterpiece. Several weeks ago, I had requested they secretly, very secretly, prepare for this trip. This was the ace I had up my sleeve And then I had forgotten which song they had prepared. I thought to myself, *Oh jeez, this could be a total disaster. Or a stroke of genius.* My heart was in my throat. I looked at Ray in the mirror. She was smiling through watery eyes, I smiled back. I owed the choir director big time, but man, these kids knew how to sing!

We were close to the restaurant now, and I timed our entrance into the parking lot with the song's completion. Big applause, most from the winners of the pool, I suspect. The legendary Rutt's Hut, home of the Ripper, perched high above the Passaic River, where Rte. 3 and Rte. 21 intersect. As the girls left the bus, I squeezed Stephanie's hand, smiled, and whispered, "Thank you."

She blushed and smiled back at me.

Ramona was the last one on the bus. She stopped in front of me, swung me around so I was facing her, put her hands on my shoulders, then on the sides of my face, then kissed me. Really kissed me, clearly not caring if there were any witnesses.

"Eet eez peety you ah such a dunski, Veelyum, and zo ah hate to admeet eet, I haff luffed you awl mah life since befaw keendagahden. Now vhat you tink uff dat?"

I stood up, my mouth open, for a few stunned seconds and finally answered her in kind. "As you ah deh luff of MAH lahff, Ramona, ah teen you muss come ovah heeah. Ve must vonce again do zees keess. Verrry nahhzah keess it vas. You say okey dokey?"

We didn't get off the bus and into Rutt's until Rafferty, of all people, came out and got us. "Willie and Ray, sittin' in a tree..." trailing her into Rutt's.

Ray and I got a big cheer from the crowd. Liam held up a Schaefer and shouted, "Willie and Ray!"

Someone yelled, "About time!" We heard the Gaels reprise, "Will and Ramona, sittin' in a tree..."

"NO GASSERS!"

Cheers and laughter. Crowd repeated the toast as Ray and I were handed beers, big smile from Sister Mary, who probably had a hand in this as well. Reverend Mather would have cast us into the eternal darkness.

The tables were laden with baskets of Rippers, hot dogs deep fried so their skins ripped the long way, fries, onion rings, chili, pickles, and other offerings of artery-clogging selections. Looking around, I saw everyone was here, even the usually sullen Pat and Mike Show. They thought they knew a secret.

The meal was a lot of fun. Monsignor made a little speech about how proud he was of St. Ethel's first basketball team and what a great job the girls had done representing the school. "Now, yez all stand up and take yer applause and let us have a good look at ya."

Applause from the parents.

"Aw, Monsignor, our hair's all messed up, and we're all skanky from the game!" Rafferty, of course.

"Mary Alice Rafferty!" yelled Peggy. "You'll apologize right now to Monsignor and Sister or I'll box your ears, I will!"

"Sorry, Monsignor. Sorry, Sister." Raffy turned purple as everyone laughed. Really, it was funny, but I felt sorry for her because now she was hung with a moniker for the rest of the season at least. And hats off to Peggy Rafferty, as I could see that raising Mary Alice might be a task which took stamina, patience, and a stout heart.

Blue and gold cupcakes for dessert finished off the evening. No cleaning up or putting away tables under the stage, but I did have to drive the bus back to Ethel with Ray as the only passenger.

I followed her up to Leonia just to hang out for a while.

* * *

"I been meanin' to ax you somethin'. Remember when you were tellin' your story and you started to talk about Victor and about that time he—"

"I didn't want to talk about it in front of Mama. I don't know if she ever knew about it," she said.

"I have a vague memory. Fill me in?" I asked.

"One Sunday, he came home drunk from Wallington and started bitchin' about his dinner, why it wasn't ready, this, that, bullshit...He got really nasty, and I thought he was gonna hit my mother," Ray said. "So I stepped in front of him and yelled, 'Don't you hit my mother! Get out of here. You're just a drunk!' I was screaming at him.

"So he grabbed my arm here, above my elbow, and squeezed really tight and pulled back his other arm like he's gonna smack me. My mother screamed, 'Noooo! Don't you hit her! I'll kill you!' And she yelled something in Russian. And she jumped on him and knocked him down.

'Go outside, Ramona,' she said. 'Don't go to Edwards. Stay in the backyard!'"So I'm outside listenin' to their fightin'. She's swearin' and screamin'. He's bellowin' like he does then somethin' crashes... and then it's quiet. Victor stumbled out of the house cursing and peeled out, drove away. My mother came out and brought me in and we're both crying."'Don't worry, 'nushka, everything will be all right,' she said.

Okay, so for school the next morning, Mama made me wear long sleeves to cover the bruise on my arm, but I hid a T-shirt in my book bag and put it on in the girls' room. Ms. Blanchard asked me what happened and I told her. She took me to Mr. Coyne's office, and I had to tell the story to the cop and the social worker. Mama came and then we all went to the police station. The cops went and got Victor. It was a court case. He was charged by DYFS, I don't know. Anyway, he took off for a month, sent us money every week. Meek as a lamb when he came home. Said he was sorry. Bought Mama a ring. I got a new bike. I never trusted him again."

"Jeez, Ray, now I remember it all. You were cryin' all the way to Union School, and cursin' when you weren't cryin'. I was cryin' too. I felt so bad for you. We shoulda just cut school that day and hung out, y'know?"

"Nah, I wanted to go and show them the bruises so the bastard would haveta pay for it. I knew Ms. Blanchard would have to report it to Mr. Coyne. F——k him, still after all these years."

"That was fifth grade, right?"

"Yeah. Let's talk about something else.

Do you remember anything about kindergarten?" she asked. "I don't know, I was just thinkin' about Washington School the other day."

"Just that the ceiling was high, but I think that's 'cause we were so little. And you had pigtails and sometimes we had nap time on our mats," I said.

"I remember recess and chasing the boys and getting into fights," she said.

"That sounds right."

"Not with you, though," she said.

"Nah, we were sweethearts from day one," I said. "Got in a lotta fights defending your honor. Not that you needed defending."

"Patience shall be rewarded in all good time. Is now a good time for you, Willieboy?"

"Why, yes, I believe it is. But first, I got a question since we were talkin' about school. Remember when we hung around with Marvin Robinson and Charlie Joe Rembert? And we got in that fight with those sixth graders at Union School?" I asked her.

"I do," she said. "We got suspended by Mr. Coyne for fighting. But, eh, we started it, right?"

"I really liked those two guys," I said, "but I lost track of them. Do you know what happened to them?"

"Marvin moved to Passaic and got in some trouble, probably dealin' to his old Rutherford buddies. But Charlie Jo went to college in Georgia, and he's a DI football player, I think Georgia State, defensive back. He done good," she said. "Might be in the NFL now. Y'know, they redhirt'm a year, so it's five years in school, then I think he got drafted as a DB, then I lost track."

"Good for him. He was a real character, funny as hell, but no dummy. He worked his ass off for football, said it was his ticket."

We were both still wound pretty tight, but we got relaxed pretty soon. Vas nice.

Rewards for planning ahead may be serendipitous, but sometimes believing in yesterday also has value.

CHAPTER THIRTY-SIX

February 9–10, 1983

I got up really early, snuck into Mama's, or thought I had until she called out, "I made some nutcakes, Vill. Help yourself."

"Thanks for that, Mama," mostly to myself. I felt like Lou Gehrig. "Today-ay-ay-ay I-I-I feel-I-I-I-i-i-k-k-e..."

Showered, shaved, only a few minutes late for seventh-grade math first period. Smiles and giggles nonetheless. Ooh, hardass Mr. Edwards would be in full regalia today, girls. Bell to bell teaching, pop quizzes for all, seat work, hard extra credit problems, homework begun at desks.

Standing at the door in between first and second periods, and as Rafferty enters, I leaned toward her and whisper, deadpanned, "Don't even think about it, Mary Alice."

At practice that afternoon, we divided the girls into guards and forwards, doing a lot of footwork and speed drills, pivoting, drop steps, jump stops, up and unders. Guards ball handling, pass and catch. Then we switched guards and forwards. Water break. Twenty minutes of five on five full court. Ten minutes reviewing some simple time and possession stuff we had been working on about twice a week. Water break. Groups-of-three shooting drills.

Escape from practice. Trudy made the first shot and yelled, "Gaels on three!"

"One, two, three, GAELS!" Wow! First time all season first shot ended practice. Good for her!

When I awoke on Thursday, it struck me that we were down to four practices and three games. Not time to mess around, put in new stuff, or change lineups. We had lost only twice, and felt we had gotten the most out of our talent and given the kids a good basketball experience. Anyway, we'll see, or as my father mustof said (I actually used to write it that way, the way I heard it until, in fourth grade, Mrs. Nearpass, used the ruler to cure me of it. In public school, no less!) "Dance with the one that brung ya, Willie lad," causing yet another eye roll from Evelyn. The saying had little relevance to Mrs. Nearpass' whacking me, but that didn't bother Frankie Edwards. His bromides, well meaning as they were, had a bit of the malaprop sewn between the lines.

* * *

We had St. Bridget's tomorrow, and we needed to have some fun today while running them a little. Bridget's would likely have gotten better, so I would talk to Sister later if she were around today.

Mama had gone to early Mass and laid out some treats for me for breakfast. I might never move out of here. Or I might have a coronary and weigh 300 lbs. by age forty. Another buzz around the school that Monsignor was hearing all confessions on Saturday and saying all weekend Masses. Now that *was* news. I would have to tell Ray. I didn't even know if she went to church anymore, and if she did, had she changed to Orthodox, or was she still with Holy Mother Church? But we did go through all the childhood sacraments together at St. Mary's in Rutherford. We'd have to talk about that sometime. I went about every other week for Mama's sake. Okay, I went every other week. Once in, never out applied to more than one organization.

School went by in a blur, less than my best effort. It would be part of my confession. At practice, we lined them all up at half-court and told them, "Okay, you each get a minute to lead in Jumping the Line. You can do any dance steps you want, but you have to jump the line, got it?"

I had brought my boom box in. "*Hit Me With Your Best Shot.*"

"Whaddawe get if we win? Guess who?" Mary Alice asked.

"What was that, Skanky—oops, forgot, can't use bad language in front of the kiddies. First up, here we go, Greet!"

All fifteen danced and jumped their hearts out, and everyone had to jump for everyone else as well, so it was a good work out. And funny. The bigs were really funny. Rafferty was a DQ, didn't jump enough, started to pout, thought better of it after receiving Ray's death stare. Applause meter had a three way tie: SJ, Cat, and Eddie. The bigger kids had no shot. Dance off, Eddie won. Big cheer. Kit Kat bar to the champion. "Okay, fun's over. On the baseline. Coach Ray will hold your Kit Kat 'cause I know you don't trust me."

"Got dat right, homes," Eddie mumbled and everyone laughed. Eddie and SJ didn't do "street" very often, but it cracked me up when they did. I think they must practice it in front of a mirror or with each other or use it just to piss off Mom and Dad. Who wouldn't?

We had them do every running and shooting drill we could devise then four-player shells with winners and losers then round-robin knockouts. Then foul shots with everyone else in the paint yelling and distracting. Then ball tag. Finally, escape. Ginna, who couldn't even see the basket let alone reach it back in November, sunk one. Did a victory lap no less. Got so excited her legs got tangled, and she went down in a heap. "Oh, my pointy bones!"

She got right up, laughing, then hands raised in the midcourt circle, yelled, as her voice cracked, "Gaels on three! One, two, three, GAELS!"

No need, at this point, for any input from the grown-ups. Ray and I just smiled.

February 11, 1983

The St. Bridget's coach was a young Sister named Veronica. We sat and had a cup of tea while the girls got changed. She said she had grown up in Ogdensburg, up in the wilds of northwest New Jersey in Sussex County. I had known a girl from there at Montclair State, "Yes, Jackie was kind of famous. Really smart, and pretty, and had gone into the Peace Corps with her husband a while ago. It was in the paper and everything. She was a few years ahead of me, and she was Ms. Ogdensburg one year. She went to Franklin, but I went to Pope John."

"Well, Sister, she worked the desk at the women's dorm at Montclair State, and my friends and I used to give her a hard time, all in fun," I said, ready to regale her with tales from college days.

Veronica had no response and made me wish Sister would show up, which, as if by magic, she did, and the two chatted away while I excused myself. I think maybe Veronica had hooped some back in the day because, as I remember, her kids were pretty well coached.

After warm-ups and Stephanie's raising the hairs on the back of my neck version of the National Anthem, a staple of our home games, we sat the kids down to go over stuff one more time. Dooney said, "I remember them, that big one had BO. Ugh."

"Good point, Doons," I said. "If we have to go man, you'll guard her…really close."

"Oh man," she complained.

"Okay, we want you to go right at 'em. Forget the score last time. They've probably gotten better. They had some good athletes. Play the scramble up, got it? Go hard and go fast. SJ?"

"Gaels on three! KSA!"

I called them back together and told them, "If I hear KSA again in a team huddle, whoever says it will sit for the rest of the game. Everyone clear?"

"Oh maaan," she whined.

"*WHAT* did you say?" I yelled at her.

"Sorry, Coach," she mumbled.

Starters went out on the floor, the rest to the bench.

"What was that about?" from Ray.

"KSA? Kick some ass?" I snapped.

"What's wrong with that?"

"Go ask Sister," I snapped again. "This is a Catholic school, Coach. These are thirteen- and fourteen-years-olds. Young girls. Maybe on the street, but not on my watch."

"Yeah, you're right," she agreed.

I almost passed out. I staggered, grabbing hold of Ray's shoulder. "Very funny. Ha ha," she deadpanned.

Not much to say about the game. Bridget's season had gone down the tubes at some point, or Sister Veronica had mailed it in. I think our seventh graders played almost ten minutes, and four of them scored. Dooney and Rafferty combined for fifteen. SJ had a goose egg, and I pulled her for pouting. Even Sister let her be. I'd tell JJ if he asked.

St. Ethel, 44
St. Bridgets, 23
Won, 15; Lost, 2

There was a lot of yapping in the locker room that went silent when I knocked. "Can I come in?"

"Yeah," Dooney's voice.

Oh boy, this didn't look good. "Someone wanna tell me what happened?"

Good ole Rafferty said, "SJ thinks you singled her out 'cause she's black."

I said, "KSA is not appropriate for junior high school girls to be using in a team huddle. End of story, nothing else to say. See you at practice Monday. One week left."

"Coach," asked Luddie, "you said there might be a tournament?"

"Don't know, Luds. Maybe we'll find out over the weekend."

Ray, Sister, and I were in kind of a hurry to get to Mama's where a Russian feast awaited us with a bottle of Smirnoff in the freezer. We almost made it. JJ and LaShonda stopped us, concerned parents. "What do we need to know?"

I said, "SJ said something she shouldn't have said. I dealt with it. That's pretty much it from my end. Let her tell you her side and then, if you want, we'll talk, okay? I'm not blowin' you off here, but we got someplace to be. I'll call you in the morning. Will that be all right?"

"Sure," said JJ.

Shots of iced vodka for Mama, Ray, and me; Jim Beam for Sister before dinner. I hadn't eaten all day, so I grabbed some nutcakes and took some for the morning. I told Ray about Monsignor's plans for the weekend, and Mama asked her to go with us to Confession and Mass.

"Ooh, Mama, it's been an awful long time. I'd be in there for hours," she said.

"Now, you know ees not true, Ramona," said Mama.

* * *

"Were you raised Catholic?" asked Sister.

"From the cradle," said Ray. "My mother is Slovak, probably more Czech. My father is Russian. He was working for the US Army at the end of the war in Moravia as translator and managed to get himself and my mother out. They would never talk about it. I guess it was awful. They came here, to this area, but they lived in Wallington first. My father worked as a translator for lots of the businesses there. And he makes deals for them. He speaks Polish and Hungarian and Slovak, too. Must speak some Czech, too. He's very smart. Then they moved to Rutherford. It was a nicer town to grow up in.

"But when I went away to college in Pennsylvania, they moved to Buffalo, that's like six years now. Weather's more like Russia, he said. He got a good job there, but I think his job is connected to

the Russian mob. I never asked. I don't see him very much, but my mother comes to visit me and Mama once in a while, maybe every six weeks or so. Mama is her mother. I don't know much about their pasts. I think they are very frightened and paranoid from having lived under the Russians and the Germans. I don't think he trusted, or trusts, the Americans either. They are very careful what they say. Except my father when he drinks."

I said, *"We grew up around the corner from each other and went all through public school together. We lived all our lives there, near the tracks. We held hands when we walked the two blocks to Washington School. All the way through public school together till we graduated from Rutherford High. Well, almost. Our mothers were friends. They spoke each other's language. I have loved Ramona since I was four years old. Okay, even when I thought I didn't! I love her mother and Mama, too."*

"And we went to CCD at St. Mary's in Rutherford, made our confirmations there," Ramona said. *"But my father was Orthodox, so he didn't go. Once in a while he went over to Wallington to Russian Orthodox Mass, but that was mostly to hang out with his friends after. He'd always come home drunk, I mean Russian drunk, and then they'd fight, and I'd run around the corner to Will's house. Didn't have no siblings."*

"Ray always played with the guys," I said, *"and when we got to junior high and high school, she'd be over there, at the basketball court, by herself for hours. That's how she got so good and how she got a full scholarship to college. Right, Ramonushka?"*

"How I got outta the house," she said.

I had done the impossible, made her blush. I laughed, but she didn't think it was that funny.

Mama shook her head and said, *"Vas not good den vit Anna and Veector. She study hard in night school to learn English so she could get job. He don't vant her to verk. All deh time fight, she tell me on phone.*

"Den she vent on her own and got part-time job at deli in Passaic vhere she could take bus and be to store in fifteen minutes. Right on Main Avenue. And zeh fighting stopped. He vas happy for extra money. She loved job, dey loved her at store,

215

put her on full-time. Ramona vas in seex grade vhen Anna start to vork and feenish high school vhen zey move to Buffalo."

* * *

"How about we take a break? Time to eat, right? All in favor? The ayes have it!" I said all this in my best Liam Dooney voice and was met with groans, but it was worth it.

The meal was to die for: borscht, pelmeni, shashlyki, and blinis. And Schaefer beer. Brought back memories of the special meals my mother used to cook for my father and me.

* * *

I chipped in, "I wanted to ask Sister something, okay? You took me up as far as your time in the convent last time we talked, remember? What happened after that?"

"Well," she said, "I started at Caldwell College. It was a Dominican college when it opened its doors in 1939, and I majored in linguistics and religion. So I speak five languages, although my Navajo has gotten rusty. My religion major was all religions, especially North American religions. It was really interesting to learn what the Catholic Church taught about Indian religions.

"Anyway, I played basketball for two years at Caldwell, and I loved it even though it was ladies' rules, I'm sorry to say. Then the war came and we all worked for the cause, but that's another story. After the war, I got my degree at Caldwell, played basketball still. Then they sent me to Columbia for a masters and PhD. I finished with that in 1951.

"I went back to Caldwell as dean of students and head basketball coach, both of which I loved doing, but the combination got to be too much. When the order wanted me to be dean of the college in 1970, I had to give up coaching just before Title IX came along. I retired from the college in 1975 and moved over here to St. Ethel. So, William, you must still call me Dr. Begay. Ray, you can call me Sister."

"Not fair. Not fair," I whined.

"Oh, hush, child," said Sister, and everyone laughed. "Many of us at the convents and the college cut back on our hours and did volunteer work for the war effort from 1942 till the war ended in 1945. Taking care of wounded GIs, running blood drives, selling war bonds, collecting clothes and blankets for the British…It was so horrible what they showed in the newsreels in the movies every week.

"It was during the war that I made my second journey back to Ship Rock to say goodbye to my mother. I got a telegram from my sister in Ship Rock to hurry if I could, and I was lucky to catch a ride on a troop train along with a group of army nurses as far as Albuqurque then caught a bus from there. It was only my second trip home since 1928. My father couldn't get home from the South Pacific though. He had enlisted in the marines to be in the Codetalker program to help with the Japanese codes and messages. He died in 1958.

"My mother died a few days after I got to Ship Rock. She hugged me and said how proud she was that I had succeeded in the white man's world. That I was truly 'God's child.' I know she looks over me every day and that my life has always been in God's hands."

Ray and I, teary-eyed and more somber than we had been an hour ago, walked Sister home.

CHAPTER THIRTY-SEVEN

February 12–13, 1983

Up early, Ray was already at the table with coffee and pastries from Strucko's. Sitting down, I said, "Four o'clock Confession, *Ramonushka. You vill be comink, no*?"

"Dah."

"Y'know," I speculated, "it's too bad we really never learned Russian. We coulda opened a store in Wallington."

"Nice try, Dollink," she said dismissively.

"No, really. How about *Ramonoushka's Splendid Blinis*? Mom and Pop, then we'll expand. We'll make fortunes."

"Stop it! Mama will hear you," she hissed but laughed.

Mama came in the room and said, "Ees nice day? Let's go for ride up to Vest Point and see reever. I buy you lunch and ve come back for confession. Ees good idea?"

"We'll clean up, Mama," said Ray, and she did. Something I had never before seen, but we worked together in the kitchen and got the room spotless. That's Will/Ray spotless. Mama would clean it all again later.

Before we left, I got JJ on the phone to check in about SJ. "Damnit, Will," he said. "She just pisses me off when she tries to pull that stuff, playing the race thing. Told her a million times 'Girl, you livin' in a white-and-black world, you been raised to know better'n that. And that ain't gonna get you nothin' but grief. You will apologize to Coach and to your teammates before practice on Monday or you won't practice. Is that clear?' They'll do it if they think it'll work. I'm glad you called her on it."

"Thanks, John. We'll check it out on Monday. You gotta go in to work today?"

"No, but I'm on call. Enjoy your day, Coach."

"You too, John."

We climbed into the Bu and drove east and then north on Palisades Parkway and 9W along the west bank of the Hudson, GWB, in the rearview mirror. It was a cold clear February day, "spotless" my mother used to say, the river a bright metallic slab to our right. Mama's idea was a good one and a good time to get away from the Gaels and all the intrigue bearing down on us. I cruised slowly, got a lot of horns and fingers. Ray gave some fingers back from the front passenger seat, her hand above the car roof, so Mama couldn't see her doing it. It was about a two-hour drive, going slow.

Once at the Point, we got out and walked around the parade ground. We found the chapel, went in, and sat and prayed for a while. The academy was always a foreboding sight and sobering experience for me. In another life, I could have been a cadet here. I really don't think I was smart or tough enough, but there was talk about it when I was still in high school. The coaches were pushing it; the recruiters showed some interest. I had grades, SATs, and sports, but my math sucked, and they never followed up. Still gives me the shivers to think about it. But the US Army did all right by me, they did.

We drove back down 9W and found a cozy-looking place with a river view that was advertising brunch and went in and feasted. To Mama's disapproval, Ray knocked back two bloodies and treated us to Beatles songs on the way home till she fell asleep in the middle of "*Eleanor Rigby*." We got home in time for confession, which, I admit, had been a long time.

"Bless me, Father, for I have sinned. It's been many years since my last confession…"Home for a nap, picked up Ray, got a burger, and went to see *Tootsie* in the movies. It was fun, but Dustin Hoffmann was one homely chick. Went back to Ray's and made out for a while, but early mass tomorrow, so I went home to Mama's. Church would be packed all day long.

* * *

Ray showed up on time on Sunday, and we all walked over to St. Ethel, got seats by the Plutarskys. A nice family, Greet was the middle child. Felt good to receive the host with my soul clean. Monsignor pulled me aside after Mass and said quietly, "Billy, lad, would you be able to stop over to the rectory about three o'clock this afternoon if yer not too busy?"

"Be my pleasure, Monsignor."

I knocked on the door on the dot, and Liam let me in. "Come on in and have a drink with us, Billy," said the monsignor, dressed in priestly black and collar. "We'll be toastin' the end of an era at St. Ethel, given today is Himself's final day at the helm. Letter has been delivered to the diocese, bags in the Lincoln, and Liam set to drive me to JFK later today. Now, waddaya think of that, boyo?"

"I think I'm happy for you, sir, and sad for all of us," I answered. "I mean my heart is broken, sir, that I'll be missing you like I'd miss my Da…" And I started to tear up…"That'll be enougha that, Billy," he said as he grabbed me in a big bear hug. "Not to be sad. I'm going to heaven without havin' to die, and I know you'll wish me well. Listen, Coach, you and yer lasses have been one of the few bright spots here the past few months. I'm speechless at the job you have done with them. Now I know Sister and Ramona have been steady for you, but those lasses play for you, and that's the God's honest truth. Am I right, Liam?"

"That you are, Monsignor. Listen, Willie," he said, "'Doons,' as she's known, would run through a wall for yah, and she's a different kid since basketball started. They all are."

"Love that kid, Liam," I said.

"So, Billy, as far as anyone else is concerned, for the time being, you know nothing about any of this. That I am leaving tonight or where I am going. And that includes Mrs. Ziska and Ramona. Is that clear, lad?"

"That it surely is, sir."

He looked at me sideways and laughed. "Ah, Billy, you'll make an Irishman someday, yah hang around here with these donkeys long enough." He let out a big laugh.

The original agreement, as it turns out, was for the monsignor to retire July 1 with all honors. Then the diocese moved it up to June 1. After some minor litigating, Monsignor acquiesced. Without telling anyone but Liam, his sister in Ireland, and Mrs. O'Toole, he packed his bags, such as they were, sent some boxes ahead, and bought his ticket on Aer Lingus to Dublin, one way, for February 13, leaving 11:00 PM.

Back at Mama's, while I was reading about Navajo history, Liam called me back and said, "Willie, you'd best be gettin' back over here. Don't ask why, don't drive either, there'll be no place to put the car. Come on now and bring Mama."

Mama was not home. Hmm...

I could feel it as I neared the rectory, dozens and dozens of parishioners standing quietly in groups, bunches of Bergen County cop cars, and NJ State Troopers cruisers lined the streets around St. Ethel. No secret send-off. The crowd kept growing, talking quietly, many holding candles in the fading light, waiting to bid goodbye to their priest who, regardless of their backgrounds, they loved and respected. A lot of tall men, both black and white, wearing their St. Peter's Prep letterman jackets were interspersed with parishoners along the sidewalks. When he came out at 6:45 and smiled and waved, there was a roar. Liam was in the driver's seat, and he motioned for me to get in as well. "Some secret, eh, Billy?" He laughed, as the caravan, led by the Staties, took off toward New York and JFK. The streets were lined with parishioners waving, and Monsignor giving blessings right and left.

He insisted we drop him off outside the terminal at JFK. He got a skycap to take care of his bags, blessed and hugged us both, told us to drop by for a pint when we were in the neighborhood, and vanished into international arrivals and departures. End of an era indeed.

* * *

And I'm sittin' in the limo thinkin', "By god, I don't know a damn thing about him. Now, that's not true anymore. Not after Hell's Kitchen, speaking Polish, and trip to Poland. He's a master of misdirection. Liam and the others think they do, but I bet they don't either. The only clues I've had the whole time were when Sister Mary let slip 'Terrence' and he let slip 'Mary.' But I'm thinkin' I'll be keepin' that to myself and that I'm soundin' more like a Harp everyday." And neither of them ever "let anything slip."

* * *

At the end of his first year of teaching at St. Stanislaus in June 1941, Terrence was (a) glad it was over, (b) humbled by the amount of work ahead of him should the powers that be decide to keep him at this school, or (c) as happy as he had ever been. Answer: all of the above.

His extraordinary abilities to concentrate and learn over long periods of time had led him to get to a conversational level of Polish by the end of September then to where he wanted, close to mastery by Thanksgiving. His Latin lessons and plans were completed and organized by the time school began. (In fact, his superiors often spoke of sending him to law school. Those conversations ended in December 1941.) He also got word through the grapevine to boys wanting to go out for basketball to report to the gym on summer mornings, etc. He liked the kids at the school, almost all of them Polish, about twice as many boys as girls. They all spoke reasonably good English, and his Polish wasn't good enough yet to teach Latin in Polish. Praise God. The kids were bright, attentive, and like all Catholic school kids from a European background stood when they spoke.

And they were in awe of an Irishman who spoke their language. Basketball had a rough start, a lot of dead wood, kids whose families had influence and who felt entitled to a spot on the team. But the team won 8, lost 6. He got to be known around Greenpoint as the Irish priest who spoke Polish and loved the cafés, delis, all of it. He cut a mean polka in the dance halls as well. And he could sing! (But he had to travel to Red Hook to find the proper environs for a rousing "Risin' of the Moon" or "Gilgarry Mountain.") The only dark spot was the unknown: the war engulfing the world both in Europe and in the Pacific. He would, of course, enlist, if FDR got us in it and if that's what the order decided. Terrence was sure he would. Get us in it. Word from the higher-ups.

The Jesuit order, in agreement with the War Department, directed him to enlist in June 1942 at the end of the school term. He spent over a year in and around Washington adding to his languages, making connections, and receiving training in the clandestine arts, as they were called. He served as an army chaplain in the European Theater. He left on a troop ship in late May 1943 and returned on the Queen Mary, also a troop ship, in September 1945, with the rank of major. He never spoke nor wrote about his service. He could now speak, in part at least, five central and eastern European languages, not including the Gaelic he picked up on his own.

Added to all that, he was, at one time, a major player in the Jesuit educational hierarchy, at least as far as I could figure, and yet settled for St. Peter's and retirement at St. Ethel. There was more to the story, I'm thinking. This was no harp off the boat from Kilarney or scrapping his way out of Hell's Kitchen, though he played those games when the situation called for it. Guys like that don't have the juice to pull off what happened in the Garden. Wheels within wheels.

* * *

In the car going back to Jersey, I asked Liam, "You grew up in this parish?"

"Family moved here from Jersey City when I was six," Liam answered. "We grew up speakin' shanty Irish, which, for the most part, we still do. Me Da worked on the docks in Hoboken, Mam did laundry for the rich folks on Ridge Road and Passaic Avenue in Rutherford. Five Dooney kids, four rooms in Jersey City. Different world then, Will. Every penny counted. The older boys were too young for WWII and Korea, barely finished high school. Kevin and I got drafted, and we were in the army. Brian enlisted in the marines and was killed in DaNang, Kevin was stationed in Japan, and I got wounded in Cambodia, but the army was never in Cambodia so I never got wounded.

"Mary Anne went to college, God bless her, and she's a teacher in Parsippany and has two kids. Kevin came out of the service, went to Bergen County Community College, and he's been a sheriff's deputy since. I love it here, so we got a bigger house, but never moved. Kevin lives in WoodRidge and has three kids.

"So, my lads, notorious as they might seem, all made it through St. Mary's, no thanks to Sister Angela. Kevin's a cop or soon will be, Sean's in Bergen County College, and Mikey's in the union at B + D with me. It's all good. I'm thinkin' Mary Grace might be the brains o'the outfit, though, like her Ma. Waddaya think there, William lad?"

"I'm thinkin' yer waxin' like a proud papa," I said, "and good for you. Mary Grace is a quick study, Liam, funny as hell, remembers things you tell her, and understands the algebra. No small achievement. She sees two or three steps ahead in basketball. Watch her. Head always moving. Especially on defense. She'll be a good high school player. And, as ye know, she's afraid of nothing."

"Sometimes I wish she was, a little anyway." Liam laughed.

"When did the monsignor get here, do ya remember?"

"That'd be 1972. I believe he'd had a heart attack down at St. Peter's. He had a big job there, y'know, and hands in a lot of pots. He was kind of a 'fixer' or a broker for the diocese. And maybe then some, y'know? He knew everybody—clergy, politicians, newspaper, and TV guys. Got things done. He asked to be sent to a more quiet parish to recover and maybe retire, so the order and the diocese sent him here. Maybe he called in a few favors, I mean, he was a big kahuna in his day. Friends in high places, too."

"Still has 'em, I believe."

We listened to oldies the rest of the ride home. Sang along to the ones we knew.

"Jojo was a man who thought he was a loner, till he found he couldn't last..."

"I was born in a cross fire hurricane..."

"I was a little too tall, coulda used a few pounds..."

We were pretty good, continuing our harmonies from the Legion.

CHAPTER THIRTY-EIGHT

February 14, 1983

I blew the whistle and "Balls in, on the baseline." I stood out in front of them for almost thirty seconds, looking around, finally landed on SJ. She stared defiantly back at me, straightened up, walked right up to me, face-to-face, looked me in the eye, and said, "I acted like a fool on Friday, Coach. I'm sorry for what I said in the locker room. It wasn't true. It's never been true with you or Coach Ray or Sister. You've been like family to me."

Turning to the girls, she shouted, "And so have y'all. I'm sorry for being a jerk. Sometimes it's hard. Bring it in. We are Ethel! We are brave! Gaels on three! GAELS!"

And damned if they didn't do just that.

So began our last week of practice. I had checked with the diocese; no tournament for junior high schools, things were a bit hectic in Paterson right at this time. But we could have practice on Ash Wednesday, which was the day after tomorrow, as long as all concerned had been to Mass. Monsignor Dan, from Our Lady of Sorrows, where we had played our development game, volunteered to take the helm at St. Ethel till the diocese got a permanent replacement, as if there could be one, for the monsignor. He would arrive tomorrow.

Good, fast, practice with lots of contact. We ran the time and possession stuff again. Had no info on Our Lady of Charity. Ended practice with the dreaded free throw game—everyone has to make a foul shot. A miss means a sprint. It can take forever, but Ray jumped in and called Escape from Practice!

Two rounds of clankers till Dooney made a bank shot. I blew the whistle and waved it off. "She didn't call Bank! Doesn't count! No basket!" And ran out of the gym with Dooney on my heels, everyone laughing. Dooney stopped, remembered, turned around. "Gaels on three!"

"One, two, three, Gaels!"

All told, we hadn't had a better practice all season and I knew, in my heart of hearts, I would miss it. I would miss the Gaels.

February 15, 1983

Bus ride to Union City, a largely Latino city now and, in that, heavily Cuban, starting right from the Revolution in 1959. My cousin used to play Connie Mack baseball there. Back in the day before that, it was German, and I think some of them relocated to that Church of the Bund where we had played earlier this season. By the way, Coach Reidelbacher had been relieved of his duties and replaced by a young sister. Today, it was Our Lady of Charity, which I guessed was all Latino.

Anyway, Father Ramon, a brown-eyed handsome man, kind-looking with a soft Cuban accent, met us at the brand-new community center next to the church. Sister right away engaged him with her Navajo-accented Spanish, and they went away chattering happily. The girls followed a manager to the locker room, and Ray and I were led to a café for a Café Americano and some tasty Cuban pastries. Ray was suspicious.

"Come on, Chiquita, ees Fat Tuesday. We can fly to the Big Easy esta noche? Leeve for Today, no?"

"I never trusted these Cubans," she claimed.

"And knowing your far-ranging and unsuperstitious Slavic mind, I know you have good solid reasons for that lack of trust. For Chrissakes, Ray, these people have been here longer than yours."

"Oh, shut up, you know it all."

"I dun shut up. *You* shut up! Yu tink yu know, yu dun know nutting." I got up and went to another table. And pretended to pray, out loud, "Now I lay me down to rest.

A bag of walnuts on my chest—"

She joined me and hissed, "Stop that, you jerk. Someone will hear you. God, you're such an asshole sometimes."

I couldn't stop laughing. "Who's a Goody Two-shoes now, All State!?"

Then a guy came in I assumed was their coach—short guy, slicked-back hair, more what I thought a Cuban would look like. Like I had a clue. He introduced himself as "Coach Alberto." No last name. Shook hands too long and made eye contact way too long with Ray, who towered over him. Jeez, here we go again.

"I see you have enjoyed Father Ramon's hospitality, for which he is famous here in Hudson County," he said.

"Nice to meet you, Alberto. I'm Will. This is Ramona, my assistant coach. Hey, do you know this Coach Ernest—oops— Ernst, Reidelbacher, from St. Anne's, Coach?" I asked.

He laughed out loud. "Oh, I see you have had the pleasure. Did you visit him at the Redoubt?"

"We did. Oh boy. Don't wanna go there again," I said just as Sister walked over. I introduced them, begged off, and they started out en Espanol. Must admit, there was something about this guy, all the Latino stuff aside, that it turned out I liked. Don't judge a book and all that. Ray put her finger down her throat and mimed gagging. Oh boy. We'll see what Sister had to say.

"I love your open mind and eagerness to meet new people, Coach," I said and laughed then said, "Go ahead. I dare you."

Gritting her teeth, she exerted some self-control.

Their girls were out warming up as we crossed the gym; they had some players, I thought, and Ray agreed. Not as big as us but quick and athletic. Whatever, we would go at 'em full speed.

Kids were ready to go after we went over everything. I called up the seventh graders to the front. "You know what to say. And say it loud!"

"We are brave!"

Which they did. Then, "Gaels on three! One, two, three."

"Gaels!"

We were up eight at the half. Rafferty and Dooney on the bench with two fouls each; Greet and Mary Pat holding down the fort. They caught us in the third and went ahead in the fourth. Dooney fouled out with two minutes left. Reenie replaced her. I called time. "How many we got left, Marcie?"

"Two, Coach." She was, as always, right on the number.

"Listen, we're only down three. Long way to go. Our ball on the side. Let's see if we can get a quick score with that play we worked on yesterday. If they line up playing us man to man. Only if they line up man, okay? My fist means they're in man. We good with it? Reenie?"

"I'm good, Coach." she replied, eyes about to pop out of her head.

"I got this, Coach," claimed Eddie. Okay then.

The sideline inbounds in our half-court depended upon them guarding us man to man, which they did. We double-screened. Eddie ran her defender into the screen and broke loose, made a layup off a pass from Reenie, down one, bench and our crowd really into the game now.

SJ made a playground steal off their inbounds, looping back and stepping in front of the girl receiving the pass, made a layup, was fouled, made the free throw, up two. Time-out Charity. A minute thirty on the clock. A small space of pandemonium. I asked Ray and Sister, "I'm listening."

"First, calm them down. Two deep breaths. I'll wait. Don't give them an inch of the floor from half-court and move the bigs up like we have done in the past. Be aggressive on D. They'll think we'll sit back." This from Sister.

"Yeah, I agree," piped in Ray.

"All right, be still," I said to the girls. "Another two slow deep ones. SJ and Eddie pick up at half-court. You know, let them cross. Trudie top of the key. Raff and Reenie foul line extended, be aggressive, don't foul. We want the ball. Got it? Reenie?"

Reenie: "I got this, Coach!"

"Gaels on three! One, two, three, Gaels!"

Best-laid plans…Charity girl beat Trudy off the dribble, made a runner, and got clobbered. No foul. Coach Carlo habloing mucho Espanol at the officials. I know some Spanish swear words and heard at least two of them. Tie game. "Where's the T?" I asked the refs but didn't push it.

We turned it over; they scored. We turned it over again, but Reenie intercepted a pass, hit Eddie long, two points. Tie game. Time-out, Charity. Clock read 0:42.

Time for gambling was over. Didn't want to foul intentionally. Though we practiced it, we hadn't done it all season, too many things could go wrong.

"Okay, pack it in. Regular two-three zone. Hands up, feet wide, no fouls. SEE THE CLOCK! What'd I just say, Rafferty?"

"SEE THE CLOCK!" they all yelled back.

"Now remember: When we get the ball, ten-second rule, right? We practiced this a hundred times. More than ten, we call time. Less then ten, what?"

"Get a shot at seven!" they yelled back.

"NO FOULS!" I yelled.

Back on the floor, Our Lady of Charity passed and dribbled around, killing the clock. Eddie and SJ darting in and out of passing lanes. God, they were such smart players, even got "tips" on some passes. One of their girls let one fly at eight seconds. Reenie grabbed the rebound, pivoted, heaved it out to Trudy, who had contested the shot and turned up court. She got the outlet between the circles, pivoted, turned, one dribble, let one fly, off the backboard, and through. Buzzer. Gaels by two! Trudy jumping up and down yelling, "Gaels on three! Gaels on three!" All too excited to complete the chant.

Then mobbed by the rest of them. Down they went, rolling around on the floor, arms raised, index fingers signifying number one. I let them be. Our parents went nuts. And, my god, Monsignor Dan, who must have driven over from St. Ethel, came trotting over, shook my hand, and said, "Well done, Billy boy," and laughed out loud. Then Sister and Ray found me, and we hugged and laughed. "Escape from practice, indeed." Sister laughed.

St. Ethel, 39
Our Lady of Chariy, 37
Won, 16; Lost, 2

Coach Alberto came over and graciously laughed and said, "Dios mio, what a game, eh? Such a well-coached team you have, Will. Very nice. I wish you all well."

"Thank you, Alberto," I said. "Stop by if you're up our way. You have a very nice club, as well."

After he left, I asked Sister what she thought of this guy. "Very humble, very Cuban, kind of out of place here. Plays in a Cuban band here in Union City. Gave me his card, in case you two wanted to catch his act. In truth, I liked him."

"There you go, Ramona," I said, holding back a laugh.

Just then, Dooney and Rafferty, throwing all caution to the wind, got in my face and yelled, for everyone to hear, "WELL DONE, BILLY BOY!" and ran away laughing.

Ray and Sister took them into the locker room to settle them down. I came in a few minutes later. I had some points to make.

"Take two deep ones," I said and waited. "Why do you think we did all that practice on footwork? On boxing out? On rebounding? On outlet passes? Escape from practice? Now, just thinking what happened in the last few seconds of this game. Reenie and Mary Pat and Raff all did their jobs. SJ and Eddie did their jobs. They did the hard work in practice. And when the time came, Reenie boxed out, rebounded, pivoted, outleted to Trudy. Trudy pivoted and let one fly. Luck? *I DON'T THINK SO!*

YOU ARE BRAVE! YOU ARE ETHEL! GAELS ON THREE! One, two, three."

"GAELS!" They all joined in laughing, jumping up and down.

Mikey's catering tonight at Ethel's. Sister was tired and I dropped her off at home. Ray and I hung around, working the room. Fitz and Mike came over, poured me some Tulamore Dew in my coffee, and Fitz said something I never expected to hear. "You have done a helluva job with these kids, Will. I apologize for what I thought, what I said, and what I did. We were eedjits and I'm sorry."

"Goes double for me," said Mike.

"Thanks for that, guys. I appreciate it. I must say, I have loved coachin' 'em, that I have, and I apologize as well," I said and meant it.

"We have to go speak to Ramona now," added Fitz. "Thanks for everything you've done, Will. I hope you'll be doin' this again next season."

Then Jan and Clara Bilotskovic caught my eye. I think they had been in the country longer than some of the other eastern Europeans, as their English was flawless. Jan said, "That was really exciting, Coach. Clara thinks it's luck. I say you practice it."

"Little of both," I said. "Trudy will explain it. I have to tell you. She has become a real basketball player in three months, hasn't she?"

"Yes, she has," Jan said, "thanks to you and Ramona, who she would follow into battle. She's even trying to walk and talk like her. Seriously, we appreciate what you've done for her. We went over to watch a St. Mary's game last week and spoke to Coach Nieman. He said Trudy would be a standout player at their school. What do you think, Will?"

"Do you want to send her to a Catholic high school?" I asked.

"Pretty sure about that," Jan said. "Why do you ask?"

"Well, word is around that Bill is leaving St. Mary's after the school year," I said. "Not sure where he's going or who is taking his place or why he's leaving. You might want to look into that. But he's a really good guy and a great coach. Really loves his kids."

"Hmm…I'm glad you told us. We have heard from Holy Angels Academy, also."

"Now that's a really good school as well. Maybe you can catch a game before the season ends and have the coach give me a call if they're interested. Let me know what you want me to do. And listen, one more thing. Trudy is a completely different girl than she was when we started, like she was afraid of her own shadow. Wow! You have a wonderful daughter!"

"Thank you, Will."

"Jan, if you are really interested, I'll buy you a beer and show how that game-winning shot was put together. Really. You can come too, Clara. Wait a minute. You mean Ramona hasn't tried to talk you into sending Trudy to Rutherford High? That's where we both played."

"She gave it her best shot, but we don't live in Rutherford," said Jan.

I found the Masaryks, for whom this whole basketball world was like life on another planet. Steve was a professor at Stevens and Mary taught Chemistry at Becton Regional HS in East Rutherford. Very smart people. "Listen, Will," Mary said, "Stephanie has spent years in singing lessons and recitals and concerts and that will be her future, but being on your team and learning Beatles' songs has been a wonderful experience for her. She just loves it all so much. Thank you for all of it."

"Mary," I said, "thank you for letting her do this, really. Her voice takes me to another world. You must be so proud of her. She is always so poised and professional."

Steve said, "Like her mother. Now *there's* a voice."

Mary blushed.

"I'm sorry, I didn't know," I said.

"Just around the house now and maybe for parties once in a while. Working on some Beatles tunes as well." She laughed. "I just love 'If I Fell' and 'In My Life.' Stephanie sings harmony with me sometimes, 'Nowhere Man' as well. Their music is so interesting, isn't it?"

"I always loved them, and they took pop music out of the G-C-Em-D7 lock it had been in, didn't they?" I said just to see if they were listening. Their mouths dropped open, they were. "Glad you like them. Well, thank you again. I have to make the rounds. But you and Stephanie are a duet I'd love to hear someday."

But when I got up, almost everyone was gone. Those left helped Ray and me clean the room. We put everything away and called it a night. I finally realized how tired I was. Ray said, "Vy dunt ju come ovah to mah plays, you handsome boy?"

My fatigue fading rapidly, I answered, "Vhy, yays, mah sveet pastila, ah veel be zere qveek qveek. Ve can continue virk on plan for verld peace."

235

CHAPTER THIRTY-NINE

February 16, 1983
Ash Wednesday

I got up really early, long before dawn, in order to get to Mama's, shave, shower, dress, and make it to Mass before school. Also needed to see Monsignor Dan about practice. He was good about it as long as they had been to Mass, as we had hammered them with all last week. He asked me to come and see him when I had some time. "Looking forward to it, Monsignor." Though I wasn't, really, not if the conversation included next year. My time in the Montclair State library had led to some interesting opportunites, both in grad school and in the military, maybe a combination of both.

After loosening them up, they each got a ball on the baseline. I told them to face left, left-hand dribble, and walk the perimeter. Second lap to jog. Third lap to run, but no passing. Fourth lap to shoot a left-handed layup when they got back to where they started. If they missed, another lap. It took a while, but it would have taken two practices in November. "Good job on that, girls, really, shows how much you've improved. Okay, rebound and outlet drill, Unseld passes, at both ends. Let's go."

Five minutes of good work then four on four shell, losers run, new kids on the floor.

We had debated all season whether to teach them taking charges or offensive fouls. Ray, of course, was all over it. I thought it was a step too far. I mean, it was rare even in high school still. Sister stayed out of it.

We ended practice with a version of Knockout we hadn't played yet. Ray and I had to shoot from the top of the key. Players still shot from the foul line. If you knocked us out, there was a Kit Kat waiting for you. I got in line behind Liz Milak, who frowned, but then I jumped back to behind Rafferty. She yelled, "Not fair, get outta here, Coach!"

But I blew the whistle and the game started. All the seventh graders went out in the first round. Dooney, Ginna, SJ, Greet, Mary Pat in the second, and then Ray missed; Trudy knocked her out, Raffy knocked Trudy out, Reenie missed, and I knocked her out. Cat knocked Eddie out. I missed, but Raffy missed, also. I missed my layup. Cat had hustled back, waited till no balls were in the air, and sank one.

Cheers from everyone. Victory laps by Cat and Trudy, chanting "Kit Kat, Kit Kat," as they pranced, arms raised, "Gaels on Three!" and leaped into the group.

Enough said.

February 17, 1983
The Last Practice

Monsignor Dan was, physically, an exact opposite of his friend, Terrence. On the short side, round jolly face that could easily be a Santa, but eyes that missed nothing. Good-natured to be sure. Long sandy brown and gray hair and a long goatee. Kind of a Burl Ives look. Played a guitar they said. Maybe we could jam.

But like with most Jesuits I had ever run into, there was that "Jesuitness." I know, that's on me. I read too much about the Inquisition at too early an age. "Give us the child and we'll give you the man." Or something like that.

But what came through in Monsignor Dan was his kindness and good nature, which I was about to test.

He summoned me to his office during my free period, lavished praise upon the basketball team and the job we had done, and then got down to business. "Where do you see yourself in five years, Will? Do you think you'll still be teaching?"

"I doubt it, Monsignor, really. Monsignor was in a bind. I was a good sub and had enough math to keep my finger in the dyke. The basketball worked out well for all concerned, but I don't see either as a career path." No use bullshitting him, as I was thinking elsewhere already.

"I'm kind of sorry to hear that. You are a very talented young man. You are not afraid to be an authority figure when you have to be, but you are friendly without being friends. That's a gift for a teacher."

"Thank you, Monsignor, you're very kind."

"Given what you've said, I don't expect you'll be looking to take education or math courses this summer or in the fall?" his voice rising.

"No, sir."

"Well, Will, we've gotten the word from on high that our teachers from seventh grade up, beginning this fall, will have to either have their NJ Certificate or show that they are working toward it. That doesn't leave us much wiggle room."

"No, it sure doesn't, Monsignor. I'm sorry."

"Not as sorry as I am or as disappointed as Monsignor Terrence will be."

"I know, sir. I owe him a lot."

"Well, son, you will be able to finish out the term, I assume?" He rose, signaling my time was up.

"I certainly hope to, Monsignor," I said, shaking his offered hand. "I hope you'll be able to attend our little end-of-season dinner Sunday evening, sir. I'm sure the parents got word to you."

"Wouldn't miss it, Coach," he said with a sly smile. I'm thinking he's thinking, "Yeah, another banquet, riiiiight..."

* * *

Rolling Stones blasting from the boom box filled the gym with: *"This may be the last time. This may be the last time...Maybe the last time, I don't know...Oh no!"*Bad taste by me, I could tell by their faces. "On the baseline," I yelled after the whistle. "You mean, you're gonna *miss* this torture?"

"You stop talkin' like a fool, William Edwards," yelled Dooney indignantly, "or we'll jump you and tickle you to death. You know your heart is breaking, as I speak, at the thought that you won't be seeing our lovely faces no more. Y'know that, dontcha?"

"Why, yes, Mary Grace, there's fourteen faces I'll be sorely missing. One...not so much."

I hadn't seen Ray come in. She grabbed me from behind as Mary Grace Dooney and Mary Alice Rafferty tackled me like they were defensive lineman for the New Yawk Football Giants. They had me locked down and they all piled on, and I took my punishment like a man, hoping like hell no parents or clergy came in.

"Enough, ye heathens. Get on the line and act like yer a basketball team and I'll forget this ever happened."

Whistle. Cariocas. Slide steps. Sprints. Drop steps. Backwards. Defensive slides. Repeat everything. "Reenie, make a foul shot, and we'll do something else." Miss. "Awww! Too bad. Rinse and repeat. Who wants to shoot the foul shot? How come not you, SJ? Oh wait, I can't single you out."

"Gimme the da—oops. May I please have the ball, Coach, sir?"

Swish! Cheers from all. SJ must have felt like the coolest kid in Jersey!

"Raff and Dooney choose teams. Pick seventh graders first."

Rafferty said, "Aww—" Death stare from Ray. "Good idea, Coach!"

240

Five on five, full court, sub for made basket, Ray and I reffed, mostly playground rules, let them play for about fifteen minutes, except called every possible foul and violation on Dooney and Rafferty. Ray and I couldn't stop laughing.

Two-minute rest and water.

Eight minutes time and possession.

Six minutes gassers. Last ones. We ran with them. I let Ray win.

Last ten minutes of practice: Captain's Choice, which I had told them this morning.

H-O-R-S-E between the coaches.

Luddie came in just then and I thought, *Damn it, they're betting on this, and I know none of them bet on me.* I blew the whistle and sat them all down, Luddie included, shaking my head in a "shame on you" mode, walking back and forth in front of them, hands clasped behind my back, Jesuit mode.

"I'm so disappointed to learn. No, disappointed isn't strong enough. I'm heartbroken. Heartbroken to learn that there's gamblin' goin' on once again here inside the walls of Holy Mother Hoops. Oh, no, Dooney, don't say that doesn't count. I already spoke to yer da about this and he'll have none of it, nor will any of the fathers and mothers. *None of it, I say!* They have told me to take all the money from Luddie and give it to the Knights Clothing Drive for Guatemala Orphans this month and that'll be the end of it. Okay, Ludmilla, bring it on up here. Oh no, Ludmilla, there'll be no grace and no salvation at St. Ethel's Holy Oasis for you on Judgement Day. Repent!"

Luddie was already heading for the cafeteria with the money before I was halfway through my rant. Even the seventh graders were laughing by this time.

Looking beseechingly toward the heavens, I prayed, "Oh, bless me St. Ethel. I have done all I can do with them. They have strayed beyond the ability of this poor sinner to save them and steer them off the path of sin. There's only one thing left to do." Long pause. I fell to my knees. I closed my eyes and put my hands together as though to pray. I opened my eyes, threw my arms up in hallelujah position, and cried, "Let's play HORSE!"

"YAAAAAAAAAAAAAAY!!!!!"

Ray and I shot fouls. First miss shoots second. I missed. Ooooh...not good.

Ray sank one from top of the key, her money shot, I missed. O-H Small cheer. Death stare from me. Ray laughed.

Ray opposite hand reverse layup. Piece o'cake for Edwards.

Ray missed from deep corner, I made. H-H.

I made hook shot from left elbow, she missed. HO-H.

Called bank from right side, made it, she missed HOR—H Sweet!

Was she throwing the game?

Let's see.

I missed from deep corner. Bad choice, shoulda gone back to bank shot.

She made from top of the key, I missed. HOR-HO.

She made from one step back. I missed HOR-HOR.

She made from two steps back. I missed. HOR-HORS.

She made from three steps back. I missed, big cheer. HOR—*HORSE!*

I feel to my knees and Salaamed Ramona, the Queen of Horse. She laughed and said to the girls, "GIRL POWER ROCKS!"

"And don't forget it! Captain's in," she yelled.

"And don't forget this either," I said. "The best basketball player in this gym is..." Pause. "A GIRL!"

Doons and Raff said, "Coach Ray! Gaels on three!" And with general pile on, index fingers to the sky, the last practice was over. "One, two, three, GAELS!"

CHAPTER FORTY

We straightened up the tables and benches, saw all the girls safely out, put everything away, and met Sister at the door.

Ray and I were taking her to dinner at Sullivans, nothing too fancy as it was Lent, and they had a special menu. It was a very cold night, so we climbed into the Bu and made the short drive. Once settled in a booth with our drinks, Sister opined: "You two know how to run a good practice."

"That's Willie, Sister," said Ray. "He's a student, and he's always thinking about this stuff. I'm just along for the ride."

"That's really the way it is," I said. "She really just gets in the way most of the time. Complains a lot, too." I paused. "No, in truth, you were a perfect match, Coach. They kids loved you but knew they couldn't take advantage. You knew your stuff and the head coach completely trusted you. You did a great job, Ramonoushka. You did."

Sister lit up. "What neither of you were very good at, until now, however, was accepting compliments. You worked together well. You knew your roles. You didn't step on each other's feet. You listened to each other. Take the compliment. Really. You've done a wonderful job!

If Navajo children spoke and acted so badly as on occasion I have seen and heard of you two, we would take them to the big hole in the mountain and leave them there."

Ray and I, eyes wide open now, took a gulp of our drinks and settled down.

"Not really," she said. "But there are four wonderful mountains that mark the corners of our land. There is a black hole, but it's somewhere else. I think it's in the Commanche country, and Navajo parents are not so sadistic as to do something like that."

"That's good for Ray to know," I said, smiling.

"I have a serious matter to discuss with you, and it is to stay here at this table. Understood? It seems that I have outlived all my colleagues or they have moved on. And now I have outlived my welcome. The diocese wants me to vacate my apartment by the end of the term so they can move in someone who will be a full-time teacher. One of Monsignor Dan's duties here will be to execute these changes because Terrence couldn't or wouldn't do it."

I started to protest.

She held up her palms to stop me and said, "It's time. It's time for me to go home. We're off from school next week, midwinter break. It would be a good time, weather permitting. What do you think, children? I really don't want to hang around until the end of school."

I jumped right on that. "Waddaya think, Ray? Can we just pack it in, give a week or two week's notice, and hit the road? Or if I take Sister back to New Mexico, Ramona? Then come back. Can I take you? We can hitch a trailer to the Bu and hit the road. Basketball will be over on Friday. The dinner is Sunday."

"Well, that's another thing, William," she said. "Yes, Dan is Terrence's longtime friend, but the diocese's hand is in this and changes will be coming. Some good, some bad. You, without credentials, are on thin ice, I am sorry to say. You need to be aware of that."

"Well, it just happens that I have news on that subject. The monsignor called me in today, and we had a chat. He wanted to know about my intentions regarding teaching next year at St. Ethel and did they include taking education and math courses toward my teaching certificate. Sorry, Monsignor, not in the picture, I told him."

"WHAT? You decided you're not coming back? And you didn't tell me?" Ray's tone was getting louder.

"Actually, Ramona, the diocese decided that, not me. I thought that was pretty clear," I said. "We had this conversation once already. I asked you what you thought about me, or us, taking Sister back to New Mexico."

"Who's Terrence anyway?" she wanted to know, smoothly changing the subject.

"Terrence is the monsignor," I said.

Sister waved to one of the Sullivan daughters. "This round's on me."

"So you would take off for New Mexico without me?"

"This all just happened today. For God's sake, can you, for once in your life, give me a break? We have time to figure out what we're gonna do."

"I don't know," Ray said. "It's not like I can just quit. I have to give notice. It's a legally binding contract. Which I could do, then join you later. But then what?"

"Don't you have faith enough in us that we can work this out, Ray?"

"Well," Sister said, "I have put a lot of thought into this. My cousin has a little place over in Farmington, off the reservation. It's a good-sized town. You could stay there till you figure out what you want to do. Or just stay for a while and then go back to New Jersey. No one will bother you, and there's lots of economic development going on now there as far as jobs are concerned. No pressure. Anyway, give it some thought. If just one of you could come out with me, and stay for a while till I get settled, that would make me very happy, and that's really all I'm asking."

"I think we can work something out, Sister," I said. "Give us a day or two? Saturday okay?"

Sister said that would be fine. Ray didn't look all that happy.

Fish and chips all around. We drove Sister home, and Ray just jumped out of my car without saying good night. She walked to her Honda at the school and drove away. I gave her ten minutes then followed her up to Leonia.

CHAPTER FORTY-ONE

I knocked and she let me right in. I couldn't tell if she was ready for battle or just to sit and talk it out. So I took the first step. "So the monsignor calls me in today and asks if I'm comin' back, and if I am, I have to start to take classes this summer to get New Jersey certification in mathematics. I told him pretty much that I didn't see that happening. Which puts us right here. I didn't know about Sister's plans to leave early till she told us tonight, but I'm not makin' any commitments without talkin' to you."

"So you'd go without me?' she asked.

"Don't think I said that, Ray," I said.

"Then *what*?"

"Listen, I loved it out there. I know you would, too. I can take Sister and come back, and we can go together after school gets out. Or I can stay, get settled, do some investigating about careers for both of us and places to live. But, hell, we can do a lot of that here at the state library. Anyway, I go now, you come in June, four months. I'm not goin' anywhere without you ever again. You are the center of my life, I will never love anyone else. I want you to love it as much as I do. It's your call, Ramonushka."

"This might take some thought, William," she said. "First, I got no reason to stay here if you're not here. I can walk away from Northern Valley and not look back. Got a problem leavin' Mama though. What about her?"

"I'm not sure she'd go, but I want her to know that I want her to come with us," I said.

"Oh, I'm so glad you said that. That's a big relief. But I don't feel good about breakin' my contract, so I'm gonna talk to the NJEA rep at my school and see what he says. I think we'll be okay, Coach Vill. I feel very relieved. If we're okay with this part, the rest is just details, right? You're the man on details, right?"

"Yeah, biggest problem is agreeing to do it. We'll need some time at liberry at Monkey State. Lots of resources there. Looks like more and different kinds of opportunities you'd never think of here. You, especially, with a physics background."

I wrapped my arms around her, looked her in the eye, and said in a whisper, "Ah teenk ju must show me vhat deez Amerikanskis call dees Hankees Pankees. You are knowing dees? Dah?"

"Dah. Come wiz me, you silly boy."

CHAPTER FORTY-TWO

February 18, 1983

This could be my last day at St. Ethel. Oh boy! Lots to do and all I could think about was mesas, deserts, Ship Rock, four big mountains, starry night skies, and Navajos. Gotta bring it today, Willie boy.

I went out during lunch and bought flowers for Stephanie (and her music teacher) so the captains could present them to her after the anthem. Then I drove over to the Rutherford Library and looked at maps. We could drive down to Carolina, pick up US 64, and drive all the way to Ship Rock on US 64, no interstates, no hurry, southern route, maybe no snow. Sister might want to go US 66; we could do that. Whoa! Horse before cart, way before. I was already gone, but I still had details to attend to with Ray.

I got back to school, put flowers in fridge in kitchen, breezed easily through remainder of the day. Felt like I was on fire. Luddie showed up after the last bell rang. "Vas is loss, Ludmilla?" I asked.

She ran off a string of German and put me in my place. Her family spoke German among their collection of central European languages. I asked if her folks were coming to the dinner on Sunday evening.

"I don't believe it, but they are! And they're really excited about it. Why do you think that is?"

"'Cause they know they've got a great kid, and they want to share an experience with her. Why do you think, dumkopf?"

"Come on, Coach," she said, blushing.

"You know I'm right," I said, tempted to give her a noogie to seal the deal.

Luddie and I headed to the gym as St. Ursula, led by a very tall, fair-haired, combed straight back, manic-looking guy entered the room. "Hey, Coach, Dennis Kazuba, head basketball coach, University of St. Ursula and all Environs. Friends call me Denny the K. Well, they would, if I still had any. Wassup, mah man?"

"Will Edwards, Coach. Welcome to St. Ethel of the Holy Oasis Junior High School for Girls. Luddie here, my chief of operations, will show your girls their spacious state-of-the-art locker room. We can go get some coffee or tea or a soda in the kitchen, okay?"

"Will, I'll tell ya, man, just got up at noon, and I've already had about six cups of coffee. I work nights so I gotta keep going, know what I'm saying?"

"So what's your night gig, Denny?" *Okay, I'll bite.*

"Willie, son, I am the man, from midnight to four, the hour for lovers on WCPR, coming to you live from Stevens Institue of Technology at 106.7 on your FM dial with all your jazz needs. Denny the K will spin you some Trane, Miles, Cannonball, Herbie, Brubeck, Diz, Phil Woods, you know what I'm sayin' man? Maybe you call in to Denny. He plays one for you and that pretty girl heading toward us right now."

He got up and introduced himself. Ray smiled warmly and said hello. "So you're a DJ in real life, Mr. K?" she teased.

Denny the K, undeterred, said, "Why, not at all, assistant coach who's name I didn't catch. I spin the finest jazz artists way past your bedtime. I'm sorry to say."

"Well, then, I expect to hear Roberta Flack tonight, Mr. K. Can you make that happen?"

"I would part the Red Sea to make it happen," he replied.

"'First Time Ever I Saw Your Face' will do just fine, around 1:00 a.m." And she turned away, heading toward a corner where I stood, mouth open.

"Holy shit, Ramona. I didn't know you could do that."

"Silly boy." Mysterious smile I had never before seen. Ramona Lisa?

Sister in the corner, taking it all in between bursts from Denny the K.

The girls were more than ready. We went over everything once. But by the time we were done, they were bouncing up and down rumbling, "We are brave! We are brave!" till Dooney and Rafferty screamed, "GAELS ON THREE!"

"One, two, three, GAELS!" And they were out the door, the thundering herd.

Sister came in, gave me a brief round of applause, reached up and grabbed the sides of my face, and gave me a kiss on the cheek. "You've done a wonderful job, William. I'm so proud of you."

"Thank you, Sister Mary. Really. Thank you. Couldn't have done it without your help and guidance," I said, starting to tear up.

We went out just as Ray was coming in. I winked at her and went over to talk to Denny. That is, listen to Denny. "So I played ball a couple of years at Monkey State. Played with the great Pete Capitano and Paul Szem, only JV though. Sister said you played JV, Coach."

"Yeah, late '70s."

"How about that? Small world. I played 62–64, I think. Was Goodie's still there on Rte. 46? Used to load up on Belly Bombs. Or go to White Castle on Bloomfield Ave. Phys ed major?"

"Nah, I was in the army for two years outa high school then to Montclair. Majored in sociology, took some math classes. I lived in Webster."

"Wonder if Herbie's python was still there? Ever hear that story?"

"Sure. Used it to scare the freshmen."

"Hey, Will, let me give you my card, okay? I do parties, caterings, magic, DJ, looking for the big break. Can you?"

"You got it. Gimme a bunch of them. I'll spread them around."

Then he broke into, *"Start spreadin' the news...I'm leavin' today..."*

Oy...Thank God the buzzer called the kids in. But you had to love it. Have to check out his radio show.

Luddie, out of sight, ready with the flowers. Stephanie, stepped to center court, unmiked, parents beaming, and let it fly. Hairs up on the back of my neck, my eyes watering, hoping I'll hear this girl sing again. When she lightly conquered "And the rockets red glare, the bombs bursting in air," I just lost it. Got my handkerchief out, pretending I had to sneeze, fooling no one.

Dooney and Rafferty managed to show some behavior appropriate, applauding Stephanie after presenting her with the bouquet and laughing at me at the same time. Stephanie came across the court to me, gave me a big hug, and whispered, "Thank you for this."

Oh man.

During the game, I think I watched their manic coach more than the action on the court; he was manic, all over the place— jumping, hand signals, arms waving, ignoring the seat belt rule (coaches had to stay on the bench), the refs finally gave him a T. He looked over at me with a Shakespearean, "Why me?"Meanwhile, back at the game, Ray and Sister were running the show. We were up seven midway through the second when Trudy, screaming, went down. Looked like an ankle from the bench. I ran out on the court, waved at Clara, her mother, who was a nurse. Sent Luddie for some towels from the bench, one under her head, one under her raised ankle.

"Ankle?" I asked Clara.

"Yes. Nothing compound. Hope it's just a sprain," Clara said calmly as Monsignor Dan came over.

"Can we help, Mrs. Bilotskovic?" he asked.

"I don't think so. Thank you, Monsignor. Is it okay if I take her to Hackensack Hospital ER? Meet my husband there?"

"He's an X-ray tech there, Monsignor."

"Clara, maybe you should go in the kitchen and call Jan and tell him you're coming," I said.

"Good idea. Come this way." He gave her his hand.

We iced Trudie's ankle and foot and compressed the foot and ankle. "Good thing it wasn't the first game, eh," I said. "My goodness, girl, what a season you've had. Much pain?"

"Thank you, Coach. Pain's pretty bad, but they'll give me something. Thanks for everything. I'll see you on Sunday."

"You sure will. Mary Alice and Mary Grace, get over here and help Trudy out to the door."

Big applause. Trudy waved and blushed. We, and she, were lucky.

Reenie and Greet and Mary Pat in for the three. Sj and Eddie picked up the slack, and the half ended with Ethel up eight.

With the kids in the locker room, I said to Sister and Ray, "Y'know, we really dodged bullets all season if this is the only time we lost a kid to an injury. Is that your work, Sister Mary?"

"On a more serious note, William, who replaces Trudy?" she asked.

"Ideas?" I said as Dooney and Rafferty came galloping back.

"Trudy was crying," said Mary Alice.

Mary Grace shoved her and said, "You promised not to tell!"

"Get in the locker room, the both of ya!" I said. "Of course she was crying. She's in pain!"

"My vote is Reenie," Ray declared.

"Can she be the rover?" asked Sister.

"She's handled it before," I said. "Let's go with Reenie, okay, coaches?"

We went in and delivered the news. Greet was not thrilled but kept it in when I smiled right at her as I made the announcement. "Play it up. SJ and Eddie at half-court, Reenie at top of key, looking for steals, okay? Be aggressive. That's our game!"

"Team!"

"Gaels!"

"Who's better on offense?" I asked after the kids went out. Both Sister and Ray said, "Reenie."

"Anna better on D?"

"Yes," they agreed.

Third quarter dragged, lots of turnovers and fouls, had to pull Dooney with four for Mary Pat, but we held on to a seven-point lead. Reenie and the guards were gassed, so we put in Anna, Ginna, and Cat. With four minutes left, we were up fifteen and two of their kids had fouled out, Denny the K moaning at his fate as though he were singing Pagliacci, received a warning from the official.

At 3:00, I called time. Our bench rushed the floor, everybody out, seventh graders would end the season on the floor, trying to get a hoop for Patsy, only kid who hadn't, as Luddie would say, "Broken into the stats." So Patsy was rover. She took a rebound from Liz and made a layup with five seconds as the home crowd acted like it was a game winner.

St. Ethel, 51
St, Ursula, 34
Won, 17; Lost, 2

Denny the K's mania had slowed down considerably. But he recovered quickly and said to me, as we shook hands, "I expect a late-night call from you, Will. I think 'Kinda Blue' would be a good choice, don't you? Or maybe 'A Love Supreme'? 'Cry Me a River'? 'Take Five'? Or somethin' from Lady Day?"

How about 'To Ramona'? by Bob Dylan, right after you play whatever Ray requested?"

And we both laughed. Denny the K, indeed.

All the parents were down on the court, smiles all around, hugs and handshakes, past slights and insults forgotten. Winning cures a lot of ills, it does. Final record of seventeen and two, what the hell, I could retire on that. A one-season wonder.

The kids got dressed and came out ot the locker room for their curtain call. Cheers all around. Trudy came in on crutches. More cheers. "Just a sprain," she said, trying not to show any tears. The kids were all going to Mikey's tonight, one last fling, on the monsignor, who would not attend but would pick up the tab but not for drinks. Wise decision. We all said good night. See you Sunday. I started to head out after we had straightened out the gym. Ray said she was beat, wanted to get home and hit the rack, set her alarm, and listen to Denny. Me too.

* * *

I couldn't sleep, so about 12:30 I turned on 106.7, and damn it, there he was. Spinnin' your favorite tunes and talking so fast I could barely follow. Denny was saying, "Got two in a row here for tonight. Will and Ray over in the wilds of southern Bergen County. They're good people, and they're doin' the Lord's work coaching a great little basketball team at St. Ethel. Have a good thought for them. It's Roberta followed by one not heard much on Denny the K, a tune from Bob Dylan."

I got up, found his card in my wallet, went downstairs for the phone, and called the station when both songs were finished. "Will, my man! I knew you'd be checking out Denny the K. Awwwwriiiiiiight!"

"Are we on the air?" I asked, still in a daze.

"That we are, my boy," Denny said, music in the background. "But not for long, not with Coltrane on."

"Okay, I'll get off," I said. "Thanks, man. You got yourself a new fan tonight, really. Good luck."

Nobody's ever gonna believe this.

Then the phone rang. "I love you, William, yes I do. And I'm *'shutting softly my watery eyes'* and going to sleep. Call me in the morning. Night."

CHAPTER FORTY-THREE

February 19, 1983

I got up early and decided to go for a long run before the snow started. I ran for an hour, picked up some pastries on the way home, and fed Mama and myself after I showered and cooled off.

I got Ray on the phone. When she picked up, I sang, "The first time, ever I saw your face..."

"You have a nice voice, you shoulda been a singa! What's up? It's early," she said.

"On my way to Montclair State library. Wanna go plan our future?"

"I'm on it. I'll be there in an hour." And she hung up.

"Yessss! And it counts!"

After I hung up, I chatted for a while with Mama about what had happened. I talked to her about my travel plans with Sister Mary, and she was both happy for us and sad to lose two friends. "Vhat about Ramona?"

"I think we're good. I'm meetin' her at the college, and we're gonna look at opportunities in the west, y'know, jobs, grad schools, see what's goin' on, y'know?"

"You can feex?"

"I think we're gonna be all right, Mama," I said. "More coffee?"

I put 880 on the AM radio to get the weather. Snow later in the day, four to six inches. "Do you want to go to confession today?"

"I vait till next veek. Go to Mass tomorrow. Home for supper?"

"I'll call, okay?"

I got up to the college about ten, met Ray at the door at ten thirty, and we really dug. Then got into grad school and the military and the Navajo. Lots of interesting-looking careers with a sociological base. I had acquired some serious analytical skills both in college and in army intelligence, and I had to think they were marketable.

Ray was deeply into the grad school catalogues, said she couldn't believe what was available. Stuff she had really been turned on by as an undergrad at Bloom. Then she found some Ansel Adams books, and it was game over. But we had lots of time.

It was three when we took a break and saw the snow falling. Damn! The Malibu could do a lot of things, but it sucked on the snow. I took out a bunch of books, some for each of us, called Mama from the library and told her we'd be home for supper. Took an hour.

"We're home, Mama," I yelled cheerfully. "Feels like time for a cocktail."

Mama had made goulash and noodles, always a favorite, so we dug out some Bull's Blood wine and feasted. Such a wonderful cook. I had seconds and made a big fuss and gave her a big hug and told her Ray would clean up. They both laughed. And I cleaned up before Mama really cleaned up.

Ray said she was going to bed early and went upstairs where she kept a set of overnight stuff in the spare bedroom. Mama watched some sitcoms then called it a night. I waited until it was quiet upstairs and tiptoed up to my room. My bedspread was all lumpy, but I took this as a good sign. *"I felt your heart so close to mine..."*Getting undressed, I said out loud, "I think I'll sleep on *top* of the covers tonight. It's kind of warm and stuffy tonight. But first I'll dive on the bed." Then I ducked behind the end of the bed and waited for the lumps to unearth themselves.

As they did, and landed on the floor, they were tackled gently. "You are under arrest by order of Czar Vilyum. Surrender or face a firing squad."

"Can't I have another choice?"

"Okay, get back in bed. Be quiet. Remove excess clothing. Dah?"

"Dah!"

CHAPTER FORTY-FOUR

February 20, 1983

Snow had stopped. I went out and shoveled and cleaned off the cars. Weather guys were close, about four inches. Everything immaculate, I went in and made coffee and started one of my Navajo books at the kitchen table till Ray came in. I got a big hug from behind. "How is my sweet Willieboy this fine winter morning?"

I got up and went to the stove. "Fresh coffee, Ramonoushka? Just delivered from Kenya. You vill lahk. Kalashi on the table."

"I got some personal grooming business to do today, Will, for the event of the season tonight, so I'll be busy all day. You givin' out any individual awards tonight?"

"Thought about it, but no," I answered, "Liam got trophies for each kid, which I told him I didn't want, but I see his point. I mean they had a hell of a good season. But no individual awards, at this level, they just create problems. Agree or no?"

"Definitely agree," Ray said. "But just out of curiosity, who's your MVP?"

261

"Trudy, hands down," I said. "Yours?"

"Same," she said.

"Most improved?" I asked her.

"Ginna."

"Reenie." We both answered at the same time. Tough choice. Glad we didn't have pick. Sister would get the deciding vote.

"Defensive player?"

We both said, "SJ."

"Mama, can you sit for a minute so Will and I can talk to you?" Ray asked her grandmother, who obliged her. "You know we're moving to New Mexico and we want you to know, once we've settled in, we want you to come and stay with us."

The old lady looked at me questioningly, and I got up from the table and hugged her from behind. "What do you think, Mama? Of course we want you to come."

"I can't come to desert. I *hate* desert. Since I vas leettle girl," she complained.

"Where we'll be isn't desert, Mama," said Ray. "It's up near the mountains in the city. It's Albuqurque, you'll see. At least, come out and stay for a while and see if you like it, okay?"

"I teenk about it," she said then looked at me and said, "Vill, you teenk ees good?"

"Yes, I do, Mama, but you have to come and see for yourself," I said. "Maybe in September, okay?"

"All agreed then?" asked Ray. "Good."

Ray got her coat, and after giving Mama and me a big kiss and hug, she took off for her appointments. Mama was making some sausage and eggs and smiled as I got a cup of coffee and sat down. "I'll be at the school most of the day. Do you want to go to Mass today, Mama?"

"You go?"

"Sure," I said. "We can go after breakfast, okay?"

"Vhat eez veazher like in Albe—oh, I can't say eet!"

"It's pretty dry, Mama, in the mountains. Not much rain, some snow in the winter and in the mountains around the city. I looked at a lot of pictures in the library, and it's really a beautiful city, not too big. Very pretty buildings. Lots of art." That seemed to satisfy her.

Ten o'clock Mass was packed, and the monsignor gave a nice homily, drawn from his days as a cabdriver in New York City. A good source. He was a good storyteller and startingly different from his old friend Terrence. *Not one to have as an enemy*, I thought. No, that's not fair. That's my ignorance.

It felt good. Things would be all right while he was in charge. I took Mama home and went back to the school to help set up for the dinner, which was being catered by "NOT MIKEY'S." There was a nice BYO bistro over in Rutherford, which had gotten some yuppie-type upscale restaurants and, here in the year 1983, was still a dry town, except for the Elks, Legion, VFW, etc. Fitz and Mike had insisted it was their treat. Given all their blackhearted dealings during the season, no one put up a fight. No alcohol, so it would be an early night, and Sullivans would be busy later.

I had bought my gifts for Sister, Ray, Luddie, and her staff. Buying stuff for females was actually something I thought I was pretty good at. Well, at least I got a kick out of it. We had a head table set up for Monsignor Dan, Sister Mary, Liam Dooney, Ray, and me, seated in that order.

Kids sat as a team, families sat together, Monsignor Dan said a prayer and blessed the meal. We saluted the flag and said the Lord's Prayer. The meal, chicken or fish, as it was Lent, was delicious and a real treat to have it served in the cafeteria, decorated by the mothers and kids. It was nice. Cost the car-dealing lads a few shillings as well.

After the meal, Sister and Ray each gave a brief talk. Liam gave every girl a trophy with her name and 17-2 inscribed on it. I guess it was okay.

I spoke. Said something nice and/or funny about every girl and about how much I loved being their coach and how I hoped they had a good experience playing basketball for St. Ethel. I spoke about how their unique mix of personalities and talents had made the season an unforgettable experience for me, one which would stay with me forever. I pointed out how tonight, civilized and pretty they all pretended to be, but that I knew better.

"Now stand up at yer table, ye heathens, and let's have the whole thing one more time. Captains!"

Dooney and Rafferty get the team up. Ready? "WE ARE BRAVE!" Then, "GAELS ON THREE."

"One, two, three, GAELS!"

"One last thing. The monsignor took a chance giving this position to a young guy with no coaching experience. We spent a lot of hours talkin' hoops, and I must tell you, he's by far the smartest man I've ever known. But I really want to thank the mothers and fathers for supporting your girls. I think I can understand the faith you have to have to hand her over to some guy you hardly know and trust that he'll do the right thing by her. I know that I'd feel that way. But you trusted the monsignor's judgment. And I thank you for that. These months we spent together, all of us, were, for me, a privilege. And I am forever grateful to the moms and dads for your kindnesses and support and trust.

"Another last thing. This team couldn't have achieved what it did without the input and guidance and the grace of Sister Mary and the teaching and examples set by Coach Ray. What a luxury it was for me to have two assistant coaches. I know I turned to Sister many times during games, and I could split practice duties with Coach Ray without missing a beat. I never beat Ray in HORSE, and the girls never beat Sister in free throws. How about that?" I led the applause and finally sat down.

Hugs and laughter and tears all around as we were cleaning up the gym. No school for a week had just hit me like a freight train. I caught Sister's eye and walked with her to the kitchen. "Got time to do some travel planning tomorrow, Sister?" I asked.

"Tuesday would be better if that's okay with you, William," she answered. "I have some paperwork to clear up tomorrow in Paterson and at the college, and Monsignor will help me with it."

"Okay, then," I said, "how about I pick you up on Tuesday at ten?"

Shaking her head, "Eight is better."

"Eight it is."

Ray and I stayed to clean up, and I followed her up to Leonia.

Donald Schlenger

CHAPTER FORTY-FIVE

February 21, 1983
Monday

First "not thinking about basketball" day since November. I went over to the school, sorted out the unis the kids had brought in last night, clean and folded, and put them away along with cleaned pinneys, basketballs, and other paraphernalia for next season's personnel. I kept the score book as a souvenier. Walked up the hill to the diner and had an omelette and coffee and went over my road maps for a while until it dawned on me that I had nothing to do. What a strange and empty feeling. Everyone I knew was at work.

On impulse, I called Ray. "Wanna go to the city?"

"When?" she asked.

"Now," I said, "I'm at Station Square." The tracks were the boundary between Rutherford and East Rutherford.

"Can't do it. Spendin' the day with the girls from school. Call me when you get back," she said.

"Good deal," I answered and hung up. I took the train into Penn Station.

It was fairly mild, cloudy, a day you could be outside all day, so I walked the forty-odd blocks up to the Museum of Natural History on 77th, found the section on North American Indians, and spent three hours checking it out.

What a story! From Asia to the land bridge to the deserts of the southwest and all the way to Chile. Maybe across the Pacific as well. Never invented the wheel, go figure. Millions wiped out over time by the whites. I thought there was an Indian museum somewhere in Manhattan but couldn't remember where, and one museum a day was my limit.

* * *

I found a public phone and called Atlantic Records and asked for Ms. Edwards in A and R. After a wait, she answered, "A and R, Celia Edwards speaking."

I sang into the phone, "Teach your parents well, their children's hell..." She picked up the harmony from that point on..."How's Cissy?" I asked her after the last "And know they love you."

"Prospering against all odds in the capitalist rat race, little Willie. Are you calling to treat your Grace Slack–lookalike sister to lunch?"

"I'm not sure, but I can go ask Alice!"

"Where *are* you, doofus?'

"Up at Natural History."

"Okay. Get on the subway and meet me at the White Rabbit Café on Christopher St. in the Village. Can't miss it. In about an hour." *Click.*

I found the subway below the museum and took it down to the Village and NYU and Washington Square. I walked around looking at old haunts from college days trying to recall the vibe, feeling suddenly old and lonely. Of course, a Monday afternoon in 1983 couldn't match a Saturday night in the Village when I was a freewheelin' senior in high school in the spring of 1976 or a college kid and army vet three years later.

Cissie showed up in a cab only nine minutes—ah, forget it. We hugged, then, at arm's length, apprised each other closely. "You *did* put on your Gracie look, didn't you?"

"Yeah, I haven't tried it here yet. Wanna walk? Let's walk around the Square and then we'll eat, okay, LB?" Little brother.

My sister was the best person I knew—smart, kind, beautiful, talented, and brave. Many of her friends and fellow musicians got swallowed up and lost in the wildness of the late sixties and early seventies in music. Cissy just walked away. There was no one else like her.

"Are you famous yet?" I asked her.

"No, you hick. I'm the one who gets to decide who *becomes* famous. Don't you get it? We're workin' on a new group now called Crosby Stills Nash and Young. You probably haven't heard of them out there in the back of the beyond."

"Nah, we're still groovin' to Danny and the Juniors. Rock and roll will never die!" I said. "Really, how are you, big sister, and Manhattan snob?" as we entered the café.

She turned every head in the place, and the hostess said, "Anywhere you'd like, Ms. Slack."

"That's very kind of you." Looking at her name tag, she said, "Jade. In the back will be fine." Cissy sat with her back to the wall, crime-boss style, I looked the place over, bodyguard sytle, Raybans and all, then joined her. "We're gettin' good at this."

"So you asked how I was. Love the job. Meet all these terrific musicians, the talent is so unbelievable, really. And they work so hard! Makes what I was involved in look like junior high school."

"You never had a decent band," I protested.

"If I was big time," she said, "someone would've found me. I was a dime a dozen, too strung out all the time. Better to be out of that life, believe me. I wasn't tough enough. There's lots of talented people who just aren't driven or tough enough. I mean, some of these people are really geniuses, Will!"

The waitress came. "Would you like some more time, Ms. Slack?"

269

"No, I think we're ready. Are you ready, Oliver? Good. I'll have a watercress and avocado salad with endive and chickpeas. Maybe some beets? Can you do that? Great! And a bottle of Perrier."

"Cheeseburger, medium, and fries for me. Cream soda. Thanks."

"They'll spend all day trying to discover who Oliver is and whether he's gettin' any."

"So why'd you walk away, Cis? All these years I never axed you."

"I didn't wanna die, Will. Really, I got too close to dyin' that one time, and it scared me. It changed me. I was smart enough at least to see I'd better get the hell outa there. The booze, the whole overdose on smack, emergency room, no one there for me. No one! They sent me to cool out and put me back on the street. I walked to Port Authority from the East Village, panhandling for bus fare on the way, and took a bus home. Talk about rock bottom. Mama broke down sobbing when she saw me. Only time I ever saw Daddy cry."

"I was so scared you were gonna die. You looked like a corpse. I cried all that night."

"I know, I heard you. I wanted to go in and snuggle like we used to when you were little, but I couldn't even move. I was so bad. Mama talked to one of the counselors at the high school, and they got me into a program, a good one. I got dried out, cleaned up, had therapy, and went to meetings when I got out. They saved my life, Willie. Did the twelve steps. Still do. That's where I met Robert."

"I like him. You take care of each other, don't you?'

"Now that's very perceptive, LB. That's enough on me. What's up?"

Just then, the meal came and we dug in. Not in the Edwards' playbook to talk and eat simultaneously.

"No, wait," she said. "Before you start. Do you ever talk to Mom and Dad? I thought not? Why not? It's breakin' her heart, Willie. Really. Why don't you call them? She says she always has to call you? What's goin' on?"

"Okay, what the f——k are they doin' in the middle a nowhere in Florida? What the hell is *there*? *She didn't wanna go.* Why did she? I was back from the army. You and Patrick were here. They were havin' kids. They coulda done the grandma-grandpa thing. Tell me! I never understood it."

"Jesus, Willie," she snapped at me, "you're still mad at Frankie Edwards, aren't ya? You been carryin' this for how long now? Ten, twelve years?"

"He was never *there*, *godamnit*! Working or parked in front of the tube or the racing form or 'drinkin' with the lads' at the VFW, never saw him at any a my games in high school. That was deliberate."

"You gotta let it go, LB. It's eatin' you up. He's a limited man with limited emotional resources. Robert picked up on that in the first five minutes he met him."

"You're makin' that up."

"Am not! And listen, it's not for you to say what's right and wrong for Mom. She owes him her life. I guess she loves him. God knows what would happened to her in the camps, y'know? Let it be. And work on your forgiving. You still go to church, don't ya? Talk to the priest. They're good at that stuff. And promise me, look at me, promise me you'll call Mom on Sunday. Say it! Good."

Meal over, coffee served. I took a deep breath. "Basketball's over, seventeen and two, I loved it, and I was good at it. Girls that age are a pisser! Whoa! Ramona was a great assistant, and more importantly, I think we patched up all the old wounds..."

"No way. No way. She broke you, Willy. How did this happen?"

Cissy and Ramona were on the "don't invite to the same party" list since May 1976. Before then, truth be told.

"I was a kid then, so was she. We've grown up. For the most part, anyway. We figured out a lot of stuff."

"There was no way she could forgive that speech you gave in the cafeteria, come on! That was historic!"

"I know, that was pretty much out of character. The chicks loved it though. Offers came flooding in, I'm tellin' ya. Had my fifteen minutes, I did."

"You were like the living dead then. You wouldn't even talk to *me* for a coupla weeks, right?" said Cissie.

"Talkin' to you helped bring me back. You always hung in there for me. Anyway, big news is I'm moving back out west. To New Mexico. Takin' Sister Mary out next month. I will have a lot of time to talk, and I promise I will talk to her about Frankie. She's retired and she's goin' home to where she was born on the Navajo Reservation. I'm gonna stay, get settled, and then Ray's comin' out when school ends. New life, Cis. Waddaytheen?

"Good for you, LB. Really, good for you. About time you got a break is what I think."

"I don't know. I feel pretty blessed, really, Cis. This time at Ethel's really been good to me. Met some really great people. Sister Mary, the monsignor, Mama, whose house I live in. Still see Angelo. Tony's only a step away from the show. I was lucky it all fell into place. You'll come and see us, won't you? Bring Robert and the kids?" I laughed, and she looked at me strange.

"No, I'm not. Pregnant. But we're talkin' about it and whether we'll stay in the city."

"You'll be a great mom, Cissy, really."

"Scary stuff, LB. Time to boogie. Got a meeting with famous rock stars you'll never meet."

"Somethin grabbed aholda me, yeah...," I sang. "Yeah, I know it's Janis."

"And it felt just like a ball and chai-ai-ain...," she responded.

"Yeah, that's exactly what it felt like...," I sang. A little treat for the lunch crowd, who applauded politely.

"Gotta go, bro."

"Enougha this, sis."

"Jade, can we have a check, please? And we'll take as many pictures as you'd like, okay?"

"Really, Ms. Slack, it's on the house. Will you be kind enough to take a—oops."

"Sure, but it's not on the house. I love the place and, of course, the name. Thank you all so much."

Poses set, pictures taken, whole crowd of customers in the act. It was fun. Check and tip taken care of by Oliver. Cissy decided to let the illusion go unrevealed. No harm, no foul. Free advertising for the White Rabbit.

"I'll cover the cab," she said. "Am I gonna see you again before the Wagon Train heads into the sunset? If not, give me a big hug and kiss, LB. Love ya like no other."

"Same for me, big sister. You're still the one."

"CALL MOM ON SUNDAY."

I got out at Penn Station; she went on uptown. If I was God, I would make sure that every guy like me had a sister like Cecelia.

* * *

Mama had cabbage rolls waiting. I called Ray. "Mama made cabbage rolls. Come on down," I said.

"On my way," she answered.

Nothing much better than Mama's cabbage rolls, old country rye bread from Strucko's, and Schaefer beer. After we cleaned up, we watched *My Darling Clementine* with Henry Fonda. Directed by John Ford, filmed in Monument Valley. *Be there soon*, I thought. Wow, what a movie!

Ray drove home after we made out a little in her car as I had an 8:00 meeting with Sister Mary.

CHAPTER FORTY-SIX

February 22, 1983
Tuesday

Once we were settled in the Rutherford library after a light breakfast, Sister asked, "William, how soon can you be ready to leave?"

"I think I have to give two weeks' notice, but I can check with Monsignor today. Do you know?"

"I shouldn't think that would be a problem. He has someone lined up for my room already, and it might as well be a math teacher," Sister said.

"Well," I said, "I would feel bad about just leaving and not saying goodbye to the kids, especially the Gaels, y'know? I mean, they did make my time at St. Ethel."

"Oh, I knew you were just an old softie, William. So let's say two weeks from this past Saturday, that would be March 5, weather permitting, okay?" she asked.

"Good. I'm sure you have ideas on routes, right? I'm all ears," I said.

Sister said, "Okay. I have old friends along the way I would really like to see and spend some time with, William, and I suspect you do as well?" I nodded. "So how about we drive to Washington the first day and stay till Tuesday. Will that be all right?"

"Sure," I agreed.

Sister: "Washington to Charlotte, okay? Two nights there?"

"Yep."

Sister: "Okay, then Charlotte to St. Augustine. Okay?"

Will: "You can drive, right, Sister?"

Sister, with some indignation: "Yes, I can. Of course I can drive. What a question!"

Will: "As Rafferty would say, 'Sorry, Sister.'"

Will: "Unfortunately, my license expired in 1968, and the Mother house on Long Island saw no need to have me renew it. As Rafferty would say, 'Not fair.' Eyesight, it was."

We both laughed.

"I always wanted to see St. Augustine. Guy I went to high school with, Tom Crosset. He's an artist, is still there I think," I said.

Sister: "Okay, then we'll stay two nights and then drive Rte. 90 along the Gulf coast to Pensacola. Catch our breaths and figure out the rest from there. Sound good?"

"Excellent plan. Beats mine for sure," I offered.

"Which was?"

"Road maps." I laughed. "But remember, I was an intelligence officer, and I can live off the land."

"You're telling this to a Navajo, right?"she said.

"You got a little Jersey in that Navajo, ah then." I laughed.

"Okay now, second order of business," she said.

"I don't like this already," I protested.

"I have accumulated more money than I can ever spend, most of which I will leave to the order. But in the case of our journey, all expenses incurred will be mine. This is clear, William."

Notice that wasn't a question.

"You wish, Sister," I wish I had said but instead went with the standard, "Yes, Sister." After all, I was, as we say, a cradle Catholic. And then, "How do you do that? It's Jedi stuff, isn't it?"

"For me to know, and you'll never find out, young man. It's a Navajo thing." And she laughed and laughed. "You thought I was gonna say Dominican, didn't you?

Next order of business," she declared, and it could mean only one thing.

"Ray and I are solid as of last night, Sister," I said. "I will stay in New Mexico, and she will come out when school lets out. We are good to go."

"Well, William, that's just wonderful news. You must have some of the Jedi magic yourself."

"Look, Sister, I have been completely and utterly devoted to Ramona my entire life. I was never seriously involved with another girl."

* * *

"Let me tell you our story and then we are done with it. You know the genesis, right? Little kids together, boyfriend-girlfriend in high school. Okay, early May of senior year, time for the prom. And this is a big deal for me. Never been to one. Worked nights and weekends as a checker at Clare's Shoprite over by Union School, you know, here in Rutherford, in the west end? Saving up my paychecks. The prom thing is expensive. So I asked Ray, she said yes, then I bought the bids. It was gonna be up at the Friar Tuck Inn in Cedar Grove, you know it? Anyway, I got the bids, ran down to the cafeteria, I'm really excited. She's at a table with her girlfriends. 'Ray, I got the prom bids.' I'm holding 'em up so everyone can see, like anyone cares.

"She laughs and says, 'Oh, Willie, I thought I told you I wasn't gonna go. Me and the girls got a good deal on a place in Seaside for that weekend, and that's the only time we can all go. So you're free to go with anyone you want, except that girl Lois from St. Mary's, okay?'

"I looked at her and said, 'You're not serious, right? You're just pullin' my leg?'""Nah, you'll be fine, really,' and she turned her back to me like I was some pesty little freshman.

"Sister, that was early May of senior year. I called to her, and she turned around and I turned, held up the bids, tore them in half, and dropped them in the trash.

"Then I stepped away, stood on a chair, and shouted at the top of my lungs to the whole cafeteria, 'Attention, can I have your attention please!' I waited till it quieted down.

'This is Bill Edwards announcing that Ramona Voytek has just blown me off for the prom. We have been together since fourth grade. Thank you. Thank you very much. I will now be leaving the building.'

"Then I stepped back over to her table, taking in all the shocked faces, leaned over her, and said to her and all her friends, 'You take care of yourself now, Ramona.'

"And I left the cafeteria. I walked out of school and walked all the way down to Memorial Field to wait for baseball practice. I never spoke to her again…till I called her from Mama's this past fall. I felt like something in me had died. She told everyone that she broke up with me and had a boyfriend from Lyndhurst.

"I had been talking to the army recruiter since I had gotten the rejection packages from Williams or Amherst or any of them other schools. I had taken the army's tests and all, and since I was eighteen, I enlisted the next day. I left for the army a week after graduation. Last six weeks of high school people thought I had a breakdown, that I was catatonic. The only thing that kept me sane was baseball. And my friends Angelo and Anthony. Ray tried to talk to me a few times, but I just stared at her or turned and walked away. Just going through the motions. My folks were worried I wouldn't graduate, that I was traumatized or would kill myself. My mother went over to Voyteks to talk to Ramona, but she just laughed it off. End of story. I don't mean to be disrespectful, but really, end of story."

* * *

Sister said, sadly, "That's a terrible story, and you must have been in terrible pain for many years. Yet I saw it lift and I saw the joy you both bring each—"

"Please don't do this, Sister. It's taken me and Ray six years to get here, Sister. I think we're gonna be all right. We know we have been in your prayers. Sometimes I almost feel it. Any superpowers you can use on me, Dominican, Navajo, Jedi, or female will also be appreciated."

"I will bring all gems, roots, potions, powders, charms, chants, and spells under lock and key. I promise. Prayers, however, and appropriate Navajo chants, I will bring," she said.

"Okay, I guess we're as set as we can be for now. I'm going to head over and make Monsignor Dan unhappy, and I'll drop you off unless you have somewhere else to go."

The monsignor was not happy. *Part of the act*, I thought, but I played along. "How am I supposed to get a teacher in two weeks?" he stormed.

"Ah, never mind, William," he said after the storm passed. "I knew Sister Mary had a schedule, places to go, old friends to see, you just caught me by surprise. Is Ramona going with you?"

"Yes, she is, sir, but not until school's out. Nontenure, two months' notice in the contract," I answered.

I shrugged, palms up. "Is it okay if I meet with my basketball team next week after school one day next week so they hear the story from me, Monsignor?"

"Of course, they'll all know by the end of business Friday anyway. Especially if you develop a thirst any night this week," he said, grinning.

"Message received, Monsignor. I will see you next week then, okay?"

"Thanks for coming in, Will, I know it wasn't easy facing the old man. Oh, listen, Monsignor left a letter of reference for you. Let me fetch it from the file."

"You know I forgot we have a student teacher over at Our Lady of Sorrows. She'd be perfect for Ethel. I'll call over there today and look into it. It'll be fine, Will."

Back at Mama's, I called my friend Angelo Lastina at his gas station in East Rutherford, and I made an appointment for service, a trailer hitch installation, and to reserve a small U-Haul trailer for March 11. Took a quick trip up to the college, dropped off my library books, and picked up my transcripts. I stopped in the Barnes and Noble on Rte. 46 on the way home and splurged on a book on Navajo culture and history. Fell asleep reading it till Mama woke me for supper and surprised me with southern fried chicken.

February 23, 1983
Wednesday

I got up early and went over to Angelo's station. I had made an appointment for service for the Bu, to get a trailer hitch, and to rent a small U-Haul for the trip west. He was not happy about my relocation to "Where the hell is Ship Rock? In the ocean somewhere? And I heard you're back with—ahh—I can't even say her name. Tell me it ain't true. I'm sorry, but she reminds me of one of the great moments of the class of '76. 'Attention! Could I have you attention please? This is Will Edwards.' Shoulda made the yearbook! And now you're back together? *MaDON! Wassamattawitchyou!*"

"Too late for that, Golden, so lighten up already," I corrected him. "I'm goin' next week. She's comin' when school ends. Deal with it, goombah."

I got my book bag out of the car and told him, "Take your time with the car. I'll be back late afternoon. I walked over to the new diner by the tracks and treated myself to breakfast then took my book to the Rutherford library, stopping to realize how many happy hours I had passed there since I was a little kid. And then a high school jock. All the ladies there and I knew each other by name.

I spent most of this day getting lost in atlases and road maps, always a fascination to me. Learning the names, the Indian tribes, the rivers and mountain ranges, towns and roads that led nowhere. Sangre de Cristo Mountains, Blood of Christ? Taos and Santa Fe sounded really cool. Anyway, I looked at the time and four hours had passed.

So I repeated the task with Arizona, then Colorado, then Utah, the whole Four Corners world. Monument Valley. Canyon de Chelley. Mesa Verde. Endless!! I killed the whole day with maps! Army intelligence, right?

I walked back over to Angelo's around five. "You're coming over the house for dinner, Arlene says so," he said. "You were in the library all day, weren't you?" I nodded, backpack full of books. "Some things nevah change."

"Good thing I don't have any plans," I said.

"Like when did you evah have any plans for anything?"

We drove over, and I called Mama and apologized.

You never had a quick bite at Arlene's table or came away hungry. They started going out in high school. She went to Becton Regional High School, which served East Rutherford and Carlstadt, and she used to help him with his work when he was at Fairleigh. Nothing, I mean nothing, got by Arlene. Now she did the books for the gas station, and they consulted monthly on investments. They were a formidable business partnership. I loved them both. They were warm and kind and generous. And I was blessed to be their friend. I hoped they lived forever and had fifty grandchildren.

Arlene gave me a big hug and kiss and put a glass of Ruffino chianti in my hand. She wanted to know all about my upcoming trip and was really interested in the Navajo part of it. She had been reading novels by Tony Hillerman, mysteries that take place on the Rez. Did I know about them? I hadn't heard about them, but when I got there, I would find out, I told her. She was that kind of woman, interested in everything, a real delight to talk to, always made you feel like the only person in the room. Hated to leave, but it got late early, as a famous New Jersey resident used to say. And she said she knew Ramona was the right girl for me. Angelo gasped, I think, as she kicked him in the shins.

February 24, 1983
Thursday

Warm February day. I called Sister and asked her, "You busy today?"

"William, as a woman of God, I am always busy. I am offended by your question," she said. Then added, "A little Dominican humor."

"Not that much, though, Sister." Bustin' chops with Sister Mary, what's better than that? Could be an interesting journey west after all. "How about a drive to the beach?"

"Ready in an hour," she said.

Then Mama. "Up for a trip to the beach, Mama?"

"Alvays."

"Leaving in an hour."

A little over an hour later, just as we were pulling away from Sister's, Ramona's car pulled up. Mama yelled, "Vill, ees Ramona!"

Mama rolled her window down and yelled across the street, "Ramona, ve are going to hocean, you can come veet us?" looking at me with a question mark on her face.

I smiled and said, "Sure."

Ramona looked at me and smiled. I smiled back. She jumped in the front seat, and we were off. Of course, the two old ladies had played me. I never even thought to ask how they both knew to get in the back seat. Ray had even brought mix tapes, but at least they were decent oldies.

I drove to my favorite old place at the shore, Asbury Park, parked near the Casino, once the grandest place on the northern shore. We walked up to the boardwalk, and I told them I would meet them right here in two hours and we would go to lunch in the old-timey restaurant nearby. "Okay?" All nodded.

"How about a run there, my darling?" I asked.

282

"Anytime, peaches," she challenged. We went over by a bench, stretched for a while, and took off southbound at a slow jog. "Running south. Set your watch for an hour, okay?" I said.

"Say when," she said.

I said, "Three, two, when," and we took off down the boardwalk.

After a few steps, Ray was galloping while I jogged at a slow pace, taking my time, sure to annoy her. "Oh, for God's sake, Willie, are you gonna jog for two hours?"

"I am not knowing dees, my sweet papooski. Ees no gut to run slow for long deestance?" I said.

Ray took off without a word.

I gradually picked up the pace, and as she had slowed down, we ran together.

Ray: "I been thinkin' a lot about going to New Mexico, y'know?"

Will: "Like what kind of thinkin'?"

Ray: "I got enough money saved I could go to grad school or at least get started. Teachin' isn't gonna do it for me, I don't think."

Will: "Me neither. I mean I like the kids and all, and I loved the coaching, but I want more, y'know? So we agree on that, and we can help each other with it too. I don't know if you can use the liberry at Monkey State, but we could spend a day at the Newark library and check out schools in the west, right?"

Ray: "That's what I'm thinkin', Willieboy. Gotta see choices and fields. I don't really like statistics, but there were classes in the physics department I had at Bloom that might prove interesting. There's some really cool research going on now, and Los Alamos is in New Mexico too. Anyway, the important thing is we'll be together. Jeez, I can't believe I'm sayin' that after all this time."

Will: "I know, Ramona. It's like a dream come true, isn't it?"

Just then, her timer went off, and we walked a ways then turned around. I hadn't decided yet whether to let her win. We took off back to meet the old ladies.

With the finish line about two hundred yards ahead, Ray was twenty yards in front of me. I still had enough gas in the tank to beat her. "Twenty bucks?"

"You're on," she yelled and accelerated, but so did I. I caught and passed her at a hundred yards then let her almost catch up. Arms raised, I did a victory lap around Ray, staying far enough away that she couldn't smack me. "Ladies and gentlemen, Montclair State Indian runner Willieboy Edwards has once again defeated the forlorn appearing Ramonoushka Voytek of some bozo college in Pennsylvania. Go Indians!"

The fortunate appearance of Mama and Sister Mary stymied Ray's reliatory strike.

"I'll get you for this," she snarled.

"That's the plan, hot lips," I said and burst out laughing. She broke down as well and then so did Mama and Sister. We had a lively dinner at The Homestead and chattered all the way home. Outstanding day.

February 25, 1983
Friday

I woke up early and made coffee, put some pastries we had bought yesterday on a tray, and took it all back into the bedroom. "Time's a wasting, come on, you're not even hungover. We have a big day ahead of us!"

"And what would that be?" she muttered from under her pillow collection.

"Not till you show your pretty, good-natured self above the covers," I singsonged.

"Oh god, go away. You are such a pest!" she growled.

"Ah dun go avay from dees playz, ees a nahz spot. You come out and enjoy. You vill lahk," I said.

Hair in a monumental tangle, she peeked from under the

covers and yelled, "Don't look at me, you jerk. Turn your head. I'll be right back!"

"Nutting could be sveeter den Ramonushka in zeh morning ven I meet her," I warbled.

"Stop that right now!" she shouted from the bathroom.

"Hokey dokies," I said. "How about 'Long tall Ramona she's built free, she got evryting dat Villyboy need, O baby...'"

"You stop that right now," she said between giggles, "but ees true."

"All de peoples say dah. Hokey dokies. Got no blinis but nice donuts and cannolis for my sveet baby," I crooned.

"So what's the plan, Stan?" she asked.

"Don't get in my way, Ray," I countered.

Would never tell Ray that Cissy and I did this. Not that Ray was a little jealous or anything.

"Clean up this mess, shower up in the water-saving mode, get some sandwiches and sodas, have lunch in the amphitheatre at State, spend another afternoon researching schools and careers in the West and Southwest. Wanna go to that little place in Rutherford for dinner, bring some wine or beer, make a reservation?"

"Wow. You knock a girl off her feet, Will. It's all good. Warm today? Good."

"Eet's a beautiful day in zeh naybuhood, von't you bee mah nayhbah?" I sang in the Rogerian style.

* * *

Another worthwhile day in the Montclair State library. I had told her if it didn't yield any new info, we would try the Newark Library, but it came through. We got more than we could digest. We were sitting in that little bistro in Rutherford, byob, with a bottle of cabernet, feeling sophisticated, and going over the day's haul.

"Wow," said Ray, "it all seems more real now, doesn't it? I mean, they're places on the map but they're pictures too, and not just New Mexico but all those other places too. It's like a dream, isn't it?"

"It's been that way for me for a long time, honey, I just never..." My eyes started to blur and I turned away. I expected Ramona would laugh at me but she took my hands, her eyes teary now as well, and said, "Dah. Ees gut."

February 26, 1983
Saturday

Ray got up early and went for coffee and pastries. There was a nice Italian bakery about a mile from her place, and she brought home some canoles.

"Ees gut habit for vimens, gettink up to get tasty food for mens. Dah," I said.

"Ees not habit for Mr. Bigpants to be getting used to," she parried.

"Just do as I say, Ray," I chirped.

"Could never do, Lou," she shot back.

"Enough of this, sis," I snapped.

"I agree, Lee." And it was over.

"You got school work to do?" I asked her.

"Nah," she replied. "How about the mall and a movie?"

"What's playing?" I asked.

"Take a look. I got the paper," she said.

Got to the movie section, big circle around *Forty Eight Hours.* I pretended to look, closed the paper, and said, "Nothing looks that good or we've already seen 'em."

"You jerk. Shopping, then *Forty Eight Hours* in Paramus at 4:30, then we'll grab a burger."

I am so outgunned.

"Just gotta call Mama about Mass tomorrow. Wanna come?" I asked her.

"Sleepin' in tomorrow, snookie, can't do it."

February 27, 1983
Sunday

I took Mama to Mass and then breakfast at Wilczynski's in Wallington, which, of course, always rated a capital B, as it eradicated the need for nourishment for at least the next ten hours. Mama was happy that Ray and I had healed our wounds.

"I'm so glad that you'll come out and see us in September, Mama. I bet you'll really like it. So much beautiful country to see, like in that movie we saw with Henry Fonda. You'll come and stay for a while, won't you, Mama? See Grand Canyon? Teach Ramona how to cook?"

"Ve'll see," she dismissed me but smiled a secret smile to let me know she would negotiate.

When we got home, I packed everything I didn't need for the next five days at St. Ethel. I would announce the team meeting for Wednesday after school and let Ray and Sister know.

Deciding to take the plunge and follow my sister's advice, I called Florida, hoping my mother would answer the phone. She didn't. "Hi, Dad, this is Will. How yez doin?"

I heard him, off the phone, yell, "Evelyn, it's Will." Silence. Didn't even speak to me.

"Oh, hi, honey," she said. "I'm so glad you called. Is everything all right?"

My mother's English was almost accent-free, but you could tell English wasn't her first language. "I'm great, Mom. It's so good to hear your voice. How are things in Florida?"

"Oh, everything's good, Will. It's so nice here. We get some cool weather in the winter, so it's like we have seasons and there are lots of veterans and folks like us so there's lots of social things to do. Never get bored. How's Mama?"

"Steady as a rock," I said. "Listen, I got some news. I'm gonna be movin' to New Mexico pretty soon. Sister Mary is retiring, and I'm gonna drive her back and stay there. Look at going to grad school and look into career possibilities as well. Ramona will come out after the school year is over. How 'bout that?"

"You've got all that straightened out with Ray finally? Goes back a long way? All the way to that ole playground, right? You and Ray stomping in puddles, remember?" she asked.

"I do, Mom," I answered, "we were just talkin' about that the other day. Are you still in touch with Mrs. Voytek?"

"We talk on the phone once in a while, and I always invite them to come down, but I don't think Victor and your father would get along too well, do you?" She laughed.

"Speakin' of which, is he all right? Didn't even say hello on the phone," I said.

"Oh, you know your father," she said. "Not much of a talker, but he loves you. Celia said you two had lunch in the city. Was that nice?'

"She's so great. Everything with Cissy is nice. Had a nice evening with Pat and AnnMarie and the kids, too. So, listen, it's gonna be a little crazy for me for a while, but I'll call when we get to New Mexico, okay, Mom?"

"That would be fine, Will. I'm glad you called. Love you, my son."

"Love you, too, Mom. Say bye to Dad. Talk to you soon."

So many things not said, so much held back. It must break her heart as much as it does mine. I know she must love him, but I don't get it.

* * *

I called Ray and asked her, "Vatcher doon, Snookie? Vanna go runnink?"

"Vhere is teenking to go?" she asked.

"Old route in Rutherford. Meet at the Cannon in Lincoln Park in an hour. Get chance to redeem self for miserable pervormanze on boardwalk. Ees gut?"

"Dah, but you are still a punk."

Of course, we tried to beat each other in sprints. Up Lincoln toward the highway to left on Pierrepont, back to town on Ridge Road, down Park Avenue, the shopping street, to Station Square, then right all the way out Orient Way, back up Pierrepont to right on Ridge. Left on Highland Cross to the park. This time, I let her win, feigning a cramp the last hundred yards. As usual, she gloated. We drove to her apartment.

"Hungry?" she asked.

"Not a bit, but hot and sweaty," I said.

"Need a shower?" she asked.

"I do. Got one?"

"Yeah, it works best for two though."

"No kiddin'? We're lucky ducks. We got two right here."

Segue into nap time.

Several hours later, I woke up and told her, "Paprikash and spaetzel tonight. Almost time to go."

She turned over and said, "You said almost, right?"

CHAPTER FORTY-SEVEN

February 28, 1983
Monday

Monday morning, so begins my last week at St. Ethel. The "lasts" are piling up, I know. I was in the building by 6:15 with coffee and pastries. I left boxes of pastries in the teachers' room, guidance office, kitchen, and for the secretaries. I had saved an official North Jersey breakfast, Taylor Ham on a Hard Roll and Coffee, for myself and took it to my classroom. Loved an empty, quiet building. Filled out plan book, graded back papers, put them in the grade book, and filled out reports for the office and guidance. By that time, the shuffle of saddle shoes had begun, kids sticking their heads in the door making sure Edwards was still here. Rafferty and Dooney walked in—no, make that marched in, as boldly as ever, stood on either side of my desk.

"There is a nasty rumor goin' round that yer leavin' us. I'm tellin'ye now fer yer own good, it better not be true." This from Rafferty. "We're havin' none of it. Captain Dooney here is about to tell you why."

"We're here on behalf of the Mighty Gaels, don'tcha know, and we now hold vast power," added Dooney, "and we intend to prevent this calamity from happenin'. In the first place, we all have plans to dance with you at the Spring Fling, as if ya didn't know this. In the second place, do ya seriously think we'd allow ya to be absent from the social event of the season? That would be our graduation of course, there, William Edwards."

"And here I'm quakin' in me boots at the threats of the Amazonian warrior children," I said in a shaky voice.

"WE ARE NOT CHILDREN!" they shouted in unison. They each stepped forward and gave me noogies. And cracked up laughing and, holding hands, skipped out of the room.

"Ya are, too! And yer devils," I yelled at their backs. What a pair!

Well, that's how my week began.

The classes were chirpy all week, even for seventh and eighth grade girls, so I taught from bell to bell, gave spot quizzes, and refused to answer any questions about the future. "The monsignor will explain everything to you in due time, that's all I can say. Now no more questions."

March 1, 1983
Tuesday

Luddie came in that morning in tears. "Close the door, Luddie," I said. "Come up here and sit down." God, this was going to be awful.

"It's all right, Coach. I'm just upset a little 'cause I heard you're leaving. I'll be okay, but sometimes I just start crying when I think what a good friend you have been. And how you changed my life." This was all in between sobs.

"Listen, Luds, everything's gonna be all right," I told her. "You and I will go and see Ms. Farrell today and have a talk, okay? I'll see what period we can spring you."

After lunch, I went to Jane's office. Luddie was already there. "Okay, Luddie," Jane started. "Next month, you will take this exam from Fordham in New York City. They are looking for the top talent in the metropolitan area in math and science. If you do well, you will attend a four week 'math and statistics' summer school at Felician College in Lodi. Questions so far?"

"How we gonna pay for this? My family can't afford this," she asked.

"Not to worry. Let me finish," said Jane, continuing. "If all goes well, you will attend Holy Angels Academy in September in a special accelerated program for eighth graders in which you'll complete five years in four, a New Jersey–approved program for about twenty top girls from Bergen County Catholic Seventh Grades. What do you think, Luddie?"

"How can I do that?" she asked. "Is that even legal?"

"Absolutely, if you apply yourself. You'll make new friends and enjoy your new school. It's in Demarest, and you'll go on the bus," Jane said.

Luddie looked at me and asked, "What's going on here, Coach, really?"

"Just what Ms. Farrell says, Luds," I said.

"You're both leaving out one big part though, aren't you?" she asked.

"And what would that be?" Jane asked with a smile.

"Well, someone's paying for this, right?" Luddie almost shouted.

"Easy does it there, lady," I said. "Yes, certainly there's someone paying for it. In fact, you've met them. Their names are Mr. Brown and Mr. Ptak. One lives near here in Livingston and works in New York City, and the other one works in Boston. You made quite an impression on them at the Garden when we were there. *All* of them, even the Knicks. They and their friends have put up the funding for your summer program and your four-year education at Holy Angels Academy on the condition that you maintain your grades. You can't tell anyone where the money came from except to say a foundation in New York and Boston. Got it? They haven't decided yet on a name, but it'll be something spiffy." I smiled at Jane but didn't get much of a reaction. Yes, things had cooled off for sure.

"And your parents have signed the agreement to this, and Holy Angels has accepted your application once you have completed an interview. That will be in April," Jane added. "So...?"

"I gotta think about this...I'll have to call Larry and make sure this is all on the up and up, but they're on the road now, so it'll have to wait. And I'll have to trust you about Coach Brown, but I know he's a good guy." She looked at me and said, "Did you have anything to do with this, Coach?"

"Listen to you, Ms. Big Stuff. 'Have to call Larry.' I just answered some questions when Larry called last week. Ms. Farrell did all the work and made it happen, Ludds. She spoke with Hubie and Bernard King as well. Apparently, you have a lot of fans in the NBA."

Luddy sprang up and gave Jane a hug, then it was my turn, then a big smile and a loud "Thank you!" Jane and I laughed, coconspirators yet again. "You're the best, Red, really. Sorry about the other night. I will miss you. You are one of the good guys."

"Thank you, kind sir. There is a rumor to that effect, I've been told."

March 2, 1983
Wednesday

All were assembled in my room after school except Ray, who we knew would be a few minutes late, so I let them gab for a while. When she ran in the door, I called for order and turned the meeting over to Sister Mary.

"Girls, I will be returning to my home in New Mexico on Saturday. I have visited there on and off over the years, but it's over sixty years since I left home. The Sisters in New York City took me in, made me a child of God, and taught me how to serve Him. But before that, I was a Navajo girl, like you are American girls. I can't be a girl again, but I can feel the desert, see the sky at night, feel the sun on my face, smell the rain coming across the mountains...I want to feel those things again.

294

"But I want to tell you this. I know I didn't enjoy a season as much as I have enjoyed seeing you enjoy and benefit from this one. Such a wonderful thing you did coming together as a team. I was so happy for you. I will miss you all, and I will pray for you every day. God bless you."

They were all crying by this time. Sister walked around the room and gave them each a light kiss on the forehead and then sat down.

Ramona stood. "Coach Will asked if I would help out, but I wasn't too sure if I would be much help. But you know what? I LOVE THIS TEAM! I LOVE THIS TEAM! You learned everything we taught you. Fundamental basketball. How to play together. It was so much fun to watch you in the games, and even when you tried to beat Will and me in Knockout, like that could ever happen, and if it did, it was because we let you."Loud boos from the crowd and then laughter.

"Seriously," she continued, "thanks for being such great kids. It was really my pleasure." And then she applauded them. And then they applauded her.

"But I have to tell you that, like Sister, I will not be back in the fall. I don't know where I will be, but it will not be in New Jersey. Time to travel on."

More tears and sad faces. Trudy was sobbing.

I stood up. God, the poor girls were getting it from all sides today.

"We didn't feel like we could just go and not tell you. We care too much and respect you too much to do that. Sister has asked me to take her home, so I am driving her home to New Mexico."

I looked at Sister, eyebrows raised. She nodded. "We are leaving Saturday morning. I will not be back."

Shock, surprise, open mouths, wide open eyes, tears...then hands over mouths and eyes...Not so much the seventh graders except for Stephanie, but Trudy, among the older kids, on her crutches, really took it hard. A double blow. She and Reenie and Greet commiserated, as did Rafferty, Dooney, and Flanagan, and the four amigas. God, I hated this. In truth, the eighth graders were all moving on and would forget about all this, as kids do, in a short time. But that was yet to come. For now, Coach Will had to weather the storm and answer the inevitable phone calls tonight. Which I would.

Not for nothing, when I was playing in high school for Rutherford, we lost a State Tournament Sectional to Newton at the buzzer. The Newton coach, an older guy, came over to our guy, gave him a hug, and said, "Y'know, Coach, they'll get over it way before you will. You and your kids did a great job against us. Really."

All these years, I've thought, "You arrogant son of a bitch." But he was right. I know I personally moved on from the heartbreak the next day when baseball practice began. Coach sat in his room watching the tape over and over. I couldn't bear it, but this classroom full of girls crying was a sight that will stay with me a long time. But not longer than Gaels on three.

March 3, 1983
Thursday

I called Rafferty up to my desk after second period and asked her to get Dooney and stop in after school if they had time. The bell to end the day had hardly stopped ringing, and they were at my door. "Get in here and sit down, captains."

"I know we kind of blindsided you yesterday, and I feel really bad about that. But we didn't want you to hear it from someone else," I said.

"We already knew—" Mary Alice began, cut right off by Mary Grace. (Raff cut off by Doons). "Shut up!" she told her.

"It's all right," I told them. "I just wanted to chat with my captains for a few minutes. Is that okay with you?"

They nodded agreement.

"Listen, let me tell you somethin'. You two were *great* captains. I know yez ain't Goody Two-shoes by any means, but we didn't need captains to be that. We needed captains we could trust to lead the team, and that's what you two did. Yez weren't afraid to speak up

296

when it needed to be done, and ye were always there when I needed you to be. You set a great example. Yeah, you screwed up, that's allowed. We all screw up, right? Well, not me."

That got their attention. We laughed. "Now c'mere and each give me a hug. I hope I'll be able to get back and see yez play in high school. Ya goin' to St. Marys?"

They nodded yes and each gave me a hug. And for once neither had anything to say. Loved 'em both. What a pair! I needed a tissue.

* * *

After school, some of the teachers had a little "farewell for the rookie" get-together at Sullivans. The school had celebrated Sister Mary's service and career a while back, but she came anyway. I had only been there six months and really didn't know most of the faculty outside of the math teachers, Jane, and a few others. Jane and I made a point of being in different parts of the room. I answered questions about our trip, but that got old early. We were really strangers still, and it didn't help that I had been Monsignor's fair-haired boy. Early night.

I went for a drive, ended up knocking on Ramona's door. No answer. Drove back to Mama's where she was waiting for me. This could go either way.

She said, "You were at Sullivans?"

"Yes," I answered.

"All this time?"

"No."

"So where—?"

"Easy there, lady."

Pause."And now I'm here," I said.

"Hungry?" she asked."Dah, for sure."

"You vant come over my place? I have nice borscht. Really."

"Eef can stay," I answered hopefully.

"Dah."

"Ees goot."

March 5, 1983
Friday

I left Ray's before dawn, a lot to do today. Showered, shaved, dressed, and had breakfast with Mama then headed over to Angelo's to hook up the trailer and bid him goodbye. "You've been a good friend to me all these years," he said to me.

"No better than you to me. I was thinkin' last night of when we stayed overnight at your Uncle Sal's in Brooklyn, and he took us to Coney Island when we were kids. Remember that? We went on the parachute jump like ten times. And the big roller coaster! I loved that day! You're the best guy I know, , and some day you'll own Gulf Oil," I said.

"That's the plan, my brother." He laughed. "Now hit the road before we get stupid."

"Listen to me, you strunze, everything you know you learned from me. Except for cars. Next summer you're gonna pile Arlene and the bambina in your new Plymouth station wagon and head west to New Mexico 'cause it's killin' you not to know what the hell I'm up to with Ramona in the West."

"You know, my friend, all of that could happen except for one thing, and you know what that is, don't you?"

We both shouted as we have been since we were twelve years old: "*NO LOUSY PLYMOUTH!*"

Angelo didn't curse and he didn't drive Plymouths. And he loved the Mets. Two for three'll get you to the show in baseball but, sadly, not in life. His only real vice was, once in a great while, he smoked one of those foul, smelly guinea diNobili cigars, but only miles away, and downwind, from Arlene. With a Juicyfruit chaser.

I pulled away yelling, "And the Adopted Bronze Guinea heads into the sunset. Hiyo Bu, Away!"

* * *

I parked in front of Sister's and began loading. There really wasn't that much, some boxes, two suitcases, an old oak chest, and bedside table. The bed and other furniture would stay, so she could stay overnight. "What time tomorrow, Sister?" I asked.

"How's six?" she opened.

"Eight's better," I countered.

"Seven it is," she said.

I took the Bu and trailer back to Mama's, parked, and got to school in time for the cup of coffee and Danish I had bought at the bakery, catch my breath, and get my head into my last day at St. Ethel. Monsignor Dan must have seen me come in or was told by a lookout that I had arrived. I stood up. He waved me down and sat in a student's chair. "I'm glad I got to know you, son. You have a gift. Terrence couldn't stop talking about you. And don't be takin' it lightly because we don't see it often. I'll be prayin' for your success in New Mexico or wherever God leads you. I loved it there back in the day, I did."

My eyes wide open, I asked him, "Monsignor, what did you do there?"

"Ah, the order had me stop there in the area in forty-six on the way home from the Pacific. I was a navy chaplain, and right after the war, kind of an emergency and crisis in the faith and I was like a fireman, putting out fires up there in the Four Corners area. Happens every once in a while among the Navajo. Sister can tell ya about it on the way west. I loved the people and couldn't get enough of the land. Woulda stayed there but the order had other plans. So I'm happy for you, William, and I hope the Dineh are as good to you as they were to me. Likely a lot of changes in forty years."

"Wow," I said. "Sister was gone by that time?"

"Twenty years gone, I believe," he said and chuckled. "You take good care of her, boyo," he said and laughed again. "Or you'll answer to Terrence, y'will."

He stood up, blessed me, and left the room.

"Thank you for everything, Monsignor," I said to his back. Wow!

299

I looked at the clock and saw I had fifteen minutes till the bell, gulped my coffee and Danish, took two deep breaths, and prepared for the onslaught.

And zoom, it was over in a blur. I couldn't tell you who said what or if I taught angles, equations, sets, or pronouns. I mustof yelled at Rafferty, wouldn't have been right not to. As soon as I made my goodbyes, I was back at Mama's loading the last of my stuff into the trailer, setting up the back seat of the Bu with a pillow and blanket for Sister. Mama had asked what I wanted for dinner, and I requested pirogies and kielbasy. Ray came over. We had a few shots and a comfortable dinner, cleaned up, left Mama with a Doris Day and Rock Hudson movie, and drove back to Ray's in her car. She told me, "Okeh dokeh, Mr. Hotsy Totsies, you so important now, ve all peasants and bow in your direction. Ees true, no?"

"Has alvays been true, Ramonushka. You just figooring dees out now?"

"Have big news for you, serious, so speak in English," she instructed me. "Turned in my resignation today, effective July 1. That's what the NJEA guy said to do. Booked a flight a week after the last day of the contract school. United 3345 from Newark to Albuqurque. Date is July 8. Will send you details once you get settled. So don't forget the date, dunski."

"Seems like such a long time," I said, "doesn't it? Then, when you think about six and a half years, it's just the wink of an eye. God help me, Ray. I love you so much. You gonna come over to Sister's tomorrow morning?"

"Come ovah heah qveek qveek," she said. "I am haffing betta ideah. You drove here vis me. Ve both drive to Mama's tomorrow. Now be still, I show you somezing."

CHAPTER FORTY-EIGHT

March 5, 1983

We got to Sister's, in Ray's car, about six. She was, of course, ready, said she had been since five. She brought out two thermoses and a shopping bag full of treats, climbed into the front with Ramona, and we drove over to Mama's. She came out with two thermoses and a bag full of treats. Many hugs, kisses, and tears. Ray and I walked off. "July 8. I will write you every day, Willieboy, you lucky duck, you. Call me when you get your telephone. And address."

"Ramona," I said, "you are the love of my life. July 8, indeed. You are now geeving me deep passionate keess. Qveek qveek, before childrens are seeing us."

"Vhat childrens?" she shouted, but I kissed her and cut her off.

Then pointed behind her and said, "*Those* childrens," who, with many of the parents, were now laughing and surrounding my car, hands raised, index fingers extended, jumping up and down except for Trudy, repeating and exclaiming in unison, "GAELS ON THREE! GAELS ON THREE!"

* * *

301

July 8, 1983
Albuqurque International Airport

From the observation deck, he stood watching the flights on their glide paths into AIA, thinking he was picking out United 3345 as it touched down. It began to taxi toward the appropriate gate, in whose direction, having scouted it all out hours ago, he was now running with increasing speed.

But as he approached the gate and the crowd waiting there, an older couple caught his eye. They were standing off to the side. He a very tall, broad-shouldered, white-haired man; she barely half his size with long white hair, likely a Navajo. His mouth dropped open as he recognized them. They were holding hands. The gate opened, people of all shapes and sizes came spilling out, and his attention was redirected. Then came a tall dark brunette, blue eyes searching the crowd. She saw him, ran in his direction, and jumped into his arms. Wrapping herself around him, she murmured, "Oh, Will."

Then he drew his head back and turned to the other couple, as did the brunette. She smiled and began to cry and laugh, as did Will. Joy and confusion. They looked at each other and laughed, made eye contact again with the older couple, and each pair began making its way toward the other through the swirling crowd. "I thought the monsignor was in—" "Never went there," Will said. "He'll explain. I was sworn to secrecy."

They met and embraced, made small talk, and headed for baggage. After it came, Monsignor suggested they find a café, have a drink, and catch up for a while over iced teas and Cokes.

"First, I never went to Ireland," he said, looking at Ray. "After Bill and Liam left, I took a cab to United where I had a flight to Phoenix. Some misdirection there, I apologize," said Monsignor.

"Not the first time," Will offered.

"Good for you, William!" Sister Mary laughed. "Here is another secret. Terrence and I have been released from our vows as of May 1. We began the process in January, knowing it would take a while, but certain it is what we wanted. We bought a house outside of Ship Rock, on the San Juan River, in a beautiful spot, with a special section for you two when you come to visit."

"Yes! Now waddaya thinka that, boyo!" The monsignor laughed.

"I don't know. We might have trouble squeezing you in with our busy schedule." Will laughed. "Released from vows, now that's a pretty big deal!"

"Oh, Mary," he said, "I think we've not seen this bold side of young Will."

"Maybe you haven't, dear, but I certainly have." She laughed.

"Do we still have to call you Sister and Monsignor?" Ray asked.

"Will does, but not you," said Terrence.

"Ah, see now, ya can take the boy outa the Jesuits, but ya can't take—" Will started to say.

"And that'll be enough a that, young Will!" Terrence sternly admonished me. Then broke out laughing. And we all did.

"Now we have a serious favor to ask you, right, dear?" she said, looking at the monsignor.

"Yes, Mary," he said. "We have decided we want to spend what time we have left as husband and wife, and we would like you to stand up for us at our wedding, be our best man and maid of honor. We would be honored if you would accept."

Ray was already crying before he finished. Will was choking up. "It would be the honor of our lives."

"Oh, that's wonderful," Sister Mary continued. "The wedding will be at a small church in Santa Fe. It's a beautiful town, and plus, there're no hotels in Ship Rock. Monsignor Dan will officiate. We have sent an invitation this week to the St. Ethel parish and to some old friends and to Mrs. Ziska as well. You both remember Sister John Damian, right? The wedding will be on Sunday over Labor Day weekend."

"My goodness, Sister," said Ray, "How long have you two known each other?"

"Very good question," said Mary, "but as Terrence has told William, asked at the wrong time, right, William? All in good time."

303

"They like secrets," Will said to Ray.

"At the right time," said the monsignor, "I am going to call the Woijahowiicz's and ask them if Luddie can come out for the wedding. I will send her a round trip ticket if she can stay with you two. Waddaya thinka that?"

"Ya gonna invite Larry Ptak, too?" Will asked, and he burst out laughing.

They had a long drive to Ship Rock from AIA after we said goodbye. Will hadn't seen them in a month or so, and it was a nice reunion. He had gotten a two-bedroom place in Albuqurque, and they were each taking classes at UNM in the fall. Meanwhile, they would be making the rounds looking at job possibilities.

He said to Ray in the car after a long kiss and hug, "Where's all your stuff?"

"Oh, you'll like this. I called Victor and told him since it didn't cost him any money for my college education, he was going to pay for my move to New Mexico. He didn't even make a fuss. Clothes, furniture, even my Honda! Vhatchu teenk of dat, snookie?"

"Ees goot. Guess what, Ramonoushka? Ve gonna live in big people's apartment! You vill lahk. New life for us. Vhatchu teenk, snookie? Ees goot?"

"Dah. Hit the road, Coach, we gotta lotta catchin' up to do."

EPILOGUE

In the glorious fall weather of New York City in October 1931, ninth grader Mary Begay of the Dominican Academy took to walking around Manhattan's Upper East Side and throughout Central Park after school. Today she had walked north on Fifth Avenue from her school on East 68th St. and turned left into the Park near the playing fields and courts on 72nd St. She found a shaded bench, took out her Latin book, and began to study grammar, hoping he would come again today. She had passed by the area several times in the past few weeks and had spotted him more than once.

Mary was a small girl with shiny jet-black hair that, when unbraided, hung to her waist in the Navajo style. She had been taken from the Navajo reservation in New Mexico by her mother in 1920 then brought by train across the country to New York in mid-1928 by a Roman Catholic Dominican sister. She was a classic Navajo beauty—high cheekbones, soft black wide-set eyes, and the classic Indian hooked nose. She was tiny, birdlike, and breathtakingly beautiful.

But Mary's interest this day was not in Latin declensions. Her attention was, rather, drawn to the tall, dark-haired, broad-shouldered boy sauntering southward on Fifth Avenue, bouncing a basketball and whistling tunelessly. She thought him to be a student at the Jesuit Regis School on East 84th St. He didn't appear to be a boy from an affluent family, though, as his face had taken some punches over the years; she could see that. And he lacked the gait and social composure that the "rich kids" had, to be sure. But she couldn't stop *staring at him as he turned right into the basketball area. It seemed to her that he felt her stare, as he turned his bright blue eyes toward her just before she looked away, embarrassed, but not mortified. She had already decided this morning, that if given the opportunity, she would be brazen.*

She turned back to her Latin, he to his loosening-up exercises, then to shooting and dribbling the basketball robotically. He was so mechanical he almost made her laugh, as though he had been taught to play by machines. Most of his shots, however, went in the basket.

They appeared to be a matched pair of sorts: both dressed head to toe in black. He almost clerical lacking the collar, she nunlike absent the headwear. He over six feet tall, she barely five feet. He in long pants, she in long skirt.

He missed a few. Then one miss bounced over to her bench, and Mary picked it up. In the same question asked around the world, he said, "A little help, please, miss?"

"Oh," she said, smiling, "so you need help, sir?"

"If you would kindly toss me the basketball, miss?" he asked again.

"Don't I get a chance to shoot it now that I have possession of the basketball, sir?" she asked, teasing him. He heard some accent or tone in her voice he had never before encountered, and he had a good ear for voices, living where he did.

"Do you think you have the strength to accomplish that lofty goal, miss?" Ah, she heard the Irish coming through though he tried to hide it.

"Well, of course I do, sir. Do you think I'd ask if I did not know I could make a basket?" She paused and put a stern expression on her face. "Sir." He was taken aback. "Well, aren't you the brash Indian maiden dressed in black?" he said and laughed.

"Where I am from, we would say, 'This boy is observant for an Anglo.'"

He looked at her and said, "Miss, I am by no means an 'Anglo,' as you say," with emphasis on Anglo as though it were a pejorative.

"*Nor am I an 'Indian,' as you say,*" Mary pointed out. "*I am Navajo.*"

"*And I am an Irishman,*" he stated somewhat defiantly.

"*Now that these things are settled and we are partly educated about each other,*" she said, "*I will show you how to make a basket.*" With a smile, she directed him to, "*Please pay close attention. It is called a reverse layup.*"

She approached him, dribbling with alternating hands, letting the ball spin into each hand, back and forth across her body, before pushing it back to the court.

"*Are you ready to defend the basket?*" she asked, now about twenty feet directly in front of the goal.

"*Why, yes, miss, I believe I am. And you have my* full *attention as well,*" he answered, bending his knees and as he did. She bent her knees, extending her right arm out sideways from her shoulder and bouncing the ball high above her waist.

She head faked and stepped toward her right. He lunged toward his left, reaching for the ball. She dribbled low, near the ground, under his lunge, across her body, switched the ball to her left hand, dribbled past him to the basket, went under it, switched the ball back to her right hand, and shot a right-hand reverse layup off the backboard and through the basket. She caught the ball and set it on the ground. Mary smiled at him, returned to her bench, primly opened her Latin book, and pretended to be interested in grammar.

"*Who are you?*" he shouted in bewilderment.

"*I am Mary Begay from Ship Rock, New Mexico,*" she answered softly. "*Who are you?*"

"*I am Terrence Patrick McEntee from Hell's Kitchen, New York, and my life will never be the same!*"

"*Well then, Terrence, I advise that you take two deep breaths. Go ahead.*" She paused. "*Good. Now do you think you have recovered enough to come sit down for a bit before the Jesuits and Dominicans come to take us away?*"

The End

Printed in the USA
CPSIA information can be obtained
at www.ICGtesting.com
LVHW092142141123
763978LV00027B/169